Dear Marc and Cheryl,

Enjoy this pageturner.

You know the protagonist
already but maybe you will
get to know her better.

Cheryl this may be a good
option for bookclub!

Happy 2014!
The Protagonist.

SINS
of the
FISHERMEN

SINS
of the
FISHERMEN

JOE DENHAM

abbott press®

A DIVISION OF WRITER'S DIGEST

SINS OF THE FISHERMEN

Abbott Press books may be ordered through booksellers or by contacting:

Abbott Press
1663 Liberty Drive
Bloomington, IN 47403
www.abbottpress.com
Phone: 1-866-697-5310

This is a work of fiction. All of the characters, names, incidents, places, organizations, and dialogue in this novel are either the products of the author's imagination or are used fictitiously.

ISBN: 978-1-4582-0738-8 (sc)
ISBN: 978-1-4582-0737-1 (hc)
ISBN: 978-1-4582-0736-4 (e)

Library of Congress Control Number: 2012923533

Printed in the United States of America

Abbott Press rev. date: 02/18/2013

To my parents,
Edward J. and Mary Margaret M. Denham,
with eternal love.

Acknowledgements

My heartfelt thanks to:

Mary Kay Denham, my sister, for her tireless efforts with transcription and edit support. This book would not have been completed without her help.

Judy Gilbert, for listening ever so closely to my transcription tapes.

Keri Gilbert, for providing safe passage of my material through the streets of Philadelphia.

Officer Robert Detweiler, one of the first readers, for his expertise in law enforcement.

West Whiteland Fire Company and West Whiteland Police Department, for keeping everyone safe.

All my law school and medical school professors, for their dedication to excellence in their disciplines.

The St. Joseph's Prep and St. Joseph's University communities. The Jesuits are the best.

Dr. Ann Marie Cahill, for allowing me to use her name. I hope you enjoy the character.

All my fellow workers at The Children's Hospital of Philadelphia, and Hospital of the University of Pennsylvania, for their dedicated service to help heal all children.

And to my wife Debbie, and my daughter Amber, who are my life.

As he passed by the Sea of Galilee, he saw Simon and his brother Andrew casting their nets into the sea; they were fishermen. Jesus said to them, "Come after me, and I will make you *fishers of men.*"

—*Mark 1:16-17*

Pegasus: The constellation which represents the winged horse that according to Greek myth came to life from the drops of blood splattered on the ground when Perseus beheaded the Gorgon, Medusa.

N.S. Gill's Ancient/Classical History

Prologue

SHADOWS DANCED ACROSS THE RAIN-BATTERED windows of Meghan Cahill's bedroom as the storm surged around her beach house. Inside her mind, Meghan struggled against another force that was stronger and evil. The simultaneous flash of lightning and crack of thunder signaled the arrival of the violent Nor'easter.

The pewter ceiling fan moved the stagnant, humid air across Meghan's face and exposed slim abdomen. Droplets of perspiration slowly moved down her flushed face and found their way against the moist bed sheets. Meghan found no comfort in her bed. She turned from side to side, disturbed by the storm but more troubled by the reality of her nightmares.

What would it take to ease her pain?

To ease her anxiety.

Her fear.

Her accusers grew in number and threatened her freedom. She was innocent. She knew it, but others didn't believe her.

She could never harm another human being.

Tainted evidence violated her innocence. Jonathan did this to her. This she also knew.

She was not a killer. She couldn't be a killer.

The police perimeter grew tighter around her with each passing minute. She had no way out. She felt like an innocent prey struggling helplessly within a spider's web—desperate to escape but even more terrified of the grim consequences of capture.

One thing was certain tonight. She accepted it now. This night, this internal storm, and her pathetic existence would soon end.

Meghan Cahill's plan was quite simple. As a research pharmacologist, Meghan had access to many drugs at the institute. She had used the narcotic, fentanyl, many times in her research work, careful to use the appropriate, safe dose. She also knew the lethal dose that would stop her breathing, cause hypoxia, and result in a quick, painless death.

At one time, Meghan Cahill was very happy and successfully employed at the prestigious Renaissance Research Institute located in Chester County, Pennsylvania. Not anymore. Jonathan had changed everything—her happiness, her life, her will to breathe. Meghan's initial resentment toward Jonathan for his many lies and deception had quickly turned to hatred as she finally realized his sadistic plan. His agenda was focused on the success of his project. Anyone who threatened his project would be eliminated— one way or another.

The police had already dismissed her desperate appeal for help. They didn't believe her innocence. Jonathan had fixed that. He would let the police and the tainted evidence destroy her freedom, her life.

Meghan had no one she could trust.

She was alone.

Meghan slowly sat up in bed and pulled her knees firmly against her exposed breasts. She lowered her head against her knees and rocked back and forth within her fragile world.

She needed one more drink to strengthen her resolve. The Jameson bottle was almost empty. She poured her final drink over the melting ice that seemed to welcome this cloak of Irish blessing as the cubes danced inside her glass.

Meghan finished her drink and instinctively reached for the filled syringe positioned between the empty whiskey bottle and a Bible. She carried the fentanyl syringe between trembling fingers and walked to her bedroom window. A soft amber glow from her antique Tiffany lamp illuminated the many rain droplets flowing down the windowpanes.

Meghan now stood at the window and stared outside at the darkness, searching for a reprieve from her self-imposed sentence. She noticed that the storm had formed streams of flowing water beneath each new droplet on her windows, as if shedding its own tears of empathy for her despair and loneliness.

It was time to end her pain.

Meghan prepared her arm for the lethal injection. Her hand trembled with each awkward attempt to secure the silk scarf tourniquet around her arm.

Meghan's final attempt was successful. She paused for a moment and stared down at her bulging veins. The tourniquet served its purpose. Many engorged veins with a characteristic bluish hue signaled their location on Meghan's forearm. Meghan took her time. She palpated each vein and assessed its worthiness.

She now focused on the chosen one.

Meghan gently wiped her skin with an alcohol pad. Why was she concerned with infection? After this lethal injection, any subsequent infection would be irrelevant.

Meghan positioned the syringe needle above the vein and now, for the first time, felt the insidious numbness ebb through the tourniquet-compressed arm.

No more delay. No more pain.

Her fingers trembled as she moved the needle closer.

Suddenly a flash of lightning filled the dimly lit room. Immediately, a thick tree limb crashed through her bedroom window, propelling pieces of jagged glass toward Meghan. Unable to escape, Meghan cried out as shards of glass tore into her skin. All thoughts of self-destruction were suddenly gone. Meghan was now fighting for her life as she grabbed the bed sheet to cover her bleeding neck wound.

Remain calm. Take deep breaths. Assess your injuries, she thought to herself.

Fortunately, her bleeding wasn't pulsatile. Meghan sat on the edge of her bed.

"My God, what was I going to do to myself?" she cried out.

Meghan released the silk tourniquet from around her arm. Her tears flowed down her cheeks with each anguished sob.

Jonathan had deceived her.

He had abandoned her when she was no longer useful to him. She deserved a better life. Her relationship with him had been an illusion, a treacherous lie. He wanted no trace of her in his life.

Meghan realized he almost succeeded tonight.

Jonathan will not get away with this, she vowed.

Chapter One

Jonathan Ashbridge had done everything right. He had graduated from the best prep school in Philadelphia and had achieved honors in chemistry and mathematics at Princeton University. His over-achieving personality had guided him further to medical school and the successful completion of a pathology residency at age twenty-eight. He then began working at the Renaissance Institute as an associate research director. Many people would have been thankful for these achievements.

Jonathan was different, however.

After ten years at the institute, he had recently been appointed senior vice president. But his goal was to be the CEO; he needed to be the CEO. With each passing year, Jonathan's resentment toward his boss,

Chief Executive Officer Jack Farraday, had grown stronger. Jonathan considered him weak and incompetent, a mere puppet for the myopic board of directors.

It was Friday, and Jonathan's weekly meeting with Farraday was not going well.

"What do you mean my drug study protocol is not acceptable for the institute? Have you even read it?" shouted Jonathan.

Jonathan was now out of his chair and pacing back and forth across Farraday's plush plum carpet.

"Let me spell it out for you, Farraday. I have, on my own, secured a three-million-dollar National Institute of Health grant for my genetics research project. I have already ordered another five hundred zebra fish and over a thousand two-liter tanks."

Jonathan finally stopped pacing and, with outstretched arms, leaned over Farraday's cherry wood desk.

"My project design will prove that I can destroy specific genes and create mutations that will eliminate certain major diseases, such as depression and obsessive-compulsive disorders."

Farraday continued to lean back in his leather desk chair, careful not to hide the sarcastic grin behind his folded hands.

"As of October 1, Ashbridge, your 'fish hobby' experiments will be removed from the Renaissance Institute's premises. We will no longer support your idiotic work," Farraday announced loud enough for others just outside his office to hear.

Jonathan stormed out of Farraday's office and ignored the startled reactions of Farraday's secretarial entourage, who couldn't help but overhear Farraday's decision.

Jonathan quickly arrived at his nearby office and muttered angry epithets as he walked past his administrative assistant.

"It's a fucking miracle this company is still solvent. That goddamn Farraday! That's the last time he calls me an idiot. I'm the genius in this company."

Jonathan slammed his office door and walked to his corner office windows where he looked out across the pristine acres of preserved Chester County land. Jonathan's heart was pounding. He took several deep breaths.

Gazing up through the midsummer haze that hung over the surrounding countryside, Jonathan caught sight of a tight V-formation of Canada geese as they effortlessly began their descent toward the designated runway on a distant patch of harvested cornfield. Jonathan admired their precision, the formation's allegiance to their leader.

Jonathan's organized and logical approach to conflict resolution had always been successful in his work at the institute. Today, however, Farraday was being unreasonable. Jonathan considered him a moron, no longer worth his time and effort. Jonathan was now more determined than ever to use his intellect, organizational strengths, and even the people around him at the institute to achieve his goal. No matter what the cost, Jonathan would become the new chief executive officer of the Renaissance Institute.

A sudden knock on the door jarred Jonathan from his thoughts.

"What do you want?" Jonathan shouted.

The door slowly opened and revealed Jonathan's administrative assistant, hesitant to enter and even more timid to speak.

"Dr. Ashbridge, can you take a call from Dr. Cahill?"

Jonathan's anger slowly subsided as he reached for the phone.

"Hi, Jonathan. I know it's only been hours since I saw you, but I really miss you," Meghan Cahill whispered.

"God, it's nice to hear your voice. I've had a horrible day—you know, my usual meeting with Farraday. I need to see you soon." Jonathan rested his six foot, well-trimmed frame in his leather chair and ran his hand through his gelled, black, wavy hair.

"You know where I am. When can you leave work?"

"I don't know. I still have to make a few more calls. Maybe in an hour."

"Well, it's 3:30 p.m. now. Do you think you could be here by 7:00?" Meghan asked.

"Yes, probably. I'll have some weekend shore traffic to deal with, though," Jonathan replied.

"You know, I'd love to have you here sooner, but I guess I can wait. I'll have one of my special dinners waiting for you."

"You're the greatest, Meghan. I don't know what I would do without you."

"See you at 7:00?" Meghan questioned.

"Promise," Jonathan assured her.

Meghan finished her call. She resumed her prone position on the deck chaise lounge, her black bikini top discarded nearby. She always enjoyed the late afternoon sun, its innocent warmth on her bronze skin. Tiny beads of perspiration slowly rolled down her slender back and found their way against her thong. Meghan appreciated the privacy of her Ocean City beach house; it gave her the seclusion she needed for such an afternoon of uninhibited tanning.

The rhythm of the ocean surf reminded Meghan of the many intimate moments shared with Jonathan. His special touch, his unique caresses that were always well received and encouraged by Meghan, served to further her obsession with Jonathan. It would be a long wait for him to arrive. His drive from Chester County would probably take about three hours, assuming there was the usual shore traffic, she figured.

Meghan stood up from the lounge chair and covered her chest with an ivory silk scarf. She paused for a moment on the deck, looking out at the ocean, blanketed by a dense summer haze reflecting the intense humidity. She was glad she didn't work every Friday at the institute since she was able to drive to the shore after work on some Thursday afternoons and avoid the hassle of Friday evening shore traffic.

Meghan's cell phone rang, disturbing her meditation. She refused to answer it. She was relaxed and was not motivated to notice the caller's identity. She also did not want to be controlled by an inanimate object. Meghan left the deck and entered the kitchen to pour another glass of Jacob's Creek Australian Chardonnay before taking her shower. Since it usually took several minutes for the warm water to flow from the shower head, Meghan would now have liquid nourishment to keep her company while she waited.

As she reached inside the shower stall, Meghan immediately felt a warm pulsating flow against her hand. *Thank God the wait was brief, allowing me one sip from the wine glass,* Meghan thought. She was ready to feel the soothing water against her body.

Meghan placed her wine glass atop the coral granite counter and gently stepped into the marble and glass shower stall. Steam slowly swirled around her and spilled into the bathroom like an amoeba searching for prey. The steam quickly claimed territory across the silver-framed mirror wall. Meghan's slender, five-foot-five-inch, toned body slowly moved in response to the pulsating flow of warm water. Her intentions were clear; she wanted Jonathan's touch and the immediate, intense pleasure each caress would bring her. She was always willing—anytime, anyplace. Anything for Jonathan. She needed him. Nervous anticipation grew as each moment passed since her brief conversation with him.

As Meghan gently spread lavender-scented body lotion across her chest and abdomen, clumps of white foam soon appeared against her deep dark skin. She gently massaged the foam across her abdomen and against her parted thighs. Her body began to move rhythmically. The wet foam felt good against her skin. Meghan slowly turned and pressed her body against the glass shower wall.

God, she wished Jonathan was with her now.

Chapter Two

*D*AMN IT. WHY DIDN'T SHE *answer her fucking phone?* Jonathan threw his cell phone against the black leather passenger seat of his BMW i8 sports car. He wanted to let Meghan know that he would be late. The traffic was worse than expected, and his meeting, which he had decided not to tell Meghan about, would delay his arrival at the shore. *Fine, she will just have to wait for me. This isn't the first time and certainly won't be the last,* he vowed. There was someone, something that needed his immediate attention.

As Jonathan approached the Philadelphia skyline, driving along the Schuylkill Expressway at rush hour, he saw the summer blanket of humidity around the pyramid atop the Mellon Building. He soon approached the University Exit off the Schuylkill Expressway and noticed a factory on the east side of the Schuylkill River. The building probably at one time boasted an impressive architectural achievement, Jonathan thought, with its multi-tiered Williamsburg brick elevation and high-pitched, gray slate roof. The tall, corroded steel exhaust pipes protruded through the roof and reached toward the pristine azure sky. The brick edifice, with discolored, broken windows, formed a mosaic design in the glare of the afternoon sun. No longer responsible for some useful manufactured product, this building was now engulfed in reckless patterns of overgrown vines.

Jonathan's plan was now set in motion. His drug study was his creation. His work of genius. He would not allow Farraday to reject and ridicule him any longer. His project would not be destroyed. Jonathan's meeting at the University of Pennsylvania's Institute of Contemporary Art would promulgate his flawless plan to eliminate CEO Farraday from the institute.

Jonathan's momentum toward Penn's campus was quickly subdued, as his black BMW came to an abrupt stop.

"Goddamn it. This city traffic sucks!" Jonathan shouted out through his open moon roof within earshot of a nearby trucker.

"Fuck you, pal. You suck! What do ya want to do about it, asshole?" shouted the bare-chested driver of an eighteen-wheel flatbed, transporting wooden crates.

Jonathan saw an opening in the traffic congestion near the University of Pennsylvania's Veterinary School and floored the accelerator. His final reply to the ignorant, obese truck driver was a defiant middle finger. Jonathan turned onto Chestnut Street and immediately found an available space not far from his meeting. He parked his car and breathed in the noxious, humid air filled with exhaust fumes. Despite his lungs begging him to return to his air-conditioned car, Jonathan hurried down Chestnut Street as he realized he was late.

Jonathan paused outside the University of Pennsylvania's Institute of Contemporary Art Museum to read the name of the current featured exhibition. Great—Apfelbaum's fabric-dyed artwork was still here. The warm, late-afternoon sun glared across the building's glass and steel elevation that encased the avant-garde artwork. Jonathan hoped the museum's air-conditioning functioned properly.

Jonathan entered the museum and immediately recognized his appointment.

The professor was focused on Apfelbaum's *Reckless*, a fabric dye on synthetic velvet display. This multi-colored palette of art was strategically arranged on the floor of a sixty-square-foot area designed to showcase such unique displays.

"I know I'm late. You know, typical Friday afternoon rush-hour traffic," Jonathan announced.

The professor didn't acknowledge Jonathan's arrival. Instead, he continued his pensive gaze on the floor display, revealing a smile beneath his well-groomed grayish auburn facial hair. The blue and reddish dominant tones running throughout the professor's tweed sport coat complemented the multi-color tones freely flowing in Apfelbaum's art work.

"How ironic, Jonathan. You called me *reckless* only months ago … you obviously failed to recognize the logic in my plan. And now," the professor continued, "we meet again at such a beautiful work of genius entitled *Reckless*."

Jonathan understood the meaning of the professor's words. The message was very clear. He wanted Jonathan and everyone else involved in the plan to recognize and accept that he was never to be questioned by anyone. The professor's authority was supreme. Of course, Jonathan accepted the fact that this sixty-year-old academician created the Pegasus Project and devised the biological theory for the project's anticipated success.

But, Goddamn it. Jonathan knew that this aging academic dinosaur came to him for his unique expertise in genetic research. Jonathan's published research in genetic coding had caught the professor's attention and led to their partnership. Without question, the professor and the Pegasus Project needed him.

"All right, you called this meeting. What is so important?" the professor demanded.

"I'm not sure, but there may be trouble for us at the Renaissance Institute," Jonathan answered in a subdued tone.

"What do you mean trouble? And what do you mean, you're not sure?" the professor challenged.

Jonathan continued to stare down at the floor exhibit, not yet wanting to meet the professor's eyes.

"Just that—trouble, maybe with Farraday. He wants to stop my research project."

"This is not our problem; it's your problem," the professor retorted.

"But this affects both of us. It's our project."

"Does he know anything about Pegasus?" the professor questioned.

"Of course not."

"Are you close to finishing our work?" the professor asked, slowly stroking his beard.

"Within weeks, maybe even days. I just need more time. If Farraday has his way, Pegasus will be dead effective October 1," Jonathan stressed.

"Listen. Farraday must be dealt with. By you, and now," the professor ordered.

Jonathan looked up into the professor's ice-blue eyes, which immediately met his own.

"What do you mean, dealt with?"

The professor paused and then said, "You must kill Farraday."

Chapter Three

JONATHAN SAT IN HIS CAR, parked along the Delaware River Waterfront. Since his meeting with the professor, Jonathan had needed time to reflect on the professor's order. *Kill Farraday.* But how could he? And why should he be Farraday's killer? Jonathan needed a drink. He knew where one was waiting for him, but he wasn't ready to see Meghan. He realized that she would already be upset with him since it was now 8:00 p.m., nearly five hours since he had spoken with her.

But Jonathan needed more time to think. Time to evaluate his meeting with the professor.

Sure, he wanted to be CEO at the Renaissance Institute. *But at what cost?* Jonathan questioned. Farraday was clearly an idiot. Jonathan always considered him expendable, but how was Farraday to leave the Institute?

Farraday was now a constant threat to the project, Jonathan decided. Farraday made it very clear this afternoon that Jonathan's genetics research would be stopped. What Farraday did not realize was his own precarious existence. He wanted to stop a project that involved many powerful people.

The professor wanted Farraday killed. Any alternative was clearly not an option.

Jonathan needed time to plan.

The darkening late-August sky enhanced the pulsing flash of neon lights that danced across his black BMW. Jonathan continued driving along Arch Street, undisturbed by the deafening police siren echoing within this ghetto of bars and cheap rooming houses. His gaze focused on the many denizens who lingered along the broken cement pavements, strategically positioned to claim a section of asphalt as their territory.

Numerous Vietnamese take-outs filled the surrounding humid air with samples of stir-fried beef and pork, and tangerine marinated duck, which easily penetrated Jonathan's BMW fortress. Vietnamese graphics displayed on the steamed kitchen windows beckoned itinerants to enter and satiate their cravings. Jonathan was hungry, but he first needed a drink. He turned into a parking space recently vacated by a pair of Harley Davidson bikes. Locking the door behind him with his remote, Jonathan entered Ladies' Choice Lounge and immediately received a friendly reception from the bartender.

"Where have you been?" Kayla asked while reaching across the parquet oak bar congested with finger-smudged glassware.

"Around. I need a drink, Kayla."

He sat down on the leather, swivel bar chair. Jonathan liked it here for a number of reasons, one of which was its discrete location and the unique bar design. The bartender was actually eye-level with the seated patrons due to the dug-out walkway behind the counter.

Kayla soon produced his drink.

"I mean it, Jon, where have you been hiding?" Kayla asked, her intense, pale blue eyes meeting his.

Jonathan easily surrendered a smile and took a healthy swallow of his drink.

"I know, it's been a few weeks."

"Try four weeks and three days," Kayla quickly replied.

"So you *do* care, Kayla," Jonathan teased as he reached for his final swallow from his drink.

Kayla turned sharply away. Her waist-length chestnut hair swirled softly across her petite frame as she strode to the far end of the bar. The dense, ambient air saturated with cigarette smoke engulfed the lounge. Alcohol fumes penetrated the nostrils of the many intoxicated patrons who begged for refills.

Jonathan sensed her displeasure with him. But what did she expect from him?

What did Meghan expect from him?

He needed another drink, but at what cost? Surely, he would not beg Kayla for another.

As Jonathan looked across the bar and into the oak-framed beveled mirror, he saw emptiness scattered across the many faces standing behind him. Fuck her. He refused to remain here and become dependent like the rest of these losers on a woman controlling their evening's pleasure.

Jonathan moved away from the bar and pushed through the aimless crowd.

He needed fresh air and time to think.

Jonathan walked toward the flashing car light controlled by his remote. He paused for a moment and noticed the many alcoholic human forms that claimed their territory amidst the discarded restaurant refuge. These citizens of Arch Street, clothed in dark hues of grime and grease, portrayed not a viable existence but rather a hopeless abyss of disease.

How desperate. How pathetic that these diseased hosts should breathe the same air with him. *Why should they live?* he thought.

As Jonathan opened his car door, he felt a callused hand touch the back of his neck. Jonathan turned quickly and instinctively grabbed his assailant's arm. Jonathan's force drove the intruder's face against a nearby wrought iron gate that enclosed a dark alley.

"I'm sorry ... I'm sorry, man! I was just gonna ask for some food money," pleaded the stranger.

Jonathan reached for the man's head and grabbed his hair that was heavily matted with years of dirt and grime. He forcefully dragged the stranger across the adjacent brick wall and stood face to face with his assailant.

My God, what a worthless piece of scum, Jonathan thought as he stared into darting, jaundiced eyes filled with fear and disease. The man's bearded face was covered with fresh blood flowing from a deformed nose that clearly had been broken many times before.

"This is your lucky night, asshole. Any other time, you wouldn't be standing right now. You'd be just another pile of garbage," Jonathan warned as he finally released his grip on the man's tangled hair and wiped his hands clean against his victim's soiled and tattered T-shirt.

As Jonathan turned away and walked toward his BMW, an eyewitness watched as the injured stranger slowly slumped to the pavement amidst broken liquor bottles. She could not believe what had just happened. How could he treat someone like that? Why would he want to ruthlessly injure that innocent and vulnerable man?

As Kayla turned away from the bar's window, she now realized that their many trips to the mountains were not moments of sincere intimacy. Jonathan showed her more about himself in those past few minutes than he had during their many hours of passion.

My God, what a fool I've been these past several months, Kayla thought. Jonathan was a stranger to her now.

She looked around the bar and for the first time felt empathy for her penurious patrons. They were either homeless and probably had begged for food money to support their alcohol addiction, or were people that simply found a temporary safe haven from the burdens tormenting their lives.

Kayla vowed to start a new life.

Chapter Four

MEGHAN REPLACED THE MANY BURNT votive candles for the third time.

She tried hard to be patient, once again, but realized he would never change. Jonathan always kept her waiting. He would always keep her waiting. When they first started dating two years ago, she would often change her clothes while waiting for Jonathan's arrival, never quite sure what to wear for him. But Meghan was always ready. Waiting for his late arrival. Jonathan would eventually show up, only to casually dismiss her insignificant concerns.

This Friday evening was no different. Meghan had prepared a special dinner: filet mignon and Norwegian salmon stuffed with crabmeat sautéed in a Louis Jadot Chardonnay. She was proud of her culinary achievement.

But where was he? Why did he not call? Jonathan was three hours late, and her dinner was ruined.

Meghan finished the bottle of Chardonnay and easily opened a second. She ran her fingers through her shoulder-length auburn hair and took a healthy swallow of the Chardonnay. She decided she needed some fresh air.

Meghan walked across the second-floor living room and through the open atrium doors that led to a spacious second-story, gray stone deck overlooking the Atlantic Ocean. She gazed up into the dark sky speckled with shimmering stars and soon felt her anger replaced by a sense of calm and wonder.

Tonight, the sea spoke softly to her as each wave gently embraced the hard sand. The ocean breeze touched Meghan with a gentleness as the cool, late-summer's breeze softly caressed her auburn hair. As Meghan walked around her deck, her sage camisole fell comfortably across her chest and revealed her slim, suntanned abdomen. Her toned thighs moved effortlessly within her silk, eggshell drawstring pants. Her body moved freely across the deck, beneath her starry refuge and within her self-made fortress.

Meghan felt safe here at her beach house. Her grandmother's beach house.

Meghan had always been close to Nana. They often had referred to each other as kindred spirits. Meghan was devastated when her grandmother died two years ago of complications from diabetes. Her grandmother had left her this spacious, six-bedroom Victorian beach house in Ocean City, New Jersey, and for the past two years, Meghan had made it her home. In fact, Nana's house had always felt like her home. During her freshman year at Yale, Meghan's parents died in a car accident during a winter storm. She rarely visited her parents' home in Malvern since the accident but often had visited Nana on weekends and had spent summers with her at the beach house.

Even as a young child growing up, Meghan would stay for weeks at a time with her in Ocean City. They would take endless walks along the beach, making new discoveries along the way. Nana would tell her creative stories about the origins and travels of the many shells and driftwood that inhabited their beach.

Her grandmother's creativity did not end with her storytelling; it was also quite evident in her painting. As a young girl, Meghan would sit for hours by her grandmother's side and watch the canvas come alive with each brush stroke. Her paintings over the years had captivated Meghan and had instilled in her a reverence for her grandmother's artistry.

Meghan turned away from the balcony, walked back through the living room, and down one step into an adjoining room that Meghan called her haven.

This room was her favorite. Her grandmother had used this special place for storytelling and painting. Meghan treasured the many hours spent here closely watching Nana, her mentor, develop an idea and then magically breathe life onto the canvas with her oil images. The windows on one side of the room gave permission for entry to an early dawn splendor that displayed its palette across the eggshell walls. The windows in the opposite wall allowed entry for a fiery sunset to complete the day's metamorphosis.

Meghan's artistic talent came honestly to her, a saying frequently used by her grandmother. Through the years, Meghan and her grandmother had worked side by side in this room. Each had critiqued the other's choice of tones or use of shadows, but they had always supported each other, especially on those days when it was difficult to express a particular concept on their canvas. To help her through a project, Nana would gently remind her never to allow her subject to control her. If she lost this freedom, her creative spirit would suffer.

Meghan loved to paint because she found an inner peace through her artistic expression. But most of all, she discovered through her painting an endless companionship with Nana. Each time she sat at her grandmother's easel, Meghan felt an inner warmth embrace her, which helped her portray her feelings of loneliness and doubt into vibrant oil images. At the completion of each painting, Meghan would remain for hours in her haven room and feel Nana's gentle spirit.

Meghan missed her grandmother.

Meghan placed her empty wine glass on an antique, tiger oak library desk. A contoured conch shell served as a coaster that protected the wood from beads of condensation that trickled down the outside of the glass. Even though there was an ocean breeze, the summer's humidity continued into the evening.

Meghan paused for a moment beside a Steinway piano and stared at her favorite photograph of her grandmother taken many years ago when Nana was in her early twenties. This particular picture captured the young artist while at work in this room at the same easel that Meghan now used. The photograph was a black and white, embraced by an antique silver frame. Her grandmother's young face was profiled with high cheek bones and toned skin that gently sloped to meet her distinctive jaw line. Her grandmother's expression seemed both calm and pensive, calculating her next brush stroke.

Meghan also treasured the painting that Nana had been working on when that photograph was taken many years ago. The finished artwork now hung against an eggshell wall that bordered the mahogany-stained Steinway. The oil painting depicted a three-mast schooner, each canvas full of wind, forging a path through a surging sea. An early dawn's light shined through each wave's crest, portraying Nana's tempera with tones of aquamarine and citrine. Meghan loved this work because it represented a prevailing strength and faith with oneself despite difficult obstacles.

Meghan's ephemeral solitude was suddenly interrupted by Jonathan's footsteps across the cherry wood, parquet floor in the living room.

"Meghan, where are you?"

Meghan's body stiffened as she anticipated her confrontation with Jonathan.

"Meghan, are you in there?" Jonathan called as he stood at the doorway leading into Meghan's haven.

"I've been waiting for hours, Jonathan. Where have you been?" Meghan responded angrily.

"I had some important things to take care of. You know, with my research project."

"Too important not to call me?"

"Listen, I know I'm late, but I'm here now." Jonathan turned and walked back into the living room.

"Yes, you are very late, and the dinner is ruined. So where have you been so late on a Friday evening?" Meghan demanded as she quickly followed him.

Jonathan found a bottle of Courvoisier XO and poured himself a drink.

"Jonathan, did you hear me? Where were you?"

Jonathan took his time. He slowly tasted the cognac and then turned toward Meghan, who was now standing in front of him.

"Look, Meghan. I can see you went to a lot of trouble making dinner, and now it's ruined. And I know you're upset. I agree, you should be angry. But you know, if I could have called you, I would have." Jonathan took another swallow from his glass.

"I was at the lab, meeting with people who are vital to my project's success. I honestly could not get away."

Even though Meghan also worked at the Renaissance Institute as a pharmaceutical researcher, she was not a member of his research team. She was not permitted to ask him anything about his work. Within the institute, Jonathan's project was considered highly classified.

Jonathan reached for Meghan's clenched hands and gently brought them to his chest. He looked into her pale green eyes.

"I should've called. I'm sorry," Jonathan whispered.

He gently stroked Meghan's face and brushed aside strands of her auburn hair that were moist with tears. Meghan's head slowly fell against Jonathan's shoulder. She was tired and didn't want to argue any longer.

Meghan held Jonathan's hand and led him into her bedroom. He smiled as he walked closely behind her.

Chapter Five

THE SUMMER HUMIDITY INTENSIFIED IN the streets of New York City. This late August, Saturday evening was filled with angry cries from city dwellers who desperately needed a reprieve from the relentless heat. The smells of roasted chestnuts and hot dogs smothered with sauerkraut made by street vendors, and the saxophone tunes from sidewalk musicians filled the suffocating air.

Even though the sounds of screeching brakes and car horns interrupted the soothing saxophone melodies along the sidewalks, the professor enjoyed the cacophonous sounds of the city.

He favored discord. Harmony was a problem for him. Dividing his academic time between Princeton and the University of Pennsylvania Law School, the professor was a bio-ethics scholar who lectured on controversial topics, such as the "Right to Die" and "Assisted Suicide." As a faculty member, he enjoyed challenging his colleagues' comfortable code of ethics. However, they never equaled his intellectual prowess. The professor was always able to effectively debate the legal and medical theories he proffered to support his positions. As both an attorney and a physician, he found the private debates and public forum discourse extremely elementary.

His colleagues sought harmonious solutions to issues, such as whether one individual should have the moral and legal right to help another commit suicide. They feared the development of a moral code that permitted assisted suicide. For them, this behavior was incompatible with their belief in the sanctity of life.

The professor also enjoyed creating unrest among his students and often challenged the ethical merits of their moral code. His students were obviously intelligent but also reticent when asked to question their self-imposed moral boundaries.

The professor leisurely walked along Fifth Avenue, glanced at his Raymond Weil Roman numeral watch, and realized he had some time before his 8:00 p.m. dinner reservation.

He window-shopped at Cartier's, found nothing to entice him inside, and walked on to Sak's window display depicting Philadelphia's Nicole Miller's fall fashion line.

He had demanded completion of Dr. Jonathan Ashbridge's research project by the end of September. No excuses. No deadline extensions would be tolerated. Ashbridge's concern that Farraday posed a threat to the project's successful completion did not worry the professor. He made it clear to Jonathan yesterday that the Pegasus Project was more important than Farraday. The professor also knew that the Pegasus Project was more important than Jonathan. Many clients were financially and emotionally committed to the project's timely completion, and the professor had no intention of destroying their trust in him. He would commit his reputation once again at this evening's dinner appointment and reassure his clients that the Pegasus Project would forever change their lives and the lives of many others.

His clients demanded revenge.

The professor was confident his Pegasus Project would not disappoint them.

The professor paused at the entrance to Giovanni's Ristorante on West Fifty-Fifth Street where a group of satiated patrons emerged, exchanging complimentary one-liners on behalf of the chef and staff.

He agreed with them. Whenever he was in the city, he always dined at Giovanni's. He appreciated the staff's obsession with detail and success with their epicurean art.

"Good evening, Professor Marguilies. It is a pleasure to see you once again," greeted Angelo, a well-built man with thick, black, wavy hair, who equaled the professor in height at six feet two.

"Your usual table is prepared and ready, sir."

The maître d' easily maneuvered among the many occupied white linen tables and escorted the professor to the Hunt Room where a table set for two stood in front of a mahogany etched wall. The professor preferred the Hunt Room for its privacy. The room housed only three other tables, all empty right now, and they were strategically positioned to allow private conversations to remain private.

"Good evening, Professor Marguilies. May I bring your drink now?" asked the waiter, who was accustomed to his usual cocktail.

"Thank you, Mario." The meeting was arranged for 8:00 p.m. The professor believed in punctuality. He trusted his dinner partner had the same ethic.

Within a minute after Mario left with the professor's order, Angelo entered the Hunt Room escorting a patron, who appeared to be in his mid-forties with gray tones woven within sandy blond hair.

Angelo presented the guest to the professor's table.

"Richard Bailey, how nice to see you again," greeted Professor Marguilies as the two men exchanged a warm greeting. "I trust your trip to the city was uneventful."

"Yes, David, it has been just that, uneventful."

Mario arrived with the professor's Remy Martin cocktail and awaited his new task.

"I'll have Tullamore with ginger ale over ice."

Mario gave a short, respectful bow and quickly disappeared beyond the atrium doors guarding the room's entrance.

"We need to talk, David," Bailey said, leaning forward in his chair.

"I know; that's why we're having dinner tonight."

"David, my clients are nervous. They need information. They deserve information," Bailey insisted.

"Listen, Richard. I understand why they are nervous. They do deserve some information, but on a limited, need-to-know basis. They will receive only enough facts that I deem appropriate. Any more right now is not acceptable. It's too risky."

"But you don't see their faces and hear their repeated demands for justice. They were injured, David. Psychologically and physically. My clients now know that the Pennsylvania Supreme Court agreed with the lower courts and decided against their class-action lawsuit. The court said the suit was without merit and was not filed within the required statute of limitations time period. Essentially, the priests got away with their crimes. The court refused to hold the priests and the Philadelphia Archdiocese accountable. I've got to do something for my clients ... give them something for all the years they have suffered."

Richard Bailey was indeed an effective advocate. Professor Marguilies recognized Bailey's strong, innate analytical talents within the first few weeks of his law school career. Marguilies was a tenured professor at Penn's Law School and was invited to lecture on the bio-ethics topic, "Right to Die" for the first-year Criminal Law Class. Marguilies remembered how impressed he was with Bailey's ability to listen attentively and quickly anticipate the direction of the lecture. Bailey was not a typical first-year law student. He confidently challenged Marguilies during his lectures with effective arguments and at times proffered a better way of resolving an ethical dilemma.

Marguilies knew that he would work with Bailey on the Pegasus Project. No other attorney could successfully manage this particular "unofficial" class action outside the judicial system on behalf of his clients.

"Well, what can I tell my clients?"

Professor Marguilies gazed down into his Remy Martin as if looking into a crystal ball to search for the right words. "I know you're frustrated with the legal system. That's why you approached me months ago about this issue. My plan to help you and your clients hasn't changed. I am committed to your cause. My Pegasus Project will be ready this fall. Our clinical trials will begin in September. In summary, your clients will see results soon thereafter."

The professor finished his drink and focused on Bailey. "You must tell your clients that they need to be patient. Our project will indeed produce our deserved goal. I guarantee it."

Mario rushed through the atrium doors and presented the Irish Whisky to Bailey.

"Excuse me, but we had such … a hard time finding Tullamore. Please excuse me for the delay," pleaded Mario.

"Relax, Mario. We'll order now," the professor said softly, placing his hand on Mario's arm to restore confidence in his friend.

The professor gestured for his dinner guest to begin. "Let's see now. I'll have the minestrone and the salmon with lemon sauce and sautéed spinach."

"Very good, sir," replied Mario.

"Mario, I'll start with the Pasta e Fagioli. Then I'll have the Carre d' Agnello al Forno. We'll also have wine with dinner."

"Excellent, Professor," beamed Mario with restored confidence.

"All right, David, I give up. What did you just order?"

"The roasted lamb is quite good, Richard. Someday you should try it." The professor smiled as he returned to his cocktail.

"You tell me that the Pegasus Project will change many lives. You also assure me that my clients will see results soon. Again, my problem rests with specifics. What can I tell my clients now that will be enough to keep them patient?"

Professor Marguilies sensed his young friend's frustration. Richard

Bailey had organized the largest class-action suit against the Catholic Church in Philadelphia.

Catholic priests had abused his clients. Injured their bodies, minds, and spirits. They were frustrated with the Philadelphia Archdiocese for abandoning their many pleas for help. The professor knew the abused victims had placed their trust in their attorney to seek justice for them and to hold the Archdiocesan priests accountable.

But Richard Bailey was angry. Angry with the Catholic Church and the legal system. The professor knew his friend well. Richard Bailey was even more angry with himself and his inability to find a legal remedy.

Unfortunately, the Pennsylvania courts refused to help them because of a legal technicality. The Catholic Church had argued successfully that the victims' grievances were not filed in a timely manner. Under the Pennsylvania Statute of Limitations Law, their class-action lawsuit was dismissed; the many victims had no choice but to follow Bailey's legal guidance. Seek retribution elsewhere. But where? At first, Richard Bailey had no one to turn to for help. That's when he remembered Professor Marguilies, his law school mentor, and hoped he could provide guidance with his dilemma.

"Richard, I understand your frustration."

"No, you don't. You can't fully understand my clients' injury."

Bailey now focused on the professor.

"David, they were irreparably damaged by the sins of priests. For years ignored by the Church. Often ridiculed and censored by the same institution that preached each Sunday for every Catholic to atone for their sins and pray for forgiveness."

Professor Marguilies looked intently into his friend's eyes.

"These sins *will* be punished," the professor vowed.

Chapter Six

Y OU HAVE AN ASSIGNMENT. CONTACT me immediately when you receive this communication.

Professor M.

Stefan read his e-mail and knew he would respond at his convenience. He had not heard from the professor for nearly three years. What could be so important?

Stefan walked back into his underground laboratory and continued the dissection of his subject's arm. Blood oozed from the man's forearm, and human screams echoed throughout the secluded estate. Stefan had the appropriate home for his eccentric interests. His estate encompassed thirty acres outside Zermatt along the slopes of the Matterhorn.

Stefan gently peeled his subject's skin away from the muscular forearm as the restrained, naked body struggled helplessly on the cold, steel autopsy table.

"Relax. Here, have a drink." Stefan offered his subject a snifter filled with Courvoisier, which the victim feverishly drank through a straw.

Stefan replaced one of the six cardiac electrodes that had become disconnected during the recent struggle. He had placed the ECG electrodes on his subject's chest to monitor the anticipated irregular heart tones associated with acute pain trauma.

The snifter was now empty, and the dissection continued.

Soon the desired cardiac arrhythmias commenced. The victim's heart was now beating erratically. First, with rapid heart tones, followed by numerous abnormal premature contractions. Stefan glanced toward the cardiac monitor that displayed bilious, green, erratic lines demonstrating his subject's lethal electrical activity. *This one won't last very long. Not like the others*, Stefan thought.

He was disappointed.

Shock had worked synergistically with the Courvoisier, quick to silence the earlier cries of protest.

Stefan continued his dissection of the man's chest under the soothing veil of Mahler's Ninth Symphony. Stefan always chose this movement while he worked. Mahler's technique of writing his own abnormal heart beats into this symphony fascinated Stefan. This symphony was an ideal accompaniment to Stefan's genius.

How unfortunate, though, his victim's music ended prematurely.

Stefan knew he would meet another.

Now what did the professor want?

Chapter Seven

MONDAY MORNING CAME TOO SOON.

Meghan Cahill arrived at the Renaissance Institute located in Chester County, Pennsylvania, earlier than usual. She needed the quiet time between 6:30 and 8:00 a.m. to catch up on work from last week.

Her research focused on pediatric cancers, such as neuroblastoma and medulloblastoma. She developed her passion to fight pediatric cancer because she had a healthy childhood and her grandmother always encouraged her to find ways to use her talents to help others. While a graduate student, Meghan often volunteered as a play-therapy assistant at the Children's Hospital of Philadelphia. She used her artistic talents to help sick children express their feelings through art, hopefully easing their pain and stress from cancer.

Meghan did like her schedule at the institute, usually Monday through Thursday, but she never looked forward to Monday. Living in Ocean City, New Jersey, required that she get up every Monday morning at 4:00 a.m. Meghan would then sit in her favorite room, the one filled with memories of Nana, for thirty minutes, drink caffeine, and prepare for her two-hour drive to Chester County. Meghan chose to live in Chester County during the week in her townhouse located in West Chester; there was no way she could survive a daily commute from the Jersey Shore.

"Hi, Meghan. How was your weekend?" a voice called out from behind an array of distillation glassware meticulously arranged on the laboratory counter.

"My God, you scared me, Dan. What are you doing here so early?"

Dan Rafferty was Meghan's lab assistant. Young, energetic, and always able to get the job done. Dan had worked with Meghan for the past three years. She remembered her first day at the institute. She had been timid about starting her first real job after completion of her doctorate in anatomy and pharmacology at the University of Pennsylvania School of Medicine. Dan was the only one who had given her a warm greeting at the institute. Meghan would always remember the kind words Dan spoke to her on that first day.

> "Welcome to the famous Renaissance Institute." Dan Rafferty smiled as he raised his arms in the air to present his laboratory domain to her.
>
> Meghan extended her hand and looked into Dan's face. His eyes were gentle and sincere. "Thank you for your kind reception, Dan." Meghan smiled. Can you show me where my office is located?"

Since that day, Meghan and Dan had developed a friendship and shared many private thoughts and opinions about life and relationships. Meghan eventually learned that Dan once had worked as a social worker at a hospital in Lancaster, Pennsylvania. After a few years of living a pauper's existence on a meager salary, Dan had decided to pursue graduate work in biological sciences. Working in the hospital, he was always impressed with the nurses and physicians who worked tirelessly for their patients. They had a special gift. He too wanted to do more for his patients. Dan had devoted several years to pursuing his master's degree in pharmacology. When he completed his degree, he began his career at the institute.

"Like you, I also wanted to get a jump on the week's work. You know, the stuff left over from Friday," Rafferty replied.

Dan stood up from behind the glassware and approached Meghan. She had always noticed Dan's physical features, but today, she saw him in a different way. Dan swam competitively in college and maintained his sleek, toned, six-feet-two frame well into his early thirties. His sandy blond hair was slightly thinning, and he was working on a beard, which had only a month's growth but already enough to cover his suntanned face.

Meghan realized she was staring and suddenly looked away. Her life with Jonathan was not a happy one. She knew that. She felt the emptiness in their relationship grow each day. She needed to let go.

Meghan leaned against the window that overlooked several acres of dense protected wetlands.

She began to cry.

Dan stood for a moment behind Meghan before he gently touched her shoulder. Meghan felt his touch but was embarrassed to face him. Yes, they were friends, but he never saw this side of her, and she wasn't sure if she could confide in him.

"Meghan, what's wrong?" Dan asked. Meghan remained silent and tried to regain her composure.

"Meg, it's me ... please tell me what's wrong."

Meghan remained focused on the thick wooded wetlands that Chester County protected as a safe haven for the many fowl and egrets living in the surrounding Pennsylvania countryside. She envied their safe haven.

Meghan valued Dan's friendship. He was never judgmental, and she trusted him for that; she had to confide in him.

"Dan, I'm sorry. I shouldn't act like this … but, I'm so tired of his lies and abuse. It's psychological abuse, and he's a master at it."

Meghan finally turned around and faced Dan. She saw kindness in his eyes, which met her own.

"I just can't take it anymore. I know he lies to me and doesn't care about my feelings. This past weekend, for example, Jonathan was late again. He kept me waiting for over five hours Friday night. The dinner that I spent hours to prepare for him was ruined. He told me he was working late in his lab. I knew it was a lie.

"We had plans for the weekend, but when I awoke early Saturday morning, he was gone. No note was left. Nothing. I kept getting his machine all weekend. Dan, I just don't know anymore."

Meghan and Dan had had similar conversations in the past. During the previous several months, Meghan had turned to Dan numerous times for advice after Jonathan had ignored her feelings making himself the priority in their relationship. Dan was careful not to malign Jonathan's egotistical behavior since he did not want Meghan to become defensive about her relationship with Jonathan and drive her even closer to him.

Dan sensed Meghan needed time and space to finally decide for herself what to do about Jonathan. This would be difficult for him, Dan thought, but he was willing to be patient with her. He had grown very fond of Meghan during the few years that they had worked together at the institute, often taking impromptu lunches at one of the many quaint, historic taverns located in the area. Their research work was intense, so it was a pleasure to take a break from the microscopes and laboratory milieu.

But Dan had to be honest with himself about his feelings toward Meghan. He realized Meghan had become more than just his research associate. More than his boss. And he hoped she would become more than a friend. Dan only wished he knew Meghan's feelings toward him.

—∭—

"This is crazy … working all weekend, and for what? I think he's lost it," shouted Dr. Luis Sanchez, who was alone in a spacious lab filled with over two hundred two-gallon fish tanks.

Luis Sanchez, a sixty-year-old Peruvian physician, with streaks of white coursing through his neatly combed black hair, began working at the Renaissance Institute fifteen years ago. He was fortunate to have his position since he could not obtain a US medical license with his foreign medical training. For the past five years, Luis Sanchez had worked for Dr. Jonathan Ashbridge as his lab supervisor.

Luis had accepted his fate. He liked his job at the institute and enjoyed the respect from his scientific peers at the institute. One thing was missing—any respect for Jonathan. Sanchez considered him an egotistical, immature American. He despised Jonathan since everything had come too easily for him. Clearly, Sanchez was certain, Jonathan had never worried when and from where his next meal would come when he was growing up.

Luis Sanchez remembered his hunger pains as a child. He remembered being six years old and the anxiety of waiting hours for the doctor to visit his gravely ill mother in their remote Peruvian village. Luis also remembered his anger when the doctor finally arrived in time to hear the missionary priest's prayers at his mother's grave.

Luis Sanchez knew Jonathan was clueless about life. But Luis also knew that he had to work with him to keep his job at the institute and support his family.

Luis Sanchez accepted his fate.

Luis continued his examination of the zebra fish embryo through his high-powered electron microscope. So far, his examination had not revealed the anticipated mutation; he was not discouraged, however. He still had hundreds of fish embryos to examine, though time was limited. "The research project must be completed within the month," Jonathan had commanded.

But why the sudden change in the protocol's timetable? Jonathan had remained elusive when Luis questioned him about the sudden urgency. Luis's two lab assistants, Emily DeHaven and Jeffrey Manion, however, did not question Jonathan early Saturday morning when he had called them into work. Emily knew Jonathan all too well; he never cared about them or their weekend plans.

Luis, however, did care about his assistants. They were individuals with lives separate from the "Sacred Institute." In fact, Luis had hired both of them long before Jonathan's arrival at the institute. He knew them well, and they deserved to be treated better.

Luis particularly liked Emily DeHaven from the first moment they met. A young, recent graduate from University of the Sciences in Philadelphia, Emily had earned her doctorate degree in pharmacology and was now ready to take on the world. Emily had impressed Luis with her sincere commitment to work long hours, and her appreciation for loyalty among her coworkers. Over the years, her enthusiasm was often a much needed remedy to revive Luis's disappointment with a research setback or failure.

On occasion, to recognize and support Luis's devotion to his work, the institute would endorse his research project that was theoretically avant-garde. Within a short time, Luis's pharmaceutical research consistently received credibility at the Renaissance Institute and in the scientific community at-large, as his projects quickly yielded beneficial results for both the institute and drug consumers.

But Luis refused to take all the credit. He recognized that his success was dependent on the close- working relationship among his coworkers. He also recognized the important role Emily often played as the devil's advocate with each proposed project.

During the monthly Research and Development meetings, each researcher was required to defend his proposed research protocol, while his peers evaluated the project's scientific merits. With her grayish-blue eyes set above soft cheek bones gently speckled with freckles, Emily would scrutinize her colleague's face while he offered her a defense. She would not interrupt at first but showed her impatience and silent rebuttal with smirks of disbelief. Her habit of then looking off into the distance and running her hands through her hair was disarming to a researcher who was not familiar with her tactics.

The analysis exercise provided valuable feedback, however, for the final arbiter—CEO Farraday. Farraday enjoyed this power. Survival of the fittest, as he termed these meetings, was good for the institute. He encouraged competition among his research lab divisions, which was comprised of three separate divisions, each of which competed for institute revenue.

Emily DeHaven's verbal assault on Jeffrey Manion suddenly interrupted Luis Sanchez's concentration on his zebra fish embryo, as the lab assistants stormed into the laboratory.

"All right, what's it this time?" Luis emitted a subtle smile from behind his microscope.

Jeffrey pleaded his case. "I'm trying to show Emily she's wrong, but she won't let me finish."

Emily strode across the ceramic floor with her hands resting comfortably in the side pockets of her pristine white lab coat. Jeffrey hurried close behind, demanding her attention.

"Emily, will you listen, God damn it. Your idiotic theory about Jonathan's project ... your claim that it will develop viruses and genetic coding to manipulate behavior and cause aggression is totally wrong. You're crazy. Our project is designed to use safe viruses to transport genes to the amygdala. At that location in the brain, these genes would create proteins that would stop synapse formation. We have already discovered, as you know, that *increased* nerve branching synapse formation in the brain, specifically at the amygdala, will cause *increased* anxiety from stress. You know ... feelings of desperate hyperactivity and loss of control. Our research will block those areas in the brain that would create that anxiety. As a result, we will discover drugs to treat and cure all forms of anxiety." Jeffrey continued his rebuttal as he waved his arms in the air as if to remove any obstacle that prevented Emily from hearing his complaint.

"Believe it or not, Emily, Jonathan's motives are humanitarian and not self-serving. Our project will, in fact, cure psychotic diseases and potentially all mental illnesses."

Emily kept her back toward Jeffrey. She knew she was right about the potential abuse of the project. Her uneasy feeling about Jonathan's work troubled her during the past few weeks.

Why did Jeffrey always dismiss her inquiries about his time spent in the quarantine lab located on the basement floor of the Renaissance Institute? At times, she noticed Jonathan and Jeffrey deep in conversation, only to abruptly go silent whenever she approached them. At first, she ignored their little secretive game. But her visceral suspicion of their covert activities kept gnawing at her.

Emily had enough. She finally turned toward Jeffrey, who continued muttering his objections to an unsympathetic Peruvian physician.

"Jeffrey, will you ever grow up and think for yourself? Or is Jonathan your appointed deity?" Emily challenged.

Jeffrey threw up his arms in disgust and stormed out of the lab.

"Once again, Emily, I think you won," lauded Sanchez.

Emily's smile, which showed her appreciation for Luis's support, soon took on a somber expression as she surveyed the lab to ensure that they were alone.

"Luis, there's something just not right."

"What do you mean, Emily?"

"I don't know exactly. There's a feeling I have about them. You know ... Jonathan and Jeffrey."

Luis pushed his chair back away from the microscope and faced Emily. "What is it?"

Emily moved closer to Luis. "I don't trust them."

Luis Sanchez had had the same concern for the past several weeks. He had chosen not to confide in Emily since she was young, and he didn't want to burden her with his concerns. But, he also didn't like to see her this way. Afraid and apprehensive.

Luis stood up and gently placed his hands on Emily's shoulders.

"I agree. I don't trust them either."

Chapter Eight

THE DECAYING, DISSECTED CORPSE FLOATED through the current within the dark depths of Lake Lucerne. The violated human form resembled a protozoan with its eviscerated bowel contents oscillating through the lake's murky water like a flagella.

A pair of warped wooden docks reached out like arthritic twisted arms onto the lake's smooth surface and seemed to embrace this abandoned human refuse and offer a final, peaceful resting place.

Stefan turned and found Maria asleep, curled beside him, her naked body warm and pressed against him. It was still very early, the last

Monday morning in August. Stefan had the entire day free. He was in no hurry to fall back asleep.

Maria had been great. She had responded to Stefan's every desire last evening. But, Stefan wanted more.

He slowly touched her slender body; she was still asleep, curled face-down against the black silk sheets. He caressed her smooth back and gently massaged her toned thighs.

Maria began to breathe heavily.

Each subtle stroke against Maria's inner thighs elicited soft, rhythmic sighs. Stefan pulled the sheet away from Maria and exposed her back. He skillfully ran his fingers across Maria's lower back and explored an area that had been covered by her thong. This area had been protected from the sun's rays and stood out in contrast against Maria's bronzed skin.

Maria responded. She slowly spread her legs farther apart and anticipated each new caress with a nervous tremor. Stefan sensed her excitement and slowly guided Maria onto her back. He moved his hand across Maria's petite but firm breasts and softly kissed her abdomen. Maria separated her legs farther apart.

"Please … I want you," Maria urged.

Maria pulled Stefan on top of her and firmly guided him inside her. They responded to each other with rhythmic artistry. Soon, Maria grabbed Stefan's arms and wrapped her legs around his lower back. He responded to her movements but chose not to reach his climax. Instead, he focused on her.

Stefan sensed that Maria was close as she began pulling him deeper inside her. Despite Maria's forceful thrusts, Stefan gently placed his lips against her moist neck and breasts.

Maria could not hold back any longer. She released a muffled cry as her tensed body repeatedly arched within Stefan's embrace. Stefan held Maria for several minutes. He felt her warm breath against his cheek and sensed her need for stillness.

Stefan would remember Maria for her sensual strength and spontaneity.

He was first attracted to her while he was on his third martini, relaxing at the unique, outdoor, thirty-foot schooner bar dry-docked at the entrance to *Mood's*, located in Zermatt, Switzerland, at the base of the Matterhorn. Maria had intrigued him last evening with her solitary entrance at Zermatt's popular bar. As she walked toward the outdoor schooner bar, her toned, petite frame moved confidently within her ankle-length, black, cotton dress. Maria found an empty chair at the bar next to Stefan and without hesitation requested *Mood's* driest Chardonnay. Soon, Stefan engaged Maria in conversation, which was rudely interrupted by a group of young, male American tourists. Stefan leaned back in his chair and enjoyed Maria's biting exchange with them, easily dominating them on content and style. Sensing defeat, the three college students retreated and regrouped for another strike at another Zermatt bar. Maria never claimed victory over her fellow countrymen but calmly resumed her last thought with Stefan.

Maria had a sense for timing. She also had a sense for intimacy. Stefan recognized these qualities, as she would place her hand first on his arm, and then on his thigh, while she was making a point on a particular topic.

Stefan often found his way to *Mood's*, a haven for reflection, located several miles from his estate. He had met Maria only several hours after his laboratory exercise had ended prematurely. She was a pleasant diversion from his obsession, his relentless need to discover the inner matrix of another human being.

Stefan quietly left his bed while Maria still slept. He knew it had been several hours since he had received the professor's e-mail. It had been several years since he had last worked with him. Stefan was curious about why his services were needed once again.

Stefan parted the lace curtains covering his second-floor dormer bedroom window and gazed out on the distant, awakening town of Zermatt.

How many lives had been changed through the night in such a few short hours? Stefan wondered.

Stefan knew he had changed three lives.

His own and two strangers'.

Each one needed excitement in their lives.

Each one experienced pleasure.

He was the facilitator.

He knew this truth.

Stefan had come to believe it.

Chapter Nine

THE PROFESSOR ENJOYED HIS Low Country hideaway along the South Carolina coast for many reasons. Foremost was the privacy created by an almost uninterrupted perimeter of oak trees cloaked in Spanish moss. Along the trees ran a narrow and solitary mile-long dirt path that led to his southern recluse.

The unpaved road resembled a serpent as it twisted unpredictably through the dense brush and marsh terrain. An evening drive by an inexperienced intruder along the dark road, bordered on each side by a five-foot precipice sloping down to a motionless marsh, would result in a quick and silent demise amid the beckoning tidewater darkness.

The entrance to the professor's reclusive drive was easily overlooked by tourists. Only a few Low Country locals knew of this road, and they obeyed the unwritten code never to disturb his privacy. The locals had created many stories about the mysterious path and what secrets lay at the end of it.

The professor would have it no other way. His Low Country haven was a three-story, gray stone house with a 180-degree wrap-around porch that overlooked his personal wildlife refuge. He was willing to share his isolation with only the egrets, herons, and other indigenous birds that, like him, sought a haven from life's turmoil.

Just as much as he enjoyed the cacophonous sounds of a late evening in New York City, the professor also found inner calm with the soft sounds of the rarely seen but often-heard clapper rail marsh hen with its distinctive, rapid, monotone *tick-tick* signals. His favorite, however, was the great blue heron. Despite its graceful and majestic presence, standing tall and aloof with its slate-blue plumes streaked with black and white, the great blue would stride effortlessly through the dark pools of the marsh in search of food, and with its bright cadmium yellow beak ruthlessly spear its unsuspecting prey with lightning precision.

The professor often gazed out upon the tidewater from his desk and admired how the heron's prey was always well chosen; its method of stalking a victim was flawless. Once the prey was chosen, whether a snake or fish or even an immature alligator, the heron's pursuit was relentless. With each graceful step carefully placed within the still water, the heron would advance closer and closer to its victim. For hours, the professor would observe this rapacious trait of the solitary hunter and wait to raise his wine glass in honor of a successful strike.

Another sunset began to shed its brilliant orange and violet hues upon the darkening tideland. This time of the evening was the professor's favorite. Taking advantage of the shadows that cloaked the marsh as evening approached, the heron gently approached its target. The distant, subtle splash signaled to the professor that a toast was due.

This evening, as was his custom, the professor ate his dinner on the wooden veranda overlooking his salt marsh treasure. With Mozart's Clarinet Concerto well underway, Professor Marguilies poured another glass of Brunello di Montalcino to accompany his medium-rare prime rib entree. He enjoyed eating almost as much as he thrived on his meticulous culinary preparation. The professor sat back in his cushioned rattan armchair, beneath pewter fans that were positioned along the entire length of the veranda's sloped ceiling. He took pleasure in his twilight collation, meditating on the eccentricities of his marsh ecosystem.

Decaying tree stalks projected their limbless existence from beneath the murky marsh toward the darkening sky, as if searching the heavens for a reprieve from nature's death sentence. The professor acknowledged a vital purpose for the marsh's jagged extremities.

Their death served a noble purpose, he thought.

Parasitic life forms used the decaying tree wood as their hideout. However, the many indigenous Low Country birds, night hawks, and plovers knew the insects' safe house and often invaded their privacy to feast on their succulent meat.

Intertwined circles of life and death were an integral part of the professor's tideland ecosystem. The professor, in fact, had designed his Pegasus Project to mirror the marshland's life and death drama. Human subjects would be chosen for the Pegasus Project with meticulous care. There was no escape for the professor's prey. His pursuit would be patient and relentless.

To feed the hungry.

Free the oppressed.

Heal the injured.

The Sins of the Fishers of Men would be gravely punished. The professor lived this truth.

The Fishermen of the Catholic Church had chosen their innocent victims with great care. These Fishers of Men, Christ's representatives in the Church, were relentless in their pursuit to devour their victims' innocence.

Their freedom.

Their sanity.

These "holy" guardians of children had used religious authority to cloak their wicked and deviant perversion. The professor knew where these guilty clerics lived, hidden and protected from the legal system; he knew of their safe house. These priests were now the prey. Their unpunished, protected depravity had received a death sentence.

The Pegasus Project was their executioner.

The professor finished his meal and left the veranda while the marsh pond still mirrored the sunset's pink and indigo hues. He entered the library, a room with floor-to-ceiling cherry wood shelves that were built into the stone wall behind the professor's desk. The shelves were filled with a collection of early Dickens books along with several works by Hemingway, his favorite. One in particular, *The Old Man and the Sea*, he had obtained from a remote, countryside bookstore in Cuba. This particular edition had an original Hemingway-signed introduction on yellow, aged paper.

The professor had traveled to Cuba several years ago, departing from Mexico City at a time when the US State Department restricted all travel to this Caribbean island. Professor Marguilies considered the restriction a mere trivial inconvenience. If he wanted to travel to Cuba, no one, not even his own country, could stop him. There were methods to circumvent this government-imposed political game. The professor knew them all.

It had been hours since the professor last checked his computer for a reply from Stefan. He had sent his original message to Stefan a week ago. He felt sure Stefan had received his e-mail. But he knew Stefan's game. His need for control. His eccentric life.

The professor faced his computer and again searched for Stefan's reply. This time his search was successful.

> *Professor*
>
> *Interesting that you now choose to contact me. How long has it been? You and I both know that answer. I see you still need my services.*
>
> *I have no commitments now.*
>
> *You are fortunate.*
>
> *A minor detail to attend to, however. Looking forward to your assignment.*
>
> *S.*

The professor smiled as he leaned back in his leather chair behind a nineteenth-century mahogany desk. There was no one else he would hire to execute the project.

Stefan never failed.

Chapter Ten

EMILY DeHAVEN WAS NOT HAPPY.

It was Saturday, Labor Day weekend, and she was confined to her lab at the Renaissance Institute, searching for a mutation within hundreds of zebra fish embryos. There was one consolation. Her friend, Dr. Luis Sanchez, was working beside her, focused on the same goal.

Emily pushed her chair away from her high-powered microscope.

"My God, why is Jonathan pushing us so hard? We work crazy hours all week only to be rewarded with working Labor Day weekend. I just don't like it." Emily slammed her fist down on the gray granite lab counter.

Luis did not like working the weekend either, being away from his family, but he chose not to react with the same emotional intensity. Luis still felt a paternal obligation to Emily. Even though he agreed with her,

Luis felt the last thing their research project needed was an emotional meltdown.

His job now was twofold: console and encourage Emily, and search for the God-damned mutation.

"Emily, you've worked long enough … you deserve a break."

Emily sighed. She didn't need any further prodding.

"I won't be long," Emily called out as she pushed against the laboratory glass-wired protective door.

Luis Sanchez soon felt a sudden wave of nausea accompany the audible hunger from his stomach. He realized he had worked through lunch, and the fact that he had eaten breakfast at 5:00 a.m., nearly nine hours ago, only reminded him of Jonathan's obsessive agenda for his research study.

But what could he possibly do about Jonathan's insane timetable? Luis only wished he had more authority and didn't feel so helpless.

Luis Sanchez moved onto the next zebra fish tank and carefully removed a group of fish eggs, which he gently separated and placed into a glass Petrie dish filled with warm salt water. Sanchez now focused his attention on what seemed to be the millionth embryo specimen. The high-resolution electron microscope slowly revealed the embryo's hidden quiescent world.

Oh my God … the mutation.

"I found it," Sanchez whispered at first and then stood up.

"I found it!" he shouted.

Luis quickly scanned the lab for Emily, who had been gone for ten minutes now. He wished Emily had found it first. It was his paternal nature at work.

Luis understood the scientific impact that this particular mutation discovery, using fish embryos, would have on future genetic research development. Traditional research had always been conducted on rodents, monkeys, and some domestic animals. Their daily care could be expensive and difficult to maintain, especially if laboratory space was limited. Luis now showed that the zebra fish, a hardy, tropical fish species, was an extremely economical research subject. Their care and maintenance required only fundamental temperature and pH control of their saltwater tank environment. And equipment was cheap. The hundreds of two-gallon tanks were purchased at a nominal price.

Not only were zebra fish more economical to use in research, their embryos allowed researchers to more quickly and easily analyze drug effects on offspring, rather than waste time waiting the weeks or months of gestation for the birth of one of the more traditional research animals.

Time, money, and productivity were essential markers used to measure success in medical research. Even though Luis despised Jonathan's obsession for personal gain, he still had to give Jonathan credit for his innovative concept and the development of a protocol to use these aquatic research subjects. However difficult it was, Luis did acknowledge Jonathan's intelligence.

Luis was lost in thought, distracted from reality with his new genetic creation. He had just found Jonathan's genetic mutation that altered the embryo's central nervous system—its brain.

"Luis, what's the matter?"

Luis Sanchez jumped as Emily's strained voice cried out. He turned and saw her standing near the doorway, breathing heavily. When she had heard Luis's shouts echo from within the laboratory, she sprinted the remaining fifty yards back to the lab.

"Luis, what's wrong?" Emily repeated. Not receiving an answer, she walked closer to Luis. His aging, small body was shaking, and his heavily wrinkled hands trembled as he clenched them tightly against his chest. His heart pounded inside his chest, which caused him to struggle for each breath. Luis wanted to speak but could not find the strength. He could only stare into Emily's concerned eyes.

Emily needed to be told about the discovery, but Luis couldn't find the words. She had to be shown instead.

Luis reached down and grabbed Emily's hands; her skin's warmth felt good against his ice-cold fingers. He then guided Emily over to his chair and pointed to the object beneath his microscope.

Emily adjusted the focus. Within seconds, the solitary zebra fish embryo revealed its secret. Emily could hardly believe it. The embryo's brain had received their drug that had been injected into its zebra fish parents. Their study drug had in fact arrived at the predicted location deep inside the fish embryo's brain that controlled behavior. Emily didn't want to look away for fear that this tiny egg would be lost, along with any evidence of their discovery.

"My God, Luis. We've done it. We've isolated the region in the brain responsible for emotions and behavior!"

Finally, Luis found strength to speak as he took hold of Emily's shoulders.

"Do you really know what this means? By being able to send our drug to the amygdala—the part of the brain that controls all forms of behavior—we can identify abnormal areas in the brain and correct abnormal brain structure and function. Emily, millions of people afflicted with many neurologic diseases now have hope for a cure. Patients with uncontrollable and dangerous urges can now be cured. Their years of suffering and premature death can be eradicated. In fact, even pathological criminal behavior can be controlled and cured."

Luis brought Emily closer to him and embraced her. Their many hours of hard work had finally paid off. This was a time for celebration, but Luis was troubled. He, like Emily, didn't trust Jonathan's motives. He feared this discovery could be potentially abused. Instead of changing abnormal, diseased regions in the brain back into normal tissue again, a researcher could use their discovery to change normal, healthy brain tissue into diseased tissue—turn a normal, healthy person into a psychotic criminal.

Luis prayed he was wrong.

He needed only to hear the word mutation and witness their reaction to know that the Pegasus Project's first stage was successfully completed.

Jeffrey Manion stood for a few more minutes in the hallway near the open laboratory door. He had chosen to keep his presence hidden and not follow Emily too closely down the corridor as she sprinted toward the lab. Jeffrey also had heard the Peruvian doctor's muffled screams. Instead of joining Emily, Jeffrey wanted to hear and observe her honest interaction with Luis. Over the past few weeks, Jeffrey had sensed their unspoken suspicion of his work with Jonathan.

His research work with Jonathan in the quarantine lab located in the Renaissance Institute's basement was off-limits to all other personnel, especially Emily and Luis. Jonathan's subterranean lab was protected by a fingerprint analysis system, which had been constructed at certain locations throughout the institute. Each person employed at the institute was required to submit his or her thumb print to a central data bank for identification and access at designated areas in the institute's complex. But not all individuals were given permission to enter the secured areas, such as the subterranean lab. Meghan Cahill was not one of the chosen few to have access to Jonathan's lab. Jonathan had seen to that. He had devised a computerized access code that recognized only his and Jeffrey's thumb prints. They were the only ones permitted inside the quarantine lab.

Jeffrey knew he must contact Jonathan immediately. It was already September 3, and Jonathan's timetable demanded completion of stage two before October 1.

His research for stage two of the Pegasus Project therefore had to start immediately.

It had already been decided that the second stage of the Pegasus Project would be performed in the quarantine lab. Only Jonathan and Jeffrey would be permitted in that lab.

Jeffrey agreed with Jonathan that Farraday was an obstacle to the success of the project. Farraday had to be removed from the institute.

Jonathan would take care of him. He had assured Jeffrey. Jeffrey's role was to focus on Emily and Luis. He was to be Jonathan's eyes and ears inside Luis Sanchez's lab.

Jeffrey turned away from the laboratory doorway and hurried down the hallway. He had to find Jonathan immediately.

Chapter Eleven

MEGHAN LOVED LABOR DAY WEEKEND at the Shore. It signaled the end of summer for thousands of tourists. The end of vehicle and people congestion. The end of annoying crowds that polluted the pristine beach all summer long.

Fortunately, Meghan's beach house was located at the north end of Ocean City, in the Gardens, where many homeowners chose not to rent for the summer. She appreciated her neighbors' mutual need for privacy; she felt safe within her Gardens recluse.

During the summer months, Meghan often avoided Ocean City's downtown area and limited her outdoor activity to running along the secluded beach near her house or along the streets of her quiet neighborhood. Her favorite run started along the beach, turned onto Gull Road, then onto Beach Boulevard, and eventually to Gardens Parkway, which took her to the Ocean City-Longport Bridge. Running across the mile-long bridge, Meghan often had to share the road with cars and cyclists traveling into Longport and other northern coastal towns. She would then turn around, usually when she reached Margate, and finish her several-mile run back at Nana's Victorian home on Gull Road.

Meghan loved an aggressive run. She often sprinted the last mile to her beach house where the smell of fresh salt air blowing in off the ocean would fill her lungs and let her know she was coming home.

To Nana's home.

To Nana. Her kindred spirit.

Meghan remained standing on her deck that overlooked the ocean, lost in thought until a sudden change in wind and current drove waves crashing against the beach below her. She wasn't sure what had caused this abrupt change in the surf since the sky remained cloudless, but she felt something was wrong.

Meghan's phone rang.

She had caller ID; it was Jonathan.

Meghan's body stiffened. She waited for the message.

"Meghan, pick up … Meghan, where are you?"

His tone was different. Not the usual self-assured, intimidating voice.

"Meghan, please call me on my cell phone. I found something … some artwork that I know you'll want. It's important."

Meghan still resented Jonathan for his abrupt departure from her bedroom last weekend. She resented his lies. His demeaning treatment of her. She had not seen or heard from him in over a week. His mental cruelty, his disregard for her feelings had intensified over the past few months. Not only did he use her whenever he wanted, Jonathan also manipulated her feelings. He seemed to have changed, ever since his business meeting several months ago near Charleston, South Carolina. Jonathan was not the same person since that week he had spent at a pharmaceutical think-tank seminar.

Dan made her realize how much she had endured during her stormy relationship with Jonathan. Meghan's discussion with Dan last week had eased some of the pain that Jonathan had caused her. Dan was thoughtful and caring. He had allowed her to vent and never became judgmental.

After speaking with Dan, she had felt a calm, healing presence enter her confused and troubled mind.

Meghan was grateful to Dan for being there for her. Recently, she began to wonder about Dan's feelings toward her. Did he only consider her as a friend? She never remembered him speak of having a current romantic relationship.

Meghan knew she had revealed her vulnerability to Dan that morning in the lab. Dan had been patient with her, never interrupting her, never telling her what she should do. He had remained quiet and listened to her angry and frustrated account of her life with Jonathan.

She deserved a better life.

Meghan wondered what Jonathan wanted now. He sounded different on the phone. His voice seemed sincere, like it was during the first couple of months when they were together.

They were good times, she fondly remembered.

What did Jonathan mean about her wanting artwork?

Jonathan Ashbridge entered New Jersey from the Commodore Barry Bridge. It was Saturday afternoon, Labor Day weekend. Most of the Shore traffic had already passed over the bridge from Pennsylvania. He knew Meghan was either at home or taking one of her runs along the beach.

Jonathan needed to speak with her now. He needed to have her in front of him.

To talk with her and explain.

She would understand his absence. His neglect.

He was sure of that.

He shifted his BMW into fifth gear and hugged the South Jersey country road with a defiant confidence that he knew would easily taunt a NASCAR competitor.

Jonathan controlled his environment. He would control CEO

Farraday's destiny. He only needed to maintain his control over Meghan.

Jonathan would give her a chance to make things right. One final chance to make it right for him.

Just yesterday, Farraday had met with Jonathan at the institute and made it very clear that as of October 1, there would be no trace of his genetic research at the Renaissance Institute. All of Jonathan's research space and allocated money would be given to Meghan Cahill. Farraday had told him further that Meghan had far more important research protocols that needed development. Jonathan's space and money devoted to his fish hobby, as Farraday termed it, would no longer exist after September.

Adding insult to injury, Farraday announced that Meghan Cahill would become the new vice president of Research and Development at the institute. Jonathan, if he wished, could remain as her assistant vice president. Or he could leave. Farraday didn't care one way or another.

The Pegasus Project was now in stage two of development. The mutation had been discovered. Jeffrey's surveillance at the lab yielded valuable information for Jonathan. Jeffrey served a useful purpose— feed Jonathan vital information that Luis and Emily may not be willing to disclose to him right away. Their drug that caused the neurologic mutation in the fish embryo's brain now required experimentation in animals. Would this drug, which was taken to the brain by their virus carrier-gene, cause the desired abnormal behavior in animal subjects? This question was vital to the project and required an answer as soon as possible. But Jonathan and the project needed more time for completion of stage two. The success of his project would be his legacy in the scientific community.

Jonathan Ashbridge guided his black sports car off Route 9 and approached the 34th Street bridge, his access to Ocean City and to the one who could ruin his life. CEO Farraday's threat to end his work and replace him with Cahill would never become a reality. Jonathan would see to that.

One solitary chance. It would be Meghan's decision whether to accept Farraday's destructive plan to end Jonathan's career or to choose life.

Her life.

Her survival.

Jonathan would give her one chance to decide. Accept his plan to remove Farraday, or die. The choice was simple. He only hoped Meghan felt the same way.

Chapter Twelve

NEARLY TWENTY MINUTES HAD PASSED since Meghan received Jonathan's message. She wanted to ignore it. She wanted him out of her life. She even tried to erase his voice from her memory, but as she stared at the red blinking light on her machine, Meghan remembered the tone of his voice. It somehow seemed genuine.

Meghan wanted to believe in him.

During their first few months together, Jonathan had always provided her with strength and encouragement. Always believing in her. Urging her to accept her grandmother's death and enjoy life. And continue to paint.

When she first met him at one of the pharmaceutical conferences, it was only several months since Nana had left her world. She was devastated by her death, lost in a world filled with meaningless work, faceless people, and insignificant details. Meghan's life had always revolved around Nana.

They were inseparable. Often, they would spend hours on the beach trying to predict the evolving color tones of the sunset and then return to the beach house to work at their easels and capture the innocence of the fragile sunset's splendor with their soft brush strokes.

Meghan missed Nana's gentle touch. She needed to hear her voice. See her face. Meghan also missed the silence they shared when they would walk along the shore, watching the gulls display their artistry as they floated effortlessly on the sea breeze. Many times they admired the avian acrobats swoop down from the clouds high above the ocean's surface and then dance across the stage of white-capped waves.

With Nana's death, Meghan's artistry died also. She lost her spirit to create. There was no purpose any longer. She merely put in time and looked at her existence with anger. Why should she enjoy life? Her best friend, her kindred spirit, was taken from her. Nana still had so much more to teach her.

About art and life.

About herself.

And then Jonathan came into her life. It was one of those moments when time stood still. Jonathan had first glanced at her from across the dining room in a Connecticut bed and breakfast where the pharmaceutical conference was held.

CEO Farraday had chosen this location as his corporate retreat for the executive members of the Renaissance Institute and its laboratory research directors. Meghan was a new director at the institute and participated reluctantly at the Connecticut retreat. She was willing to comply with the institute's directive to attend only because it gave her the chance to revisit her "second home." Meghan loved the time she had spent at Yale, driving along the coast with friends to discover another quaint restaurant or to paint in one of the many fishing towns nestled along the Sound.

The weekend retreat was a welcome surprise for Meghan. She expected three days and two nights of boredom, sequestered with academicians and corporate over-achievers. Instead, the weekend flew by. Since meeting Jonathan, her time was always occupied. Not just with the meetings and New Age corporate games, but rather, a return to her former life in Connecticut. Only this time, Jonathan was a part of her life.

He wanted to know everything about her world.

Everything about her life.

Her desires and passions.

Meghan believed in him.

—⋙—

Meghan's phone rang again. She knew it was him. Should she allow Jonathan back into her life? Could she trust him?

Meghan answered the phone.

"Hello." Meghan tried to sound confident. She did not want Jonathan to hear any emotion in her voice. Not sadness. Not loneliness. She wanted Jonathan to hear a mature woman. Happy with her life. Confident without him.

"Meghan, I hoped you would be home. I called earlier and left a message … Did you listen to it?" Jonathan paused a few seconds to allow Meghan a chance to speak. He viewed her continued silence as her way to control him.

How naive she was to think she could manipulate him.

She was an amateur.

Jonathan played along. He had to see her to resolve the issue with Farraday. Jonathan began his portrayal of the guilty and remorseful lover.

"Meghan, I'm really sorry for hurting you so many times. I wasn't fair to you. You deserve better."

Jonathan paused again. This time he heard Meghan sigh deeply. He sensed he was gaining some ground with her. The artwork. Jonathan decided it was time to tell her about the artwork.

"Meghan, I have something important to tell you. You won't believe it, but I found an oil painting that you must have. I saw it at an estate sale in Chester County."

Jonathan waited a moment for her response.

"Meghan, did you hear me?"

"I'm listening." Meghan remembered his earlier message about some important art piece. Jonathan did share her interest in painting and probably found a unique work that he would use as a peace offering.

Jonathan continued.

"The oil painting is quite striking. It shows a young girl sitting on a jetty, staring out on the ocean at a passing sail boat. And Meghan, you know the artist."

Jonathan took a breath.

"Meghan, it was painted by Nana."

"What did you just say?" Meghan felt her heart beat faster.

"It was Nana's painting. Meghan, remember the one you told me about when we first met? You were seven years old, and you remembered Nana sketching you as you sat by the ocean one early morning waiting for the sunrise. You told me you never saw the completed work. You always thought Nana had probably completed it years later while you were away at college. You thought she may have given the painting to your parents as a gift. But, you told me that you never were able to find it after they died. Somehow the painting was sold at their estate sale shortly after their car accident." Jonathan sensed Meghan's excitement as he heard her breaths hasten and become more shallow as the story unfolded.

"Meghan, I've got the painting. I gave an antique dealer a deposit to hold it for a week."

Meghan was overwhelmed with the idea that she would finally see this treasured painting of Nana's. Meghan realized that she was equally excited with the realization that Jonathan really did care for her.

"Jonathan, my God, I can't believe it. You are so good to me. How can I ever repay you for this surprise?"

"You know that's not necessary. I simply love you very much and need to give you this special painting. You need to have it after all these years."

Jonathan paused to allow Meghan to absorb the meaning of his words.

"Meghan, I just arrived in Ocean City. Can I come over to see you?"

"Of course, Jonathan. Please hurry."

Jonathan slowly maneuvered his BMW through Ocean City's congested Labor Day traffic. Jonathan wasn't surprised with Meghan's reaction. He was always confident with his ability to know people well and identify their basic needs for survival and happiness.

Meghan's character was not complicated.

He learned her basic needs early on in their relationship. Jonathan knew what Meghan needed to survive.

Chapter Thirteen

Jonathan's BMW cruised down Central Avenue into Ocean City's Gardens section, where he was pleased to find a respite from the Labor Day weekend traffic. He could see why Meghan preferred to live in the Gardens. It was quieter here. The homes were spaced farther apart. People were able to breathe here. The sea breeze always seemed to be a bit stronger in this northern section of town.

Jonathan liked it here. If things worked out the way he planned, Jonathan saw himself sharing Meghan's beach house with her.

But only on his terms.

Jonathan turned onto the white pebble, circular drive in front of Meghan's home. As he expected, she was standing on the front porch waiting for him.

Waiting for him once again.

"Jonathan, my God, what took you so long? It doesn't matter. You're here now." Meghan ran down the gray stone porch steps and embraced Jonathan with a forgiving touch. He felt her petite body press firmly against him. Her ivory cotton sundress with its low-cut lace neckline exposed her suntanned chest. Her petite but firm breasts softly revealed themselves through the thin cotton material.

"God, I missed you," Jonathan whispered.

"Let's go inside," Meghan urged. "I have some chilled wine waiting for us out on the deck. There is also a nice cool breeze off the ocean. Jonathan, it's a perfect afternoon."

Jonathan smiled. He had to admit that Meghan did excite him. Meghan always responded to him with honesty. Even though her touch was always sincere, Jonathan still questioned whether he could continue this relationship with her. Farraday planned to give Jonathan's research money to Meghan. He now must know if Meghan would be loyal to him and refuse Farraday's offer.

Jonathan knew he would have that answer soon.

Meghan would be allowed only one choice.

She would decide her fate.

Jonathan felt comfortable on Meghan's deck overlooking the calm sea as he relaxed on one of her cushioned chaise lounges. Meghan walked onto the deck and handed Jonathan a glass of Jacob's Creek Chardonnay. Meghan took the last sip from her wine glass and placed the empty glass on the E.P. Henry gray-brick deck floor. She turned and faced Jonathan as she leaned against the black wrought iron gate that formed a half-wall around the deck. The warm late-afternoon sun enticed Meghan to lift her sundress up around her waist and expose her thighs. The ocean breeze was a welcome relief for Meghan as the cool air softly soothed her skin.

Jonathan stared at Meghan and liked what he saw. Her pale green eyes revealed her innocence, her vulnerability.

Jonathan remembered the first time he looked into her eyes—into her soul. It was in Connecticut at the institute's conference. Her presence in the bed and breakfast lounge seemed surreal to him. She moved gracefully amidst the crowd of corporate suits, who did not notice her as they lobbied one another for their own research agenda.

But Jonathan did notice her. She was different from the others. Even though her body moved before him across the room, Jonathan sensed her mind—her spirit—was someplace else far away. It was as if her body was on loan only to perform the perfunctory duty of attending the institute's New Age think-tank workshop.

This woman intrigued him. Jonathan needed to know more about her. He wanted to know where she really was at this moment. He needed to talk to her now. Not lose the moment; not let her slip away. That evening in Connecticut was the first time he stared into her eyes.

Innocent and vulnerable.

Jonathan liked what he saw.

"Jonathan, I can't wait any longer. When can we pick up Nana's painting?" Meghan asked as she walked across the deck and sat beside Jonathan.

"Soon. I told the woman at the antique shop I'd probably be back next weekend. Maybe on Saturday."

"Can't we pick it up any sooner?" Meghan pleaded.

"No. Something about her closing her shop for a few days to bid on estate antiques somewhere in Vermont."

Meghan was disappointed. She poured another glass of wine and walked back to the edge of the deck where the wrought-iron fence provided her with the only protection from a two-story fall to the beach below.

Jonathan stood up and walked toward Meghan. He allowed a few feet between them before he paused and gazed out beyond her toward the sea that now churned its waters into white-capped waves.

His hands gently touched her shoulders and pulled her closer to him.

She had one chance to decide.

"Meghan, there's something I have to talk to you about. It's important ... it concerns Farraday."

Meghan saw an abrupt change in Jonathan. He looked worried.

"Farraday wants to take away all of my research money. He intends to contact NIH and have them rescind my research grant."

Jonathan tightened his grasp on Meghan's shoulders. "He even wants our board of directors to withdraw all Renaissance support for my research."

"But why does he want to do that to you?" Meghan asked.

"Farraday wants to ruin me. He sees me as a threat to him. He thinks I'm undermining him. Farraday is convinced the board of directors will give him a vote of no confidence at their next meeting in October and appoint me as the new acting chief executive officer. Meghan, he's crazy," Jonathan's voice cracked. His eyes slowly filled with tears.

Meghan felt her legs weaken, shocked at this sudden display of emotional distress. She had never seen Jonathan distraught. In fact, she had never seen him worry about anything. Meghan raised her hands and gently held Jonathan's face.

"What can I do to help?"

Jonathan paused a few seconds and then whispered his rehearsed reply.

"I don't know if there is anything you can do, Meghan. Actually, I haven't told you the whole story."

"What do you mean?"

"Farraday plans to take my research money and give it all to you. He wants to give you more support for your research projects."

"Why?" Meghan asked.

"For two reasons. One, he thinks your projects deserve more attention and more financial support than they've received so far. Meghan, believe me, I think he's right about that. You're doing great work at the institute."

Meghan quickly dismissed the compliment. "And the second?"

"Farraday wants to reward you at my expense. I've told you he sees me as a personal threat. It's true; I have constantly challenged his effectiveness. I think his philosophy for the institute is archaic and will eventually ruin the institute. Meghan, I won't stand for that."

"But Jonathan, I don't understand—what could I possibly do to help?"

"Refuse the money. Stand with me and fight him. Help me expose his incompetence."

Meghan moved away from Jonathan.

She needed her space.

She gazed out at the surging sea and felt the sea breeze gust across her face. The cool wind stung as it fell against her face. Meghan knew what her answer should be, but she needed time to find the right words.

Jonathan poured himself another glass of wine and waited for her decision. Her one chance.

Meghan didn't feel right about the whole thing. She didn't want to hurt Jonathan, but she also couldn't harm Farraday. He had always been fair to her and supportive of her research.

She decided she must remain impartial.

"Jonathan, I don't want to see you get hurt. I really don't. But I just can't destroy Farraday. He has always been honest with me. I'm sorry."

Jonathan pressed his lips together and nodded, amused with Meghan's misguided loyalty to Farraday.

How pathetic she looked. *How fucking naive can one person be?* Jonathan thought.

Farraday was the wrong choice; he would not be able to save her now.

"Meghan, I understand. I really do. This is my problem and not yours. It wasn't fair to expect you to risk everything you have at the institute over this dispute between Farraday and me. You shouldn't have to choose." Jonathan finished his lines, confident he had not over-acted.

Meghan's eyes welled with tears. This was the Jonathan she had first met—gentle and kind and understanding. Meghan embraced Jonathan and dried her tears against his cheeks.

"Meghan, we can't forget about Nana's painting. Remember, I told you we can go next weekend to pick it up. I told the shopkeeper I would confirm a time. Do you think we can send an e-mail from your computer?"

Meghan had almost forgotten about the painting. She gently kissed Jonathan on his cheek.

"Yes ... of course," Meghan whispered.

They walked arm in arm across the deck, back inside her house, and passed by her haven. This is where Nana's painting would be placed. Safe inside her haven.

Meghan sat in front of her computer located in the study at the front of the house. Jonathan waited beside her as she confirmed her password that had been saved from her previous use. Meghan typed the confirmation for next weekend, Saturday, September 10, and sent it to the antique shop's e-mail address that Jonathan gave her.

"You look tired, Meghan. Why don't you take a shower? I have some work I need to finish. Afterwards, we can go out for dinner."

Meghan agreed. She was tired. She felt as if her emotions had been on a rollercoaster—first, with the painting, and then with Jonathan's problem at the institute.

"I won't be long." Meghan kissed Jonathan and walked toward the doorway. She had walked only a few feet before turning around.

"Jonathan, I love you. I'll never forget what you did for me today ... with Nana's painting."

Jonathan smiled. "I know, Meghan. I love you, too."

When Jonathan heard the shower water running from the third-floor bathroom, he decided it was time.

Time to get to work.

And yes, Meghan, you really won't forget this day.

Chapter Fourteen

JONATHAN REMOVED THE COMPACT FLASH drive from his jacket as he stood behind Meghan's computer. He carefully connected the electronic device to the computer's USB receptacle. The sound of a click signaled the start of the removal of Meghan's computer files into the tiny rectangular device.

On several occasions, Jonathan had seen Meghan work on her computer and knew she usually saved her password. It was simply convenient for her to do this, she often had said. What Meghan did not know was that her saved password was stored in her computer files. In fact, few people were aware of this, Jonathan thought. Only the more sophisticated hackers would know what he was doing.

The short process of retrieving the files was now complete. Jonathan removed the flash drive and placed it back inside his pocket.

Jonathan now had Meghan's password.

He controlled her computer identity.

Jonathan's work wasn't finished. Before Meghan came back, he had something else to do.

Jonathan walked back into the kitchen where he had seen Meghan leave her cell phone. It was still there on the counter. Jonathan realized he did not have much time left before Meghan returned. He quickly removed the back cover of Meghan's cell phone and removed its electronic SIM card. He replaced it with another SIM card from an identical cell phone model he had purchased earlier.

Jonathan now had Meghan's cell phone identity. He would place her SIM card into his identical cell phone model. He would then be able to make calls and send text messages to others from his phone, showing the other person who received the message that Meghan was the sender.

Jonathan was almost finished. He needed to do one final thing.

Meghan quickly descended the third-floor stairs with renewed energy and entered the kitchen where Jonathan stood facing the granite countertop.

"Jonathan, I'm finished. Taking a shower was a great idea. I feel like a new person."

Jonathan had not heard her come down. He was able, however, to subdue any startled reaction. As he turned to face her, he palmed the small SIM card and casually placed his hand into his pocket.

"Great, I've missed you," he replied.

"I wasn't gone that long, was I?"

"No, but I still missed being with you," Jonathan assured her with a smile.

"That's nice of you to say," Meghan replied as she walked closer to Jonathan and pulled his arms around her.

"Now it's my turn to take a shower. I won't be long. I promise."

"You better not. I'm famished." Meghan smiled.

Jonathan hurried up the stairs and locked the bathroom door behind him. Soon he would be finished with Meghan.

Jonathan removed a small Ziploc bag from his pocket and scanned the bathroom for DNA samples. He knew what he needed.

Hair.

Skin.

Saliva.

DNA evidence from Meghan. *Each sample will be easy to obtain,* Jonathan thought.

Hair brush.

Skin shavings on her razor blade.

Toothbrush.

Jonathan now had Meghan's DNA.

He controlled her identity; soon she would regret her decision.

Jonathan's plan to destroy Farraday was now set in motion. Even though Meghan had chosen to remain neutral and not support him, she would still become instrumental in Farraday's demise.

Jonathan felt sure his preparation to ensure the survival of the Pegasus Project would interest the professor. He would inform the professor of his plan to neutralize Farraday's threat to the project during their dinner meeting on Sunday, September 11, at Vickers Tavern in Chester County. The professor would also receive an update on the mutation discovery.

Their September meeting, however, had another purpose. Jonathan understood that the professor wanted him to meet someone who was contracted to execute the clinical stage of the Pegasus Project. His identity was not known to Jonathan. The professor would only say he was a foreigner whom he trusted to get the job done. Quickly and successfully. The professor had told him he would trust no one else. But he also had warned Jonathan his life would never be the same after working with this professional.

The foreigner's existence—his inner force—was very dangerous, the professor had warned.

Evil nurtured his life.

Chapter Fifteen

"WE WILL BE ARRIVING AT Philadelphia International Airport in thirty minutes. Please fasten your seatbelts for our descent into the Philadelphia area."

Stefan finished his Beluga caviar, which had been served nestled in a glass dish over crushed ice within a fluted, crystal caviar server. He then cleansed his palate with a chilled glass of Stoli, the only true Russian liquid accompaniment, Stefan believed, that enhanced the eggs' delicate flavors. Whenever Stefan traveled to Russia on an assignment, he preferred using the term *ikra*, the native Russian word for caviar, when ordering this delicacy. Even though most people considered caviar a name that described the Russian appetizer, Stefan knew only a few people realized that the word, caviar, really had its derivation from a mix of Italian, French, and Turkish origins.

Stefan took one last look at the front page of the Zermatt newspaper.

> *Dissected Body of American Female Student*
> *Found Along Lake Lucerne's Shoreline.*

Stefan would fondly remember Maria.
At least until the next one.

———ɯ———

Stefan had agreed to meet the Professor at Chester County's historic Vickers Tavern. Professor Marguilies had said that he needed to speak with him as soon as possible. The assignment was crucial and required a non-negotiable timetable, the professor stressed.

Without hesitation, Stefan had accepted the invitation since he had no commitments. No other projects could equal the intense sensual pleasure Stefan experienced with the professor's assignments.

One assignment, in particular, Stefan would always remember. His first with Professor Marguilies. A project in which the professor gained insight into Stefan's world. By his own admission, the professor was a changed person after that project.

Stefan had revealed to the professor, his obsessions, his atrocities, his motivation for living.

At first, Professor Marguilies abhorred Stefan's behavior. The professor was disgusted by his horrid acts against humanity. Sickened by his work ethic. An assignment initially designed to serve a noble purpose had deteriorated into acts of decadence and wanton disregard for the sanctity of human existence. Stefan enjoyed the professor's eventual transformation from a life once based on a strict moral code to an existence of ungodly eccentricities. The two men now shared a common purpose in life.

Stefan never feared his own evil potential. To fight evil and win, he had to know evil—know his enemy. *Become his enemy.* Stefan always accepted his fate as it slowly, piece by piece, ingested his body and soul.

Stefan knew the professor at one time devoted his academic life to promulgate a respect for mankind's desire to die with respect. The professor honored mankind's right to die only when life's malignancies insidiously violated one's treasured health and happiness.

Now, Stefan expanded the professor's vision for human existence. *Certain people must die to atone for their sins and the sins of others.* This was Stefan's monstrous moral code. It soon became the professor's as well.

How the guilty died was Stefan's work.

Stefan now grew impatient, waiting to satisfy his appetite.

Stefan hoped the Pegasus Project would satiate his craving.

Indigo clouds sprayed with pink and orange hues cloaked the autumn sunset as Stefan arrived for his meeting with Professor Marguilies at Vickers Tavern. The Chester County countryside was not foreign to Stefan. Even though it had been several years since his last visit, the surrounding tree-lined hills painted with autumn's foliage reminded Stefan it was also autumn when he last visited Chester County. When Stefan last worked here. An assignment which had convinced the professor that Stefan's work was thorough and effective—multiple murders still unsolved in Chester County's Great Valley region. All victims surgically dissected, their rigid flesh eventually found scattered across the nursing home grounds.

Diseased hosts with the right to die.

Stefan entered the Tavern's dark vestibule encased in antique oak walls that displayed nineteenth-century paintings depicting the tavern's historical significance. They were oil images of displaced slave families searching through the dark valley for a temporary safe house that would protect them from their pursuers—angry Southern torchbearers atop a nearby hill. Stefan admired the professor's decision to meet at this location since Vickers Tavern had played a vital role in the nineteenth-century Underground Railroad slave movement. This restaurant had provided a haven for the tired, oppressed slaves who had struggled to free their families from their inhumane, abusive life in the South. Without the Underground Railroad system, these ravaged and forgotten children of God would have been destined to suffer a cruel existence.

Slavery. An evil power that thrived on destroying the souls of mankind. Stefan had always considered the United States government hypocritical—a country, founded on the principle of freedom, had condoned slavery and imprisoned the minds, hearts, and souls of an entire race.

The professor had told Stefan that the Pegasus Project would free many young men, abused as children, from their own prison filled with years of dark memories and guilt—free them from the abusive horror inflicted on them by so-called righteous men.

These clerics, the guilty ones, must atone for their sins, the professor had stressed. Their evil power had destroyed the young souls of innocent boys.

Stefan was needed now, the professor had urged. Stefan's work was vital to safeguard the future of God's children. However, Stefan needed to learn more. The professor had assured him that the meeting tonight would explain everything. He had promised that the Pegasus Project would be Stefan's most satisfying contract. The professor had guaranteed it.

A woman slowly moved through the shadows of the candle-lit vestibule and offered Stefan a gentle smile as an apology for waiting. As she came closer, Stefan saw a young woman in her early twenties with black braided hair, gently pulled back to reveal soft olive skin that accented her pale green eyes.

A face of innocence, he thought.

"I'm so sorry for keeping you waiting. I hope you haven't been here long," the young hostess offered.

"Not a problem. I only arrived a few minutes ago," Stefan reassured her. Her shy demeanor attracted him.

The young woman retreated behind the reservation book and looked up.

"I have an eight o'clock reservation—under Marguilies," Stefan said, meeting her eyes with a smile.

"Yes, of course, party of three. Would you please follow me."

The hostess escorted Stefan along a narrow corridor that led toward a room that seemed to Stefan too crowded and inappropriate for a discreet dinner meeting. The young woman sensed Stefan's hesitation and gently touched his coat sleeve, guiding him through an arched doorway that avoided the noisy, crowded dining room. She led Stefan down a steep stairway that responded with nineteenth-century creaks, as if their descent awakened each aged wooden step. The stairway brought them to a room dimly lit by candles seated on pewter holders, anchored to thick, oak walls.

"This is our private dining room, which also serves as our wine cellar," explained the young hostess.

Stefan's eyes soon adjusted to the subtle lighting afforded by the flickering candles. Numerous wine bottles rested horizontally, secured in multi-shelved columns made from the same period oak wood as the staircase. As the hostess led Stefan through the maze of wine shelves, he heard two distinct voices, one of which he knew well. Their location was not yet in view. The hostess turned a corner in the wine cellar and presented Stefan to his dinner companions.

"I hope you'll find your dinner this evening quite relaxing and suitably private." Stefan nodded his approval to his attractive escort as he stood before a solitary dinner table with two guests already seated and engaged in discussion. Noticing Stefan's arrival, the professor disregarded Jonathan's ongoing discourse and immediately stood up and welcomed his associate with a lively and sustained handshake.

"Stefan, my God, how long has it been? Two, maybe three years?"

"It'll be three years next month. I'm sure you remember that time in October. In fact, we last met just several miles from here."

"Yes, I do remember." Professor Marguilies softly spoke as he stared into Stefan's ice-blue eyes.

Stefan grinned. "It was at Yellow Springs Inn. Another secluded restaurant. You do have a flair for choosing discreet and historic locations, Professor."

Jonathan remained seated. He remembered the professor's vague description of Stefan's work.

Effective.

Thorough.

Professional.

We'll see, Jonathan thought. He did not appreciate the professor's disregard for hearing more of his intricate plan for Meghan Cahill. Jonathan was determined not to allow the professor to undermine him. He could see Stefan was clearly the professor's friend and admired business associate.

The professor had insisted Stefan's work was crucial to the success of the project. Jonathan would not, however, permit anyone to forget that the Pegasus Project was his creation—his scientific discovery.

"Come join us, Stefan," offered Marguilies. He sensed Jonathan's uneasiness. Professor Marguilies smiled at Stefan as he guided him to a seat across from Jonathan.

"I want you to meet Stefan," announced Professor Marguilies.

Jonathan acknowledged Stefan's arrival with a subtle nod as the two men exchanged a brief handshake.

"Stefan, what?" questioned Jonathan.

"Just Stefan, for now."

"Well, Professor Marguilies hasn't told me anything about your unique services or how you intend to help us," Jonathan asserted as he sat back against his antique oak arm chair and resumed drinking his wine.

Stefan stared across at Jonathan.

"You may not have heard me, but I would like to know how you can possibly assist with our project," challenged Jonathan.

Professor Marguilies took another sip from his wine glass and leaned forward to enjoy Jonathan's attempt to intimidate Stefan.

"First, I want to compliment you on your excellent meeting location." Stefan offered a weak smile to Jonathan.

Stefan paused.

"Now, Jonathan, you may tell me about your Pegasus Project."

Stefan never looked away.

Jonathan shifted in his chair and shot a glance toward Marguilies, expecting him to reply instead; hiring this guy was his idea. The professor could certainly give him the details. Jonathan refused to play along with Stefan's tactics.

Sensing Jonathan's hesitation, Stefan chose another approach. "I understand from the professor that the scientific research for the project is entirely your idea. In fact, I'm told your work is genius and unparalleled. I'm very interested to learn the project's design and its applications."

Jonathan focused his attention back on Stefan. *You're right, my work does reflect my genius,* Jonathan thought.

Jonathan decided to answer. "My research at the Renaissance Institute will provide the method to successfully achieve our client's expectations. In the laboratory, I have discovered a way to chemically manipulate a subject's central nervous system, the brain, and thereby cause that subject to perform violent acts. Uncontrollable, reckless acts. Behavior that would normally never occur from that subject. The professor has recommended you to help us with our human trials. To test my chemical on humans before we use it against our targets. As you may know, our targets are two priests who are quite influential in the Church."

Jonathan finished his drink. He now leaned forward against the table.

"Our client is an attorney who represents several men who were injured as boys by three priests. During several years, these three clerics repeatedly violated their bodies by performing horrific sexual acts on them." Jonathan's voice grew more intense.

"These men of God destroyed their innocent minds and ravaged their souls. These children trusted these priests who manipulated their lives to serve their own perverse sexual obsessions." Jonathan's voice became louder.

"The attorney has attempted unsuccessfully to sue these priests and the Philadelphia Archdiocese for damages and monetary relief to help atone for these injuries and crimes. The attorney is frustrated because the legal system has failed to help his clients. Even the Pennsylvania Supreme Court, on appeal, rejected his clients' cause of action because their claims were not reported in a timely manner and therefore failed to meet the state's statute of limitations. In essence, the courts hid behind this legal technicality because, in our client's opinion, they're afraid of the Catholic Church. If they allowed their lawsuit to continue in Philadelphia, the Supreme Court argued, a floodgate would be opened, which would potentially allow millions of dollars to be levied against the Philadelphia Archdiocese." Jonathan sighed and noticed Stefan's eyes had not moved off him.

Jonathan continued. "This attorney did not have anywhere else to go. Even though he filed a claim in federal court, he said he was not optimistic. He wants revenge against two of the three priests. A bishop and a monsignor. The third priest was defrocked by the Church. The attorney wants us to pursue these two clerics who used their influence in the Catholic Church and avoided punishment. They had devised a plan to force the senior priest, now in his seventies, to plead guilty and take full responsibility for all of their heinous acts." Jonathan sat back and took a swallow of wine.

For the first time since sitting at the table, Stefan turned and faced the professor, probing his face for verification of Jonathan's briefing. Professor Marguilies leaned forward and met Stefan's eyes with the familiar, unwavering stare that assured Stefan his expertise was desperately needed.

"Imago Dei requires your help once again. The bishop and his monsignor have violated their oath to God."

The professor now directed his attention back to Jonathan. "As Christians, and especially as members of the clergy, they failed in their duty to do good for their fellow man. Since all humans were made in the image of God, to help one's fellow man is to do good for God , who will determine man's ultimate destiny. This fundamental theological doctrine is clearly substantiated in Matthew's Gospel and in the Acts of the Apostles." The professor saw disbelief etched across Jonathan's wry smile.

"Where is this theology lesson going?" Jonathan questioned.

"Be patient and just listen," the professor admonished. "Our work, the Pegasus Project, is concerned with more than just the punishment of these priests and the completion of the contract for our client, the attorney. My life's work with the secret Catholic organization in Rome—Imago Dei—shares the sworn allegiance with Stefan and with many others around the world to seek out those individuals who are without self-consciousness and who have rebuked God's desire for them to nourish spiritual reflection and moral growth. As reflected through Christ's teachings in the Bible, all humans are called to bring the Doctrine of Imago Dei into their daily lives and thereby strive to live faithfully as creations in God's image. Those individuals, such as Bishop Torrey and Monsignor Brannigan, who have rejected this sacred and fundamental doctrine of Christian faith will suffer the consequences. Imago Dei will determine the destiny of all offenders."

"Hold on. I don't understand what you're saying. I thought you only intended to use my drug research to physically impair our targets. What gives you and Imago Dei the authority to execute these so-called offenders?" Jonathan challenged, leaning his arms across the table toward the professor.

"Your question should not be *what*, but rather *who* gives us the authority."

"Fine. Then *who* authorizes Imago Dei's secret agenda?"

"God has ordained it." Professor Marguilies paused as Jonathan withdrew into his chair, his brow furrowed. The professor continued now that he knew he had set the hook. "There are numerous biblical references to support Imago Dei's work. Beginning in Genesis, God proclaims man is made in his image and thereby authorizes man to rule over every living entity on earth. There are similar references in Romans

8:29, 1Corinthians 15:49, and 2 Corinthians 3:18, and Psalm 8:5. In fact, St. Paul uses Imago Dei as the basic structure for his teachings."

"Okay. So what if man is made in God's image. This concept still doesn't give support for what you are planning to do."

"You need to hear more. In James 3:8–9, Imago Dei is used as the foundation for condemning the utterance of all hurtful words from one person to another. And again in Genesis 9:6, God proclaims that *whoever sheds man's blood, by man his blood shall be shed; for in the image of God, He made man*." Even though he knew he finally had Jonathan's full attention, still, the professor saw confusion etched across Jonathan's face.

"Let me explain further. This last Genesis reference that I mentioned ultimately validates our sacred mission with the Pegasus Project and with all of our other projects around the world. *Whoever sheds man's blood*—the crimes of the bishop and monsignor against the innocent children—*by man his blood shall be shed*—our organization must seek out the offenders and 'shed their blood,' thereby condemning their existence—*for in the image of God, He made man*—the secret and holy organization, Imago Dei, must thereby fulfill God's command."

Jonathan Ashbridge remained silent. His taut and empty expression was etched across his ashen skin. His eyes, devoid of any life, reflected the solemn realization of what he was just told. He interlaced his fingers and lowered his head against his clenched fists.

"Stefan, Imago Dei needs you. The children need you," the professor whispered.

Chapter Sixteen

B EFORE THE FIRST RAYS OF sun burned their golden splendor through the eastern, wooded hills surrounding the 200-year-old seminary, Monsignor Patrick Brannigan hastened down the pristine marble-floor hallway that led to the prefect's office.

This morning, Monsignor Pat, as he was commonly referred to by the seminary's administrative hierarchy, was running late. It was close to 6:00 a.m., and he was already behind schedule.

His early morning assignment was simple. He was to deliver various national newspapers along with his critique of relevant stories affecting the Church. He would routinely accomplish his task by 5:30 a.m., which allowed enough time left over to grab a quick breakfast at a nearby bagel store and return in time for his 6:00 a.m. meeting.

This morning allowed no such freedom. Monsignor Pat had overslept and had resigned himself to struggle through the morning with hunger. He could not be unprepared for the 6:00 a.m. briefing.

The bishop would not tolerate it. He demanded efficiency and loyalty from the monsignor; tardiness and an unprepared briefing were evidence of disloyalty. The bishop was not a person to cross.

Monsignor Pat Brannigan sat in his assigned chair positioned in front of the bishop's massive eighteenth-century oak office desk that rested upon a plush cardinal-red carpet.

The monsignor patiently waited for the arrival of His Eminence.

Soon, distant echoes of footsteps emanated throughout the hallway, announcing the bishop's arrival.

Draped in Venetian lace, the double French doors parted as Bishop Timothy Torrey strode into his office.

"What do you have for me?" asked the bishop. Monsignor Brannigan was already out of his chair.

"There are several major newspapers covering the trial here in Philadelphia. Some are objective and fair. However, most are very critical of the Church."

"Doesn't surprise me. The quality of newspaper writing these days isn't worth the paper it's written on. You do know, of course, all the major newspapers and journals are out to get us. They hate us for what we stand for." Monsignor Brannigan nodded as Bishop Torrey poured himself a cup of coffee from the warmed pewter coffee urn.

Another expected duty successfully completed early this morning, thought Monsignor Brannigan.

"Have we heard from the Vatican?" the bishop inquired.

"Not yet, sir. It's still too soon for their assessment."

"You're probably right, Pat. The trial just got started a few days ago. Apparently, the DA's office has several weeks of testimony to admit into evidence." The bishop carried his second cup of coffee over to his chair and stared down at his image reflected in the thick glass that covered the top of his oak desk. He focused on his right hand, which boasted a ruby stone encased in a thick, etched gold ring, which he had received when he became bishop.

The bishop, however, wanted more. He knew he deserved more from the Church than his present title.

He deserved to be Cardinal Timothy Torrey.

To wear the cardinal's ring and become a Prince of the Church.

He also knew he had to act quickly. Pope Luke was gravely ill, and soon a successor would be chosen. Bishop Torrey needed to be a cardinal when the vote for successor to His Holiness occurred. He knew that in the history of the Catholic Church, it was rare for a non-cardinal to be elected or appointed pope—not since 1378 when Urban VI, who was not a cardinal, was elected pope.

The bishop had many friends in the Vatican—important friends. Strong lobbyists who were already committed to support his quest to become the next pope, the Catholic Church's representative of St. Peter.

But, he first needed to be appointed cardinal.

Bishop Torrey understood that his appointment to this holy inner circle—the College of Cardinals—depended on the outcome of the trial in Philadelphia. Bishop Torrey's political advisors in Vatican City had warned him that if the vicar were convicted, the bishop would never see Vatican City as a cardinal. His advisors further warned that if convicted, the vicar promised them he would implicate an American bishop—with connections to the Vatican—as a criminal who was equally guilty of the charges against him.

Child molestation.

Bishop Torrey knew the vicar all too well. They had worked together during the early eighties with numerous parish grade-school retreats. Young inner-city children were often brought to the seminary to enjoy the country air, play in the acres of ball fields, and explore the densely wooded fields.

The bishop knew he shared the vicar's guilt. The only difference between them was that the bishop had used drugs to blur the innocent children's tragic memories. No child was ever able to identify him. He had escaped prosecution once again. Several years earlier, the bishop had avoided prosecution on yet another occasion that had resulted in the conviction and twenty-year sentence for another parish priest who had worked with the bishop organizing CYO athletic programs. That priest had taken the fall also.

This time, however, Bishop Torrey was concerned. What could he do to assure his friends at the Vatican he would not be brought in as a co-defendant in the Philadelphia trial?

What could he possibly do to avoid the parish priest's accusations? Avoid culpability?

He needed to be a cardinal. But at what cost? The bishop simply knew the priest must be silenced.

But how could he guarantee that silence?

"I'm sorry, Your Excellency, what do you need to do?" asked Monsignor Brannigan.

Bishop Torrey was not aware he was actually speaking. His private, troubled thoughts had somehow managed to escape.

"Pat, you and I know we were lucky with the incident in Boston several years ago. We were never criminally charged. The Church also found no credible evidence linking us to those two boys. Our friend, however, wasn't that fortunate." The bishop turned away from his desk and stood beneath the stained-glass window that depicted Christ's Agony in the Garden.

"You remember, Pat, we did the same things to those boys that Father Mike was held accountable for by the Church and the City of Boston. Drugs that we used had obscured our identity and involvement with the Boston matter, and again with the claimants in Philadelphia."

"Yes, I know, Eminence. But why are you troubled?" asked Monsignor Brannigan as he walked toward the bishop.

"We could be faced with a crisis if our vicar is found guilty in the Philadelphia trial."

"I don't understand. The Church found no credible evidence, and the

DA's office exonerated us and removed all suspicions surrounding our involvement in that case." Monsignor Brannigan felt uneasy defending their innocence. Did the bishop know of new evidence that would change everything?

Removal from Church duties?

New criminal charges?

An embarrassing trial?

And even worse—incarceration?

"What do you know?" pleaded Monsignor Brannigan.

Bishop Timothy Torrey turned and faced his longtime friend. He saw fear in his friend's eyes. He only wished he could lessen the impact of what he was about to tell the monsignor.

"Pat, our problem is simple but complex. My associates at the Vatican have warned me that if the vicar is convicted in Philadelphia, he intends to turn on us and become a witness for the DA against us. Remember, Pat, he knows about the amnestic drug, Midazolam, that we used. He also saw us with those two boys in the seminary." Bishop Torrey gently placed his hand on his friend's shoulder as the monsignor slowly raised his hands to hide the anguish etched across his face.

"Pat, if the vicar testifies against us, we're ruined. Everything we've worked for together over the past twenty years will be destroyed—our plan for me to become cardinal and eventually pope, with you closely at my side. As cardinal, my Vatican supporters assure me that I could become the next pope. Currently, there are many divisive factors within the College of Cardinals. The Italians want to regain the papacy, while the other European, Asian, and African cardinals demand their equal voice," Bishop Torrey continued.

"I've been told by many inner-circle supporters that now is the time for a fresh voice, perhaps from the West, to bring modernization and solidarity within the Church. The Christian world needs an intelligent and compassionate pope who will no longer ignore the Muslim countries but acknowledge their vital message and their importance, not only in the Middle East but in the western hemisphere as well."

Monsignor Brannigan knew some of the influential Vatican clergy from whom the bishop received valuable support. The monsignor had been assigned to Rome for three years, during which time he saw more political maneuvers than in the Washington DC Beltway.

There was one other monsignor similar to him in age and seniority whom he had befriended during his tenure at the Vatican. Monsignor Brannigan soon learned the extent of his influence. If a task was deemed insurmountable and required discreet ingenuity, this Swiss theologian was the one to get the job done. Monsignor Brannigan had kept in close contact with him over the years and had strengthened their relationship during brief visits to Rome over the past several years.

"Pat, we must guarantee the vicar's silence. The Church needs us. The world requires our success."

Monsignor Brannigan needed to hear the bishop's recitation of their divine plan. *Yes, it is a divine plan,* believed Monsignor Brannigan.

The bishop and he were entrusted with an austere and sanctified mission.

They had worked hard toward that goal.

They had prayed tirelessly for their success.

No one, not even a vicar, would stand in their way.

Monsignor Brannigan continued to look at the bishop and admire his conviction. The bishop had chosen him for his similar driven personality.

The early morning sun slowly showered its rays through the eastern tree-lined hills that offered protection to the secrets born within the seminary's 200-year-old gray stone walls. Monsignor Brannigan focused on the stained-glass window behind the bishop. The rays glistened through the windowpanes and highlighted the drama portrayed in the stained-glass scene.

The once-dark halo of holiness that surrounded Christ's head in the predawn now blazed with a glorious aura that captivated the attention of Monsignor Brannigan. With each passing second, the dawn showered its splendor across the stained-glass depiction of Christ's Agony in the

Garden. Monsignor Brannigan saw the fear, the anguish etched in Christ's face. He now saw subtle beads of sanguineous sweat flow from Christ's body. He also saw Christ's followers, who swore their nocturnal vigilance, but now slumbered helplessly in the garden.

Bishop Torrey was indeed a representative of Christ. Monsignor Brannigan renewed his sworn allegiance to his bishop. The monsignor was determined not to sleep as Christ's disciples had done that dark night.

They were useless and helpless.

He would remain vigilant. He would protect his future pope.

Monsignor Pat Brannigan vowed he would silence the vicar.

Silence him at any cost.

Chapter Seventeen

A HARSH TONE CHIMED THROUGHOUT THE Swiss cleric's bedroom, interrupting his sleep. It was 2:00 a.m. in Rome, and Monsignor Hans Reuss was not happy as he reached for the phone.

"Who is this?" Monsignor Reuss knew who the caller was *not*. If he was needed at the Vatican, his pager would have gone off. He had just worked a twenty-hour day—longer than his routine sixteen-hour day—and he was exhausted.

"Did you hear me ... who the hell is this?"

"Hans, it's me, Pat Brannigan. I'm so sorry about the time," Monsignor Pat humbly replied.

"Pat Brannigan ... Is that really you?"

"Yes it is ... I'm so sorry ..."

"Forget it. My God, how the hell are you?"

"I have a problem. It's very serious, and I don't know what to do about it," Monsignor Brannigan replied anxiously.

Reuss heard Monsignor Brannigan take several deep breaths.

"It'll be okay, Pat, just take your time," Monsignor Reuss offered.

"It's actually a serious issue affecting not only me, but Bishop Torrey as well. Our problem concerns a trial in Philadelphia where a parish priest, actually he's a close friend of ours, is accused of performing certain indiscretions with several children. We're told if he's found guilty, the priest will implicate the bishop and me in those offenses. Hans, we can't have this happen to us. Too much is at stake. You must already know about the efforts to make Bishop Torrey a cardinal and a candidate to become our next pope." Monsignor Brannigan paused and sighed deeply.

"Hans, please help us."

Monsignor Hans Reuss listened to each word. He was trained to study closely the words chosen by various people he encountered in his work at the Vatican. As a scholar in canon law, Monsignor Reuss considered every spoken word to be highly relevant.

"Pat, will you be honest with me?"

"Yes, of course."

"Regarding these indiscretions, what do you really mean?"

There was a moment of silence.

"Child molestation," Monsignor Brannigan whispered.

"I see. How do these charges involve you and the bishop?"

"Hans, we'll be ruined just by the accusations. You know as well as I that the Church will not like the publicity, let alone support Bishop Torrey's appointment as cardinal. Hans, the Church will defrock us, remove us from our ministry … our life's work … and refer our case to the Philadelphia District Attorney's Office for prosecution."

Monsignor Reuss's question wasn't answered. Monsignor Brannigan knew that. He also knew his friend needed to hear the truth.

"Pat, you need to be honest with me. Is there any truth to these accusations?" Monsignor Reuss probed.

What seemed like several minutes of silence to Monsignor Brannigan was actually only a few seconds.

How could he admit his guilt to his friend? He had never wanted to do those things to the children. The bishop had forced him. Their victims were innocent, not deserving of those heinous acts of abuse.

The bishop, however, had defended his behavior; the monsignor had heard his rationale many times. The bishop had insisted that his intense devotion to the Church and his many years of hard work for the benefit of the Church had burdened him with stressors that needed release.

The bishop had lured him into a delusional existence nurtured with alcohol, drug, and child abuses. The bishop had insisted their behavior was exempt from society's laws. He had argued their important religious work cloaked them with an immunity from the sinful secular laws. Their acts were not acts of perversion. The laws of society were in fact the source of perversion.

Monsignor Brannigan had desperately tried to free himself from the bishop but knew it was too late. Too many acts, too many wrongs had been committed.

Monsignor Pat Brannigan was ashamed.

He now found the courage to speak.

"Hans, the accusations are true. I have sinned against God ... and against children who trusted us with their faith ... with their lives ... with their innocence."

"Pat, I understand that—"

"Wait a minute, Hans. You don't understand. I don't deserve exoneration for my behavior. I knew better. I must be held accountable for ..."

The Swiss theologian heard his friend's confession through his muffled cries. He felt sorry for Pat.

Hans knew the bishop's personality well. During his many visits to Rome, the bishop had been a bastard—difficult to work with, and even worse to interact with socially.

Hans was also aware of the bishop's "special needs." His abhorrent behavior had found nourishment at the many nearby schools in Rome.

Monsignor Hans Reuss empathized with his friend's anguish.

"Pat, I can help. I know someone. He's reliable and very discreet." Monsignor Hans Reuss spoke with a calming tone.

"Hans, what can he possibly do to help us?" questioned Monsignor Brannigan.

"Do you trust me, Pat?"

"Yes."

"Then trust me when I tell you he'll remove your problem."

"What do you mean?" asked Monsignor Brannigan.

The Swiss theologian spoke in a calm voice.

"The parish vicar on trial in Philadelphia will never be a threat. He'll never accuse you of anything. My associate will guarantee it."

Monsignor Reuss knew he could easily remove this burden from his dear friend's shoulders. He was also confident that he could not save Monsignor Pat from Imago Dei's death sentence.

Chapter Eighteen

SEPTEMBER 15

JONATHAN PRESSED HIS THUMB ON the identification scanner outside the entry door to his Special Project Lab located in the basement of the Renaissance Institute. As the soft tone quickly approved his access, the thick, steel door that guarded Jonathan's Pegasus Project slowly opened. Jonathan turned toward Stefan and motioned him to enter first.

The subterranean lab emitted a strong, decaying odor that hung heavily in the thick, humid air. A dim, red florescent glow attempted to permeate the stagnant air and offer its visitors guidance through the long, narrow work benches.

Stefan inhaled deeply. The foul odor filled his nostrils and satiated his taste buds.

Stefan was very familiar with this smell.

This taste.

A fresh kill—death was not a stranger to Stefan.

Jonathan followed his Swiss associate into the subterranean lab. Even though he worked closely with his assistant, Jeffrey Manion, in the lab, Jonathan still found the odors repulsive and considered this environment beneath him. Jonathan reminded himself, however, he was the only one who could ensure the success of the project, so his presence in the lab was necessary. The Pegasus Project was his creation. He didn't trust anyone, not even his assistant who had worked with him for many years at the institute. The stench was just a necessary byproduct of his valuable work, Jonathan acknowledged.

"Jonathan, I'm over here," Jeffrey Manion called out.

As the two men walked toward the voice, Stefan noticed several stainless steel animal pens on the floor. As he walked closer, the smell of decaying flesh became more intense.

Stefan paused and looked down into the roofless steel enclosures. Even though the dim florescent light hindered his view, Stefan still was able to discover the source of the laboratory's rancid odor.

Thick, red clumps of sawdust scattered throughout one of the stainless steel pens partially covered a dark, motionless form.

Stefan moved closer.

Dark coagulated blood covered the exposed, disfigured head of a small dog. Pieces of flesh torn from the animal's neck remained stuck against the stainless steel walls.

What mutilated this animal? Stefan thought. He did not have to wait long for an answer.

"Jonathan, I just finished with another animal experiment. Our drug is working just as we predicted," Jeffrey Manion announced.

"What animals did you use this time?" Jonathan asked.

"Dogs. I gave the drug to one of our beagles. One that was never aggressive."

"And the victim?" Jonathan asked.

"The beagle's target was a pit bull. Jonathan, it was an extremely aggressive one," Manion answered as he stared at Stefan, who continued to examine the lifeless animal.

"Where is the beagle now?" asked Jonathan.

Manion led the two men to an aluminum wire crate placed on a nearby examination table. As Stefan stood in front of the crate covered with plastic panels, he could see through the wired front-gate a form that moved restlessly in the darkness. A sustained guttural noise vibrated from within the blackness, pausing at times to allow for several panting breaths.

Stefan moved closer and peered through the wire door.

Suddenly, the form hurled its body against the front gate, forcing the crate to slide across the table toward Stefan. Blood-soaked teeth gripped the wire gate, trying to tear apart the barrier and claim another victim.

Stefan never moved away. He stared into the beagle's bloodshot eyes, which became fixed on Stefan's eyes. He did not see anger. He did not see evil.

Stefan recognized fear in the eyes of this ravaged beast. He had seen this fear many times before in the faces of men and women whom he had cleansed with their own deaths.

"What did you give it?" asked Stefan as he turned and realized that both Jonathan and his assistant had retreated several yards behind him, away from the beast.

"It's all right, Jeffrey, you can speak freely. Stefan is part of our project," Jonathan reassured as he sensed his lab assistant's apprehension.

"I used our drug. The one Jonathan and I developed in our lab upstairs using zebra fish embryos. We found that this drug, when tagged with our carrier-virus, can be sent to a specific location in the brain. The drug then stimulates a special part of brain tissue that is responsible for the creation of impulses. Essentially, too much stimulation at this site results in intense, pathological behavior." Jeffrey turned to Jonathan for approval of his presentation.

"What you really mean to say is that your drug causes uncontrollable urges, impulses. As we discussed earlier in our meeting at Vickers Tavern, your plan, Jonathan, is for me to give this drug to our human targets. Right?" Stefan asked.

"Yes, that's right."

"Are you sure you don't want me to simply kill the clerics?" questioned Stefan.

Jonathan's purpose for the drug, for the Pegasus Project, was twofold. He needed to perform human clinical trials. Human experiments. Demonstrate the drug's ability to cause uncontrollable impulses. If he could prove that his research could create these pathological urges, he could also demonstrate to the scientific community that the same drug, when made weaker, could lessen or in fact cure all abnormal urges. Diseases such as alcoholism, drug abuse, in fact, all obsessive-compulsive behavior would be eradicated forever.

The second purpose for the Pegasus Project was to punish two clerics who had abused innocent children. Once young boys, now scarred young men, living in limbo, torn between their wounded, shameful childhood memories and their agonizing search for retribution.

"No, Stefan. The bishop and monsignor must not simply die. They must atone for their sins. They must suffer," Jonathan commanded.

"I understand." Stefan nodded.

Jonathan continued. "But there is one problem. We're not sure how you can give it to them. You know, by mouth, intravenous, or by skin contact."

"How did you give it to the dog?" Stefan asked.

"It was an intramuscular injection," Jeffrey replied.

"How long did it take to work?" Stefan questioned.

"About twenty-four hours. Why?" Jeffrey asked.

"What I need to know concerns the drug's absorption rate. You know, I need to know how long it takes for the drug to work. From the time it enters the body until it causes the desired effect. I prefer a quicker effect; twenty-four hours is simply too long," Stefan asserted.

"Well, what do you suggest?" Manion challenged.

"Have you considered our targets inhaling the drug?" Stefan questioned.

"Can it work that way?" Manion asked.

Jonathan walked toward Stefan, ignoring his assistant's question.

"How can the victims inhale our drug?" Jonathan asked.

"That's simple. The monsignor and bishop won't even know what hit them. I have a plan," Stefan replied.

Chapter Nineteen

JONATHAN ASHBRIDGE WAS TROUBLED. EVEN though he admired Stefan's confidence, he still could not accept Stefan's cold detachment. Jonathan was not like him. He knew he could never become the type of person Stefan was—a hired killer, devoid of any emotion or guilt.

Jonathan and Stefan exited the Renaissance Institute and walked across the black macadam parking lot toward their cars. When the two men arrived at their cars parked adjacent to one another, Jonathan stared out across the sixty acres of tan cornstalks that covered the perimeter of the property. He paused for a moment and studied the unique spray of colors that moved across the western sky.

Jonathan was troubled. There were only two weeks left until the October 1 deadline.

Jonathan needed more time.

And then there was the matter with Meghan. Farraday wanted to destroy him and reward Meghan for her loyalty.

That was unacceptable to Jonathan.

He needed to stop them. But how? He did have a plan to eliminate Farraday and to discredit Meghan, but he wasn't sure he could be the one to carry out the plan. *He was not like Stefan.*

"What's wrong?" Stefan asked.

"It's Farraday. We only have fourteen days until he puts an end to my work. In fact, I don't trust Farraday will even give me those two weeks. The Pegasus Project needs more time. You still need to test the drug on human subjects. The success of my research depends on those human experiments. There's still so much more to do," Jonathan pleaded.

"If you're allowed to work uninterrupted, without interference from Farraday, could you have your drug ready for me in a couple of days?" Stefan asked as he calmly lit a cigarette.

"Yes, I'm sure of it. But what about Farraday? I don't think I can ..."

"Listen to me. When do you want him killed?" Stefan asked.

"What do you mean?"

Stefan walked closer to Jonathan and stared into his eyes. "Just that. When do you want Farraday killed?"

"You would kill him?" Jonathan anxiously questioned.

"The professor warned me about you. Wanting all the glory is easy, but you aren't willing to pay the price. Yes, Jonathan, I'll do it, but I will need a separate contract." Using his thumb and index finger, Stefan extinguished his half-smoked cigarette and placed it inside his coat pocket.

"Wait a minute, Stefan. I do have a plan. I think a good one. We can take care of Farraday and also eliminate my competition at the institute. Meghan Cahill will not take over my lab," Jonathan declared.

Stefan was amused at Jonathan's sudden display of confidence. "If you insist, Jonathan, let's hear your plan. Then I'll decide its worth."

Chapter Twenty

M EGHAN STOOD ALONE ON THE sandy banks surrounding the lake, partially hidden behind a dense perimeter of oak and pine trees about a half mile from the Renaissance Institute complex. Meghan often chose this location as a retreat from her intense work schedule since she could easily walk the short distance from the institute down to the lake, spend time to reflect, and then return to her lab before anyone noticed her absence.

Her short hike had brought her along a path formed through the surrounding acres of seven-foot high cornstalks that led to her "lake of serenity," as she once described it to Dan Rafferty. Even the time spent walking along the path through the cornfield was calming.

It was Friday afternoon, and Meghan realized it had been two weeks since Labor Day weekend when Jonathan had visited her in Ocean City and had told her about her grandmother's oil painting. Two weeks in fact since she had last seen him or heard from him. Her many attempts to meet him were unsuccessful either because he was too busy with his research at the institute or because he had travel commitments that took him out of the area.

Why was Jonathan ignoring her?

Why was he treating her like this?

Meghan remembered how excited she was when Jonathan first told her about the painting.

Jonathan had promised her the painting. The painting that she had never seen would finally be with her. By having this painting, she would feel Nana's presence even stronger in her beach house and in her life.

But, she had not yet received the oil painting, and Jonathan was not returning her calls. Why then did he ever claim to have found Nana's painting?

Meghan now accepted the truth—there was no painting. Jonathan was a fraud. Their whole relationship had been a lie. How could she ever have been such a fool? Meghan chastised herself.

Was there even any love between them? she wondered.

Maybe at first. There had to be at least some value in her two-year relationship with him.

Meghan wiped the tears from her eyes and realized she should return to her lab. She had left Dan back at the lab over an hour ago, telling him she was going for a short walk outside. As Meghan turned to leave, she heard a rustle through the cornstalks, which grew louder as the hidden intruder approached her.

"Meg, are you there?" a familiar voice called out.

"My God, Dan, you scared me. I didn't know what was coming toward me."

"I'm sorry, but I was getting worried when you didn't return."

"What do you want?" challenged Meghan. As soon as she spoke, she felt the harshness in her tone. Dan did not deserve this treatment.

"I'm sorry, Meghan. I was just worried. I didn't see you outside on the grounds, so I thought I might find you down here." Dan slowly walked toward Meghan. He stopped a few feet in front of her.

"Are you okay?" Dan asked.

"I don't know. It's just not right … what he's done to me," Meghan said.

Dan knew what was wrong. "Tell me what I can do to help you."

"I can't hold it together any longer. I don't know what to do. Jonathan is not good. I hate him."

Dan held her trembling hands. "I can help. Please … let me," Dan softly replied.

Dan looked into Meghan's weary eyes. "You're right. Jonathan is no good. He has controlled you and manipulated you for a long time. He has hurt you, and I have felt the pain he has caused you."

Meghan remained focused on her friend. "I've been so foolish … to have stayed with him for so long. What can I do now?"

Dan gently squeezed Meghan's hands. "I care about you, Meg. Call it silly or immature, but I've had these feelings for you ever since that first day you walked into the lab."

Meghan's eyes began to tear up again.

"I promise, Meg, your life will be better without Jonathan in it."

Meghan brought her hands to Dan's bearded, tanned face and gently stroked his sun-bleached hair with her fingertips. Time seemed to have stopped for Meghan as Dan embraced her.

Dan broke the silence.

"I have an idea. Let's have dinner tomorrow night. There is so much more I want to say to you."

"Yes, I'd like that. There's just one thing I have to do Saturday evening."

"What's that?"

Meghan relived with Dan her two-hour meeting earlier in the day with CEO Farraday. Jonathan was right; Farraday did want Jonathan gone. He wanted to take away his corporate title as vice president of Research and Development and all of his research grant money and lab space. Farraday's plan was to give it all to her—Jonathan's corporate authority, his money, and his lab.

Dan Rafferty listened intently. "What did you say to Farraday?"

"At first nothing. He was doing all of the talking, and I was just listening. Then, after he finished, he finally asked me my opinion. At first, I spoke in support of Jonathan. I tried to separate my personal feelings for him and give Farraday my honest opinion of his professional strengths. Believe me, Dan, that was difficult for me to do."

Dan nodded. "What did Farraday have to say then?"

"Exactly what you would think. He acknowledged my professional loyalty to Jonathan but insisted I tell him my real opinion of Jonathan. I tried to be fair. But Farraday was determined. I think he wanted to see if I could function successfully as the new vice president of R&D. I just don't know for sure."

"Did you accept his offer?" Dan asked.

"Yes, I did. I also told Farraday that I thought Jonathan was too focused on his own research agenda and did not support the other research divisions, mine included. I also assured Farraday that I would work fairly with all of the institute's associate directors to support their individual research projects."

Dan heard confidence slowly return in Meghan's voice. He liked this quality in her. Despite all the harsh treatment that she had endured, Meghan was a fighter and had the courage to speak her truth.

Dan smiled. "Let me then be the first to congratulate you as our new vice president and director of research. Meg, you've earned it. More than anyone else here. You've put in more time than any of the other associate directors. Trust me, I see the value of your pediatric cancer research. Hell, the value of our research. We're a team, right?"

Meghan smiled and wrapped her arms around Dan. She held onto him and felt a calm, loving strength.

They left the lake and walked back through the cornfield to the Renaissance Institute.

"Tomorrow evening, right?" Dan asked.

"I'll give you a call when I'm finished here at the lab. I have to meet with Jonathan's assistant, Jeffrey Manion. He wants to talk to me about something important. It has to do with Jonathan's special research project. Something I think he called Pegasus Project."

"He can't meet with you this afternoon?" Dan asked.

"Apparently not. Jeffrey told me he's worried about Jonathan's Project. Also, he doesn't want Jonathan to see us together. He thinks that Saturday evening would be best since Jonathan is supposed to be away on business over the weekend."

"All right, but be careful. I don't trust Jonathan or anyone associated with him."

"Don't be silly. I can take care of myself. Especially, as the new vice president. Don't worry. I won't be long."

"Then, tomorrow evening it is. I should be at home. Call me, okay? I mean, call me if you need anything. Promise?" Dan urged.

Meghan smiled and nodded.

Chapter Twenty-One

"It's about time you got here. I was giving you just five more minutes before I left," CEO Farraday announced as Jonathan quickly maneuvered his way through the crowded bar. Jonathan had chosen this meeting place for its proximity to the Renaissance Institute; the restaurant was located just three miles from the institute and half that distance from the institute's lake.

"I'm sorry. I was delayed at work. You know, trying to tie up loose ends before I leave at the end of the month."

"Good to hear that. Now what critical information about the institute do you need to tell me on a Saturday night?" Farraday said, trying to be heard above the cacophonous conversations of the bar patrons.

"Before I leave the institute, you need to know something about the real Meghan Cahill," Jonathan answered.

"What do you mean, the real Meghan Cahill?"

"My friend at the Justice Department in Washington recently gave me some background information on her."

"Stop right there. You're trying to discredit Meghan because she's taking your job. You're a bastard." Farraday started to get up from the lounge table when Jonathan grabbed his arm.

"No, you don't understand. I've had it with you and the institute. I want to be far away from that pharmaceutical whore house of has-been researchers. I deserve better. I have nothing to gain by what I have to tell you."

Jonathan loosened his grip on Farraday and continued. "Listen, you're right about one thing. In the beginning, when you told me about Cahill taking over my lab and getting my grant money, you're right, I was angry. Angry at you and resentful toward Cahill. It was then that I contacted my friend in Washington to do a background check on her. I wanted to discredit her, ruin her professional life at any cost. However, over the past few weeks, I've realized my work deserves international recognition. The institute is wrong for me, and I've accepted that now."

Farraday was now back in his seat, waving at the waitress for a refill in his empty martini glass.

"I'm listening." Farraday nodded for Jonathan to continue.

"My friend just called me a few hours ago and gave me this information. Cahill is under federal investigation for the illegal sale and possession of the narcotic fentanyl. The feds think she is the source for drug dealers who are now mixing fentanyl in the heroin they're selling on the streets."

"What? I don't believe it," Farraday scoffed.

"Believe it. The government has been watching Meghan since grad school. I was told she's also been selling drugs while working at the institute. It's been easy for her since she controls our narcotic supply as part of her job. Admit it, Farraday. She's good. She's been stealing our narcotics to sell to drug dealers, and we never had a clue."

Farraday leaned back in his chair and sighed.

"I don't know what to say. I was going to give her your job. God, she had me fooled. I need that drink," Farraday demanded as his eyes searched the crowded lounge for the waitress.

Jonathan emptied his glass of Louis Jadot Beaujolais and glanced at his watch. It was 7:45 p.m.

—◊◊◊—

"I know what you must think, Meghan. How could I remain loyal to Jonathan and be involved in this type of research? Well, I don't know why," Jeffrey Manion said as he ran his fingers through his hair, staring down at the blood clots splattered across the subterranean lab floor.

Meghan still could not believe what Jeffrey had just shown her.

Ravaged canine victims entombed in their blood-soaked cages.

Psychotic dogs—salivating for their next living meal.

Meghan had just heard Jeffrey's detailed account of Jonathan's secret experiments. He had told her about Jonathan's research that would empower him with international prestige. Jonathan was convinced of this, Jeffrey had told her. Jonathan was obsessed with gaining international acclaim for his work.

Jeffrey had had enough. He couldn't do this work any longer. These experiments, these tortures repulsed him.

Jeffrey grabbed Meghan's arms as his knees buckled from the strain.

"You must help me. I can't just walk away. Jonathan would never allow me to leave. I know too much. Please, you've got to help me," Jeffrey pleaded.

"All right … I'll help you, but we have to report this immediately to Farraday."

"You're right. We do need to report this," Jeffrey responded. He glanced at his watch as Meghan turned away and walked closer to examine one of the bloodied, motionless forms.

It was 8:00 p.m. Jeffrey realized it was time for him to act.

"Meghan, I need to use the bathroom. I'll be right back," Jeffrey called out as he left Meghan alone with the odors of death.

"Farraday, can I use your cell phone? I left mine in my car. I want to call the airport to see if my flight is on time tonight," Jonathan asked.

"Where are you going?"

"A job interview in Switzerland. I told you, I'm finished with the institute and ready to move on."

"Yeah, here." Farraday checked for messages before he handed his cell to Jonathan. There were none.

Jonathan dialed the number for the airline's international flights. It was 8:00 p.m. His call was timed perfectly.

Jeffrey dialed Farraday's cell phone. He was relieved when he heard the recorded voice of Farraday requesting that a message be left.

Jeffrey replied with a text message:

Mr. Farraday, I must see you immediately.

It's urgent. It involves Jonathan and his work at the institute. Please meet me at once at the institute's lake. I'm here inside the institute. The building may not be safe. Please come. I will wait for you.

M. Cahill

Jeffrey placed the phone that contained Meghan Cahill's SIM card back inside his trousers and returned to the basement lab.

"Thanks. My flight's on time." Jonathan returned the cell phone to Farraday, who again checked for messages. This time he had one.

Text message received at 8:00 p.m.

Caller ID was Meghan Cahill.

Farraday read the message as Jonathan stood up from the heavy oak table and walked toward the bar.

Farraday trusted his instincts. He never liked Jonathan and was glad to have a reason to disbelieve Jonathan's accusations against Meghan's integrity.

Farraday believed in Meghan. She must have discovered something important about Jonathan and now needed to meet with him.

He also needed to meet her.

Now, at the lake.

Chapter Twenty-Two

THE GRAY CLOUDS ROLLED ACROSS the western sky and soon extinguished the few remaining rays that struggled against the suffocating cloud cover. It was nearly 8:30 p.m., and Farraday decided it was now safe to leave Ship Inn. He had given Jonathan almost fifteen minutes, plenty of time for Jonathan to get to his car and leave the premises. Farraday didn't want to risk the chance of Jonathan following him to the lake.

Even though Meghan's message was somewhat cryptic, Farraday believed she was in trouble; her fear of Jonathan was real.

Farraday parked his car in a remote corner of the institute lot, near the field of aging, crisp cornstalks. As he hurried along the path through the dense cornfield, Farraday hoped Meghan was safe at the lake awaiting his arrival.

Shortly after Jonathan had departed Ship Inn, Farraday had attempted to contact Meghan and had thought it odd that she didn't answer her phone. He would have felt better had he been able to speak directly with her. He texted her to let her know that he would be at the lake by 8:30.

Farraday had received an immediate text reply: *Thank you, M. Cahill.*

As Farraday broke through the dark and silent labyrinth, he hastened toward the lake, past rows of aged oak and pine trees positioned as if they were a fortress safeguarding secrets hidden within the silent and dark water.

Farraday finally arrived at the lake's shore—breathless—and strained his eyes to search for Meghan in the darkness that surrounded him.

Suddenly, Farraday heard something moving toward him. He could tell that it was moving quickly and was headed directly toward him as each hastened step became louder and louder.

"Meghan, is that you? It's me, Farraday."

When he received no reply, Farraday called out again.

"Meghan … it's me … Farraday. Can you hear me?"

Again, no answer.

Farraday slowly walked backward; he wasn't sure who or what was rapidly approaching him.

Where *was* Meghan? She said she would be waiting for him.

Suddenly, a dark figure emerged from behind a cluster of trees and stood directly in front of him. Farraday immediately recognized the human figure, but everything was wrong; he was not supposed to be here. Jonathan Ashbridge was not expected to be here.

"Good evening, Farraday. Out for a lakeside stroll? You should be more careful. It's very dark, and the water is quite murky—thick with algae and mud."

"What … what are you doing here?" Farraday stammered as he slowly retreated.

"I'm here for one reason—to see you die."

Jonathan quickly took one step aside. Suddenly, another human figure appeared from behind Jonathan, now standing face-to-face with Farraday.

This person was a stranger to Farraday. Unsure of what to say or do, Farraday turned toward Jonathan, searching for some explanation. As Farraday stared at Jonathan, Farraday felt a sudden, sharp burn enter his abdomen. His mouth opened, emitting a guttural gasp. Farraday looked back at the stranger, who now grabbed the back of his neck and pulled him closer along the entire length of the steel ice pick.

The stranger held Farraday for another second and then twisted the steel weapon 180 degrees inside Farraday's liver.

Farraday's mouth remained open as several spastic gasps flowed from deep inside his lungs' air sacs; these small areas of lung tissue had already begun to rapidly collapse.

Finally, the stranger released his grip on his victim, and Farraday's lifeless body collapsed onto the moist, moss-laden ground surrounding the dark lake. Pools of dark blood from the motionless form slowly ebbed across the earth and found their way to the water's edge.

Blood and water.

Stefan took it all in.

They pierced Christ's side with a sword, and from the wound flowed blood and water.

He admired the artistry that he had just created.

Stefan took a deep breath and smiled. He bent down over Farraday's body and retrieved Farraday's cell phone. Stefan then grabbed Farraday's right thumb and carefully placed it against the cell phone identity pad. A green light came on signaling that the phone was now activated. Using Farraday's right index finger, Stefan quickly entered an emergency call message into the phone and forwarded it to the Renaissance Institute's security office.

help me, farrady ... stabbed ...

lake ... m cahl

Stefan noticed Jonathan had remained motionless during the assault on Farraday, standing nearby as a weak, awestruck bystander. *How pathetic he looks,* Stefan thought. Even in the darkness that surrounded them, Stefan saw more than fear in Jonathan's eyes—Stefan saw terror. A look Stefan had seen many times in his profession.

"Have you seen enough?" Stefan asked.

"I don't know what to say, I never …" Jonathan whispered as he slowly shook his head.

"What … you never expected it would look like this? Isn't that right, Dr. Ashbridge?" Stefan taunted.

Stefan grabbed Jonathan's arm and led him away from the lake and the Renaissance Institute toward an abandoned railroad trail located several hundred yards away that eventually would lead them back to their cars.

They had not walked far before Stefan heard someone approach them.

Stefan paused and pushed Jonathan behind a thick oak tree. Stefan hid just inside the edge of the cornfield.

The approaching footsteps grew louder.

Stefan quietly removed the red-stained steel weapon from the plastic bag.

He sensed impending pleasure.

He would soon have another victim.

Within seconds, a tall man who appeared athletic to Stefan came into view. Stefan did not miss his chance. With one effortless thrust, the steel weapon was advanced between the fourth and fifth ribs and angled enough to violate the victim's pericardium. Within seconds, inside the victim's chest, bright oxygenated blood fled the victim's aorta and filled the sac surrounding the heart. The increasing flow of blood into the heart sac quickly compressed the failing heart, impeding its ability to function and pump blood to vital organs.

Soon, Stefan witnessed the anguish in the young man's dying eyes.

He liked this work.

He finally felt satisfied.

At least, for tonight.

Chapter Twenty-Three

MEGHAN CAHILL SWIPED HER ID badge across the electronic sensor that permitted her exit from the Renaissance Institute. As Meghan raced across the parking lot toward her 320i BMW sedan, she recalled what Jeffrey Manion had shown her earlier in the subterranean lab. She needed to tell someone about Jonathan's secret work. She had to expose Jonathan's project.

Meghan turned on the ignition and glanced at the green digital clock mounted on the car's ceiling above her rearview mirror. It was 8:55 p.m. As she stared at the clock, her eyes were distracted by the distant red and blue lights that filled her mirror. Probably a serious accident, Meghan thought, as she pulled away from the institute and the approaching screams of police sirens.

Meghan was desperate. She needed to see Dan tonight. She needed to tell him about Jonathan's horrible experiments. She knew Dan never trusted Jonathan and his assistant, and for that matter, anything they were involved in. In fact, Meghan remembered how worried Dan had become when she had told him about her meeting with Jeffrey Manion tonight.

Meghan drove to her nearby townhouse located in West Chester. For the first time tonight, she felt her eyes burning as she tried to focus on the road. She was glad she had a place near work where she could unwind. As she entered West Chester off of Route 202, Meghan decided she should call Dan, who also lived in West Chester. He would be expecting to hear from her.

The green digital clock showed that it was now 9:15 p.m., not too late, Meghan thought, as she dialed Dan's cell phone number. After several unsuccessful attempts to contact him, Meghan decided to leave a voice message.

Even though she desperately wanted to see Dan and tell him all about the horrors she had witnessed in Jonathan's subterranean lab, Meghan was resigned to wait until tomorrow morning.

But why did he not answer? They were supposed to go out tonight.

Chapter Twenty-Four

SEPTEMBER 17
SATURDAY EVENING

THE RENAISSANCE INSTITUTE'S SECURITY OFFICE received Farraday's cell phone call at 8:40 p.m. At first, the security officer thought it was a hoax. All too often, the security office had to call the local Valley Creek Township Police to respond to teenage trespassers who would use the institute lake's privacy for an evening party. It was only after the security guard finally decided to look at the caller ID that he realized the call had come from the institute's CEO.

Panic suddenly filled the seventy-five-year-old retired policeman.

CEO Farraday needed his help.

The aged security guard's response was a hurried and confusing 911 call to the Chester County dispatcher. "This is the institute reporting a crime ... we need police here now ... a man ... Mr. Farraday is hurt ..."

"Calm down, sir. Now tell me who you are," the female dispatcher responded.

"Goddamn it ... send the police here right away ..."

"We will, sir, but please tell me exactly where you are."

"I told you ... the institute ... I mean the Renaissance Institute. This is Officer Mantucci. I just got a call ... Mr. Farraday has been attacked ... down at the lake. I need help ..."

"Sir, remain on the phone. I've dispatched an emergency call to Valley Creek police. You'll also have other nearby township police respond as well."

There were several seconds of silence. "Sir, did you hear me? Sir, are you there?"

The retired police officer couldn't wait any longer. He radioed his night shift coworkers for assistance.

Mr. Farraday needed his help now.

It was on his watch, and he was determined not to let Mr. Farraday down. As Officer Mantucci pushed open the heavy, thick glass front doors of the institute, he noticed a young woman, approximately a hundred yards away, sprint across the parking lot from the direction of the laboratory located near the cornfield. Who was she? Had she come from the lake? Mantucci quickly pulled out his notepad and scribbled his observation.

Blue and red lights flooded the two roads that led up to the Renaissance Institute, signaling the arrival of numerous police vehicles.

The overweight security guard ran breathlessly across the parking lot toward the cornfield that obscured any view of the lake. A thick mist surrounded the dense cornstalks.

As the security guard entered the cornfield, he groped at his gun holster that hung well below his distended abdomen and struggled to release the .38 caliber revolver. Despite his difficulty seeing the narrow path through the stalks, he managed to free himself from the corn maze and finally reached the clearing around the lake.

The guard's determined focus to rescue Mr. Farraday had numbed any pain he normally would have had from the many scratches he had received across his face and hands from the sharp edges of the aging cornstalks.

"Mr. Farraday ... Mr. Farraday ... it's Officer Mantucci. Where are you? I'm ..." The half-mile run from the institute had finally taken its toll on the overweight security guard. Mantucci suddenly fell to his knees, sinking deep into the mud, struggling to find a breath. Within seconds, a sharp, crushing pain tore through his chest as his diseased coronary arteries struggled to keep blood flowing to his dying heart muscle.

Mantucci released the death-grip he had on his weapon and grabbed at his shirt as if to manually extract whatever it was that was crushing his chest.

It was futile. Mantucci fell forward, lying prone in the thick mud.

The dense mist had obscured his view. Officer Mantucci lay dead only several feet away from Farraday's stiffening body.

Chapter Twenty-Five

THE MAPLE TREES HAD ALREADY given up their summer cover and now gently released their golden-red leaves, which fell against the red and gray cobblestone street.

It was Philadelphia's Old City section, and Friar Anthony Salvo was taking his usual early morning walk. He was required to remain downtown during his trial, always accessible for his Center City defense attorney's questions and trial preparations. But each early morning, he would set out in defiance, on his walk from Center City through historic Philadelphia to the Delaware River.

Friar Salvo felt like a whore. He felt used. Yes, he was guilty, but there were others.

Friar Salvo was convinced that if the jury found him guilty of child abuse crimes, he would immediately cop a plea. His life was certainly worth something. Bishop Torrey and his spineless assistant, Monsignor Brannigan, would also take the fall.

Salvo was certain of that.

The Capuchin Friar strode across Philadelphia's Independence Mall and gazed up at the historic steeple clock that stood atop the birthplace of the Declaration of Independence. Friar Salvo compared the time displayed on the weathered clock to the time on his pocket watch. It was 4:45 a.m. Independence Hall was the halfway point, and both clocks confirmed his energetic pace for his five-mile walk through the city.

As Friar Salvo turned onto Walnut Street and headed east toward the Delaware River, he sensed that the surrounding city buildings shared his restlessness. Despite their sturdy brick and stone cover, the predawn autumnal wind swirled its rage into the buildings' tiny crevices and across their exposed glass panes, which surrendered subtle crackling cries. Sporadic street lamps stood as sentries and illuminated Salvo's cobblestone path, while an occasional lamp flickered its dying yellow beacon along the deserted street.

Friar Salvo soon arrived at the park adjacent to the Delaware River, where he heard the hulls of several docked boats rock against the wood pilings. He looked down at his pocket watch and realized he had walked a little quicker this morning. Perhaps it was the chilled wind at his back that quickened his pace. Or maybe it was his nervous tension, his anxiety, that caused adrenalin to surge through his body.

Tomorrow, Monday morning, the jury would meet again to deliberate the facts of his case.

They were the trier of fact. At least in theory, they were. On Friday afternoon, the Philadelphia common pleas judge had read the jury detailed instructions that were composed of language submitted by the assistant district attorney and the friar's defense attorney. The judge had reminded the jury panel to consider only the evidence presented in the case. Their responsibility as jurors required them to weigh the evidence, make judgments about factual discrepancies, and ultimately render their decision.

To search for the truth, the judge had instructed them.

What do they know? Friar Salvo thought. *This jury was only given half-truths.*

Finding him guilty was not achieving the truth.

As the trier of fact, this jury would legally decide his fate, Salvo knew.

As a Capuchin friar, a parish vicar, he held the power to decide the fate of the bishop and monsignor.

He would be *their* jury.

He would decide *their* fate.

The friar stared up at the dark, cloudy sky that draped its moonlit shadows on the Delaware River and across the park bench where he sought a moment's rest.

Rest from his trial. His burden.

Here, in the isolated park, not all of the shadows were created by the cloudy moonlit night. One shadow moved with purpose. The dark form flowed instinctively across the grass, toward the bench where its unsuspecting prey sat in silence. Each warm, exhaled breath filled the darkness, signaling the shadow's approach toward the priest.

Suddenly, Friar Salvo spun around to see what had disturbed the crisp, fallen leaves. Just as the full moon broke through the shroud of black clouds, the shadow's strike was quick and deliberate.

A dense cloud of anguished breath slowly left Friar Salvo's mouth as the steel blade ripped into his upper abdomen.

The friar's final gasp signaled his departure from earth and acknowledged his pursuer's successful completion of yet another assignment.

Chapter Twenty-Six

THE WARM, MORNING BREEZE SOFTLY parted the lace curtains covering the two ceiling-to-floor windows in Meghan Cahill's bedroom located on the second floor of her historic townhouse in West Chester. Soft, rhythmic flashes of sunlight found their way through the flowing ripples of lace and gently awoke Meghan from her sleep.

Meghan raised her hands and covered her face. She slowly rubbed her eyes, which ached, reminding her of last night's restless sleep.

How could I possibly sleep after visiting Jonathan's subterranean lab last night? Meghan thought. She needed to tell someone immediately— someone she trusted. *My God, where was Dan last night?* They were supposed to go out after she finished her meeting with Jeffrey. She never dreamed she would be shown the horrible effects from Jonathan's experiments with dogs, which, she was told, would culminate in the destruction of human lives.

At first, she refused to believe him. It was all too surreal. But when she saw for herself the many ravaged canine bodies and smelled the blood, she knew it was not a dream.

It was a nightmare.

Last night, it was her nightmare. Jonathan's work horrified her. She remembered standing in the lab; her stomach churned, sending waves of nausea up into her throat. She had tried to swallow, but it was no use. She could barely breathe, but she needed to remain in the lab and hear Jeffrey's confession. She had tried to ask him several questions, get more specific information from him, but was unsuccessful; his head hung down against his chest, and his shoulders slouched—ashamed and defeated.

Jeffrey was distraught over his association with Jonathan, as well as his decision to finally inform an outsider.

Meghan had seen more than shame in Jeffrey's eyes.

She saw fear. Jeffrey's fear of Jonathan.

Somehow, Meghan felt empathy for Jeffrey. She felt his same fear, afraid of what Jonathan would do to them if he ever found out. But why was she kidding herself?

Jonathan would find out about their meeting; there was no doubt. Somehow he would learn about Jeffrey's disloyalty. She had to report Jonathan to the institute's board of directors.

And whatever happened with Dan? Meghan questioned. She desperately needed to talk to him.

Meghan sat up in bed and tried to run her fingers through her tangled, auburn hair. The bells from nearby St. Agnes Catholic Church tolled throughout the historic neighborhood of West Chester, ending on the eighth resonating note. Even on a weekend, she was usually awake by 7:00 a.m. But not this morning. Whenever she stayed at her West Chester home, she routinely ran an early-morning twelve-mile course along the Chester County countryside on Route 842, which she would turn onto from High Street near the Chester County courthouse.

This Sunday morning was different. She was exhausted and felt like she had never gone to sleep. Her mind was full of racing thoughts. Thoughts mixed up like a jigsaw puzzle with its many pieces of varied shapes and sizes strewn across the floor.

Meghan desperately needed help. She needed Dan's calmness and logic to help her.

Meghan felt drained. She slowly lowered herself beneath the warm bed sheets and pulled her comforter on top of her. She would rest for just a few more minutes, she decided.

Meghan raced from the dark, silent lake through the brown cornstalks toward the building's parking lot lights that glowed against the green-tinted windows of the Renaissance Institute. The faster Meghan ran, the farther away the research building appeared. Suddenly, the thick stalks seemed to reach out and wrap themselves around her as they swayed in the cold, damp autumn wind.

Soon, the hard ground beneath her feet grew soft and muddy, slowing her escape from the secrets at the lake.

Meghan knew she had to get away.

Her every effort made to pull her legs out of the deep, thick mud was useless. Her breathing grew heavier. Her chest ached as she struggled for her next breath. She felt herself sinking deeper and deeper into the mud pit. Images of earth worms slithering across her face and through her hair sent waves of panic throughout her body. The smell of wet soil sickened her as she fought against the sustained spasms tightening in the back of her throat.

Dead cornstalks burdened with decayed cornhusks covered her head, pushing her deeper into her living tomb. Her final view, just before her burial was complete, showed her flashes of red and blue lights accompanied by piercing sirens that echoed deep within her head.

Meghan finally struggled free from the damp, tangled bed sheets and quickly sat up in bed. She was home, safe in her townhouse, but her heart still pounded. Outside her bedroom windows, Meghan could hear an approaching police siren. How long had she slept? Her nightstand clock showed that it was almost 9:00 a.m.

Suddenly, Meghan heard a soothing and familiar sound. St. Agnes's church bells began their "Ave Maria" rendition as a prelude to the nine resonating chimes.

Meghan reached for her cell phone. Dan had not left her any messages while she had slept.

She decided to dial Dan's cell phone once again. After the fourth ring, Meghan was about to hang up. Suddenly she heard a man's voice. She knew it wasn't Dan.

"Hello … hello. Who is this?" Meghan remained silent despite her urge to demand where Dan was.

"Did you hear me? Identify yourself," the voice insisted.

Meghan quickly ended the call. She sat for a moment and tried to identify the foreign voice on Dan's phone. She pressed redial and saw Dan's number on her screen. She hadn't misdialed. But who was that man answering Dan's phone?

She chose not to speak because she didn't want to reveal herself to a stranger. Why did another man have his cell phone?

Meghan tried to control her questions before they suddenly became her fears. She resolved to remain calm. Dan would want her to be calm. Meghan's mind quickly raced to an acceptable explanation.

Dan must have lost his cell phone.

Meghan stood up and walked across the bedroom floor toward her bedroom windows overlooking High Street.

That's right.

He probably left it at work, and someone turned it into security.

Meghan dialed Dan's home.

After five rings, Dan's voice answered. *Thank God,* Meghan thought.

> *Hi, I'm not available to take your call. Please leave a message, and I'll return your call as soon as possible.*

Meghan sighed. She realized this was the first time she had heard his voice message. Where was he?

> *Dan, it's me, Meghan. It's 9:10 in the morning. Sunday morning. Where are you? Please give me a call right away. I've got to see you. I'm at home, in West Chester.*

Meghan sat back down on her bed and stared at the lace curtains of her bedroom windows. Earlier, they had flowed gracefully away from the windows, moving like angel wings across her bed. Now, they desperately clung to the screens as if some unknown force was trying to drain all energy and grace from them.

Were her curtains the victims of some mysterious power? The wind had simply shifted direction, Meghan assured herself.

Nothing mysterious. Right?

Meghan quickly stood up and rubbed her eyes. Everything would be fine, she told herself. She would go for a long run, unwind, and be back to hear Dan's phone message. They would meet, and she would tell him everything.

They would develop a strategy to finally hold Jonathan accountable.

Chapter Twenty-Seven

"W HO WAS ON THE PHONE?"

Detective McManus ignored the young police officer's question and pressed the caller ID button on Dan Rafferty's cell phone.

Jeffrey Perseus.

Who was this person? A friend of the murder victim? Or maybe a coworker.

Detective McManus scribbled the name on a sheet of paper torn from his pocket-size notebook and handed it to his fellow Valley Creek Township police officer.

"Here, run this name through our computer. Also check it with our list of employees at the Renaissance Institute."

"Probably just a wrong number," offered the rookie who had just completed his first year on the force.

McManus slowly raised his eyes over his tortoise-shell reading glasses that rested against the lower part of his prominent Irish nose and glared at the neophyte cop. A twenty-year veteran of the Philadelphia Police Department, McManus now enjoyed the less hectic police work of his ten years with the Valley Creek Police Department in Chester County. What he didn't particularly enjoy, though, were these sophomoric observations made by the inexperienced police staff. McManus accepted these rash comments as a trade-off for working in this pristine Chester County suburb of Philadelphia.

"Listen closely. I'm only going to say it once. In our work, everything that happens is relevant. Only after you think first ... did you hear me, Officer ... think about what you have seen and heard, should you begin to eliminate the irrelevant crap."

McManus enjoyed the rookie's uneasiness with the lecture as the young cop repeatedly grabbed at his leather gun belt, not to readjust its weight, but to reaffirm his status as a law enforcement officer.

McManus continued. "That wasn't a wrong number. The person who called intended to speak to our victim. I know that because most callers who think they've dialed incorrectly will either immediately hang up or admit they misdialed. This person was different. Not only did the person remain quiet on the line while I spoke, the caller's breathing actually became more rapid."

McManus continued his lecture. "In fact, I'll even bet this wasn't a social call. I think the caller *needed* to speak with Dan Rafferty and was frightened not to hear his voice."

"All right, I get your point. Anything else, sir?" The young patrolman grew impatient. He didn't like being treated like one of McManus's police academy recruits. Thank God, he wasn't permanently assigned to him, he thought. His chief had assigned him to assist McManus during the preliminary investigation of the Renaissance Institute murders. He could do this. Just as long as it was a temporary assignment.

"No. That's all. Just get back to me about the name." McManus had heard something on the cell phone that was interesting to him. He paused for a moment, prepared to tell his novice assistant about what he had heard but decided it was a waste of his time. This young cop had a lot to learn. McManus was willing to teach him, but only on his terms. He had no time for a rookie who was impatient and showed no interest in learning from his experience.

Detective McManus took out his notepad and scribbled an entry:

Sept. 18, 9:00 a.m.—cell phone call
Church bells—"Ave Maria."
Police siren.
Jeffrey Perseus?

Chapter Twenty-Eight

JEFFREY MANION STOOD UP AND looked down at the subterranean lab's freshly scrubbed linoleum floor. It was 7:00, Sunday morning, and Manion was not surprised that, since he had been working nonstop all night erasing every trace of evidence of the project from the floor and examination tables, evidence of a thick ammonium odor saturated the air in the lab.

Jeffrey felt it difficult to breathe. He quickly lifted his wet T-shirt and wiped the beads of sweat that flowed from his matted hair. He had hoped he could temporarily escape the pungent odor as he buried his face against his shirt.

No such luck. The smell only got worse as Jeffrey realized the ammonium vapor had also saturated his sweat; he had spent too much time cleaning the lab. Manion quickly gathered the tainted scrub brushes and buckets used to remove traces of splattered blood stains and animal hair and stood back to critique his work.

One final look. He was satisfied Jonathan would be pleased.

Suddenly, the high-pitched rhythmic tone from Manion's cell phone echoed against the sterile, cement-white laboratory walls and reminded him that he had forgotten to check in with Jonathan.

Their plan was well orchestrated. Timing was crucial. Manion was confident he had successfully performed his part last night.

Meet with Meghan alone.

Call Farraday at Ship Inn using a cell phone that contains Meghan's identity SIM card.

Get Farraday to the lake.

Manion did his part, but what happened last night?

Did Farraday show up at the lake?

If he did, what did Stefan do to him? Forget that. Manion knew what was going to happen to Farraday. He just wanted to know how Stefan killed him.

"Hello?" Manion answered hesitatingly.

"Why haven't you called me?" Jonathan challenged.

"I was going to call … this morning, but I've been down here in the lab since last night. You know, cleaning. There was a lot to clean up." Manion knew he initially answered Jonathan somewhat sheepishly. He didn't like how easily Jonathan could make him feel defensive. Manion felt he finished his reply more confidently.

"You've got to be joking. You mean to tell me that you're still at the institute? What the hell have you been doing all night?" Jonathan demanded.

"I told you. I've been—"

"Shut the hell up. Did you forget that Farraday has been lying dead down there at the lake?"

"No, I didn't forget. But I needed—"

"You needed to get the fuck out of there last night. Be far away as possible from the institute. The whole perimeter is now a fucking crime scene!" Jonathan shouted.

"All right, all right ... I get the point," Manion tried to calm his boss.

After pausing a few seconds, Jonathan inhaled deeply and said, "Look, I'm sure the police have not only found the bodies by now, but have also started their search around the premises."

"What do you mean, bodies. I thought ..." Manion's voice cracked as he tried to regain his composure.

"Quiet. There were two victims last night. Farraday and some other asshole. You don't need to know who it was. You just need to get out of there, now. And without anyone seeing you."

"I'm sorry, Jonathan. I'm leaving now. There won't be any more slip-ups. Trust me." Manion wanted to hear a reassuring word from Jonathan. What he heard instead was the sudden click from Jonathan's phone.

"What a pompous ass. I hate him," Manion murmured.

Jeffrey decided to exit the institute from the east side doorway since he noticed that the police had focused their investigation at the lake and surrounding cornfields on the west side of the complex.

As he approached the east side's exit door, Manion gave a sigh of relief. No security guard. His cryptic call made earlier to the security office, posing as a police officer requesting assistance, had indeed worked. No need to secure the east side of the building, Manion had advised. The security officers were all too willing to do real police work.

Manion retrieved an electronic card-key from his jacket pocket, but before swiping the card, he stared down at the card's photo of the institute employee. She was his cover. If Jeffrey had used his card, the security office would know that he had been at the lab. All card swipes were electronically recorded and stored in the Security Department's data bank.

Manion couldn't afford being placed here.

His coworker, Emily DeHaven, would be his cover.

DeHaven was always argumentative with him and constantly

challenged him about his work with Jonathan. She deserved the problems that would arise with the use of her ID card. He was confident that instead of his identity recorded, the data bank would show that Emily DeHaven was at the institute throughout the night.

Manion was also confident that Emily was at home alone working on a research grant proposal assignment that Jonathan had insisted be completed and submitted to him by early Monday morning. To ensure she was at home alone Saturday evening, Manion had called her shortly before he used her access card to enter the building.

He enjoyed his few minutes of one-sided conversation—taunting Emily with her last-minute assignment.

Emily had one comment before she hung up on him. *Don't you have anything better to do tonight than to harass me?*

Jeffrey would remember her rhetorical question. How naive she was to think she could dismiss him in such a way.

He did, in fact, have something better to do that night. It would involve her in such a way that would forever affect her life.

Her happiness.

Her freedom.

Chapter Twenty-Nine

DETECTIVE SEAN MCMANUS LEANED BACK in his black leather desk chair and stared up at his office ceiling, stained with fresh water marks from last night's heavy rain storm. McManus knew that one day part of the Valley Creek Township building's second floor would eventually collapse and bury his office. He only hoped he wasn't working at his desk at the time to witness his own demise.

McManus slowly rubbed his eyes and mentally reviewed the evidence he had so far on the Renaissance Institute murders.

He had just returned from the coroner's lab where he witnessed the autopsies.

Two men were murdered. A third, found dead. A security guard with a bad heart. Their deaths occurred between 7:30 and 9:00 p.m. At least that was the preliminary time-frame the Chester County coroner had given. "Remember, Detective, it's only an approximate time," the coroner had announced in his monotone voice.

McManus was amused. The coroner actually admitted he had the luxury of knowing the time of Farraday's death based on the time Farraday had dialed the 911 call from his cell phone down at the lake to the Renaissance Security office.

However, McManus was worried. He knew never to assume anything about a crime scene. He was concerned, therefore, about the county coroner's depth of experience. How many murder victims had Dr. Swope, the seventy-three-year-old medical examiner, examined in Chester County?

McManus was confident with his own level of experience. His expertise had developed over the many years he had spent working homicide cases in Philadelphia. Many hours—no, many months—had been logged in at the Philadelphia medical examiner's lab located at University Avenue and Currie Boulevard in West Philadelphia. He would always personally attend every autopsy of the victim he was working on.

Not only did he admire the Philadelphia Chief M.E.'s unique background and expertise, McManus also liked him. Dr. Evan Hawthorne was a decent, hard-working M.E. who paid no attention to the clock but focused for hours on one goal. Find the exact cause of death and investigate any and all forensic clues left behind at the crime scene. Hawthorne instilled confidence in all of Philadelphia's homicide detectives, and especially in the city's district attorney's office.

One group of professionals, however, despised him. They felt he was too thorough.

Too prepared. Too confident.

When they learned Hawthorne was working the case, defense attorneys would flinch. What worried them the most was that Dr. Hawthorne was more than just a well-trained forensic pathologist. Hawthorne was also an experienced attorney, a seasoned litigator who had decided after ten years of criminal defense work to finally get out. He realized he had lived and breathed enough scum. He had had more than his share of defending criminals, most of whom he knew were guilty of the crimes and deserved the worst punishment. Hawthorne had turned his back on a multimillion-dollar-a-year legal career and had pursued his medical education and training at the University of Pennsylvania Medical School.

His goal was to become Philadelphia's chief medical examiner. At the age of forty-five, he finally reached his goal. His five years of experience now as the chief M.E. only enhanced his drive to become better with each new homicide case.

What McManus liked most about Hawthorne was his honesty. He knew how to talk to a jury; he was always comfortable explaining things without appearing condescending.

Defense attorneys hated him. They hated how juries listened to every word he spoke.

Juries trusted him.

Detective McManus knew he could call Dr. Evan Hawthorne anytime to review the physical evidence with him. In other words, get a second opinion on whatever the Chester County coroner theorized about the murders.

McManus continued his review of his notes on the two victims' autopsies.

> One victim, fifty-five years old, verified by driver's license ID, with good overall muscle tone sustained a single stab puncture wound to upper abdomen below the sternum, extending up into the chest through the sub xiphoid area.

McManus had been impressed as he witnessed Dr. Swope's external examination. He had probed his slender and agile fingers deep inside along the stab-wound tract. McManus then had braced himself as the county coroner reached for his scalpel and firmly pressed the steel blade against the cold, rigid skin. Within seconds, Dr. Swope had performed the customary Y-incision across the torso and prepared for a quick entry into the victim's abdomen and chest.

McManus had witnessed Dr. Swope's latex-gloved hands quickly begin their exploration through adipose tissue and then further beneath the modest layer of dissected fat downward toward the muscle layers that had tried to protect the victim's vital organs. Dr. Swope quickly focused his attention on the stab-wound track and meticulously pursued the cause of death.

> Upper abdominal entry wound penetrated the liver and extended upward into the chest and into the heart's pericardium. The heart's sac was punctured by a fine-point sharp object, approximately 15 centimeters in length, which had been removed along the same track without causing any other trauma to the surrounding tissue.

Detective McManus read Dr. Swope's cause of death ... *massive hemorrhage from liver trauma, acute heart failure, secondary to cardiac tamponade due to acute trauma to pericardial sac.*

Detective McManus tossed aside the Chester County M.E.'s autopsy report on CEO Farraday. He now turned his attention to the second victim's autopsy report.

> Thirty-seven-year-old, six foot two, sandy blond haired male, excellent muscle development with suntanned skin, sustained single puncture stab wound to upper abdomen, through sub xiphoid area that extends into pericardial sac.

McManus knew that it was no coincidence.

Both men were killed by the same stab wound technique.

And both victims were probably killed with the same weapon.

However, Detective McManus still had many unanswered questions. Were both men murdered by the same assailant? Was there more than one killer?

What was the motive or motives for these murders?

And, what connection, if any, did the victims share?

McManus questioned the Chester County M.E. as to how long each man could have lived after the assault. Dr. Swope paused during his dissection of the second victim's heart sac and slowly raised his heavy-browed eyes to meet McManus's. Still holding the victim's grayish-red heart muscle, Dr. Swope answered.

"It depends. If the victim was in poor health, death would occur immediately. There would be no cardiac reserve to sustain such a person beyond a few seconds. However, if the victim was healthy, I mean to say, in excellent shape like our two victims, then death would probably occur after a few minutes." Dr. Swope gazed down toward his hands and carefully cradled the victim's heart.

"Let me explain further. Once the sac that surrounds the heart is penetrated by a sharp object, such as a knife or pick, blood from the heart quickly fills the sac and presses against the pulsating heart muscle. As the pressure of blood increases in the sac, it soon becomes difficult for the heart to contract, and thereby difficult to send oxygenated blood throughout the body. The victim will experience a decrease in blood pressure, and his awareness diminishes since blood flow to the brain is compromised."

McManus liked what he heard. He already knew the answer to his question. He just wanted to assess Swope's expertise with chest trauma. He had to admit, Dr. Swope wasn't as inexperienced as he had thought.

But could the Chester County M.E.'s office effectively analyze the DNA evidence? There had been numerous samples collected.

Hair strands found on each victim. Traces of skin found beneath Farraday's fingers.

Samples of body fluid found on the victims' hands.

McManus had the experience to know that many criminal cases were either won or lost based solely on DNA samples. Fortunately, he was present and in charge at the crime scene when the samples were discovered and collected, and he had ensured that the chain of custody for this evidence was not violated.

However, there was one aspect of the investigation that was beyond his control—the laboratory techniques used to analyze the DNA.

McManus knew that the collection and storage of DNA evidence was vital to a police investigation. Also important in a homicide investigation was the procedure for DNA testing. The country also quickly became well aware of this fact, as they became armchair experts glued to their TV sets, watching the O. J. Simpson trial unfold.

Based on years of experience working with the Philadelphia medical examiner's office, McManus was certain that the courtroom demeanor and testimony of the M.E. was even more crucial to the prosecution's case. Even if the evidence clearly pointed toward a guilty verdict, an experienced defense attorney could weaken the strength of the D.A.'s case if the jury was shown that the medical examiner was not credible.

McManus still had doubts about Dr. Swope. Even though the Chester County M.E. knew about chest trauma and physiologic effects of cardiac tamponade, McManus still had a feeling Dr. Swope would not be effective in the courtroom. Call it a hunch, he thought. What he did know for certain was that the Philadelphia M.E.'s office boasted an experienced staff and a highly effective conviction rate.

They were his reference, his standard of expertise for a prosecutor's successful scientific basis for a successful guilty verdict.

Dr. Evan Hawthorne, the chief medical examiner for Philadelphia, was Detective McManus's gold standard for professionalism, honesty, and credibility in the courtroom.

Defense attorneys hated him. McManus admired him.

McManus was resolved to call Dr. Hawthorne for assistance with these double homicides. He knew, however, he would first have to officially clear it with Dr. Swope.

He didn't expect a problem with the Chester County M.E. He was confident he could convince the elderly coroner to consider it professional courtesy. McManus grinned.

Chapter Thirty

Professor Marguilies quickly reached for his cell phone as it sent vibratory tones across the etched glass-top table, disrupting his solitary silence as he pondered life from his porch overlooking his private South Carolina marshland.

"I'm alone. What do you have for me?" said Professor Marguilies.

"Pegasus continues to soar. The threat has been eliminated," Stefan's confident voice replied.

"Very good." The professor exhaled a subtle sigh of relief.

"There was one more matter that I had to take care of," replied Stefan.

"Yes, I'm listening."

"Soon after I completed the contract, there was another individual that required my attention. Some guy named Rafferty. He was a potential witness. Trust me. He won't be a problem for us anymore," Stefan assured him.

"Well, that is interesting. We were not expecting him to be a problem. I presume you will need some further financial satisfaction from our associates." Professor Marguilies spoke with a detached tone.

"Normally I would. However, another matter has recently benefited me. You can tell your associates there will not be any increased financial expectation." Stefan paused.

"Consider it my professional courtesy to you." Stefan enjoyed the leverage he now had over the professor. Stefan continued.

"Contact me when you want me to begin the clinical trials for your drug. I have already chosen the human subjects."

The professor recognized the cold, impassionate tone in Stefan's voice. He *was* the right choice for the Pegasus Project, the professor reflected.

"Answer the God-damned phone," Professor Marguilies muttered as he waited for Jonathan Ashbridge to pick up. It had been several days since he last spoke with Jonathan. Much had happened since that time. The professor didn't care that there was a second victim last night at the lake. He trusted Stefan's judgment. If he had decided this guy— Rafferty—had to die, so be it. He had worked with Stefan before; the professor knew his style. Even though at first he was sickened by Stefan's killing methods, over time, Professor Marguilies rationalized that his Swiss associate's techniques were justified since they were the necessary means to achieve the desired goal.

But did he view Stefan's nonpareil work as something more than bizarre examples of someone's detached professional life? Marguilies asked himself many times if he was beginning to adopt more of Stefan's philosophy of life. As a bioethicist known and respected throughout the world, Professor Marguilies had challenged many traditional ethical tenets, which had always supported the sanctity of life, at any cost.

At any cost? No, not to support life at any cost, but instead support a higher, more noble cause than life itself.

Execute the means necessary to attain the more ethical end.

Yes, Professor Marguilies had often times tried to convince others through his writings and law school lectures that sometimes a situation called for lives to be punished and sacrificed in order to benefit that more noble cause.

His Pegasus Project. Designed to help the abandoned. The oppressed. The project would sacrifice lives in order to punish others.

Even human subjects would be killed during the project's clinical trials. Stefan would see to that.

Priests would also be killed. They would atone for their sins through suffering; these religious fishermen would suffer justifiable mental and physical anguish.

The Pegasus Project's drug would see to that.

Now where is Ashbridge? Professor Marguilies thought. He decided to try Jonathan's phone again.

After the fifth ring, Jonathan decided he had kept Marguilies waiting long enough. He still resented the professor's condescending attitude toward him when they had their first meeting with Stefan at Vickers Tavern in Chester County. He deserved more respect. Without his pharmaceutical research and discovery of their drug, there would be no project. The professor owed a great deal to him. Jonathan was resolved not to let the professor forget it.

"Hello, Professor. How are you?" Jonathan tried to sound sincere.

"I've been just fine. Why haven't I heard from you?" said Marguilies.

"I've been busy, Professor. You do remember what Jeffrey and I have been doing during the last week?" Jonathan rebutted.

"How can I remember something that you haven't told me? You were supposed to keep me informed each day regarding your work on the drug's effectiveness as a vapor. *You do* remember that obligation, don't you?"

Jonathan forced himself to inhale deeply and slowly exhale his contempt for this aging academician.

"Professor Marguilies, my drug is ready," Jonathan replied with contempt.

For the first time since Jonathan and the professor had met at the University of Pennsylvania Medical School more than fifteen years ago, Jonathan now felt he was finally in control of their relationship.

Excuse me ... you mean ...," stammered Professor Marguilies.

"You heard me. My drug is ready for human trials," Jonathan answered.

Chapter Thirty-One

MEGHAN SPRINTED THE LAST MILE of her run through the Chester County countryside outside West Chester. Her run had become longer than she had originally planned since the weather was too perfect to turn around. The cool autumn breeze slowly guided the silver-lined clouds across the blue sky above her, as if following her along the way.

As Meghan raced the last several hundred yards along Route 842 before she would turn onto High Street in downtown West Chester, she thought of the graceful sojourn of the clouds across the azure autumn sky. She wanted to be part of the sky. Meghan felt her cloud cover was a kindred spirit, protecting her from all harm and encouraging her to reach beyond her self-imposed limitations.

As Meghan turned onto High Street, she wondered what had drawn her so intensely to her clouds.

Of course, she knew.

It was her grandmother, Nana. Nana's spirit had talked to her. She should have known this right away, but she was too distracted with everything Jeffrey had shown her last night at the Renaissance Institute lab.

Strive beyond your potential, Nana often taught her, not only with her painting, but also with life.

Never allow your art subject to control you.

Meghan could still hear Nana's gentle voice, guiding her to become more self-assured in her personal life, not in her professional life as a pharmaceutical research scientist. Meghan's reputation for research in the pharmaceutical industry was excellent. During her employment at the institute, she was well-published; her academic credentials boasted a dual PhD in Pathology and Pharmacology. The board of directors and especially CEO Farraday knew about her reputation at Penn and also knew that they needed her unique expertise at the Renaissance Institute.

Where Meghan struggled, though, was with self-confidence in her personal life. The shock of suddenly losing her parents in a fatal car accident while she was at Yale, and then the sudden death of Nana were losses so profound and traumatic that Meghan found it impossible to recover.

Meghan struggled with relationships now. At one point, she honestly believed Jonathan Ashbridge could change everything for her. Help her renew her self-confidence. Believe in herself.

Meghan now realized that Jonathan's affections and commitment to her had been a lie.

He had manipulated her.

Never allow your subject to control you.

Meghan needed her grandmother now more than ever. God, she wished that Nana were still alive, teaching her, guiding her.

Meghan arrived back at her townhouse, and as she unlocked the front door, she heard her phone ringing. She sprinted up the five steps that brought her to the first-floor landing of her living area and prayed that it would be Dan finally calling.

Before reaching her phone positioned on an antique mahogany stand beside an earth-toned cloth recliner, Meghan paused and inhaled deeply, not merely to catch her breath, but to garner enough inner strength to simply answer the phone.

"Hello," whispered Meghan, hesitant to ask who the caller was.

"Meg. Is that you?" the female caller asked.

"Yes … it is." Meghan's hope that it was Dan was now quickly shattered.

"It's me, Emily. Are you alone?" Her voice was soft and guarded.

"Yes, I am. What's wrong?"

"Have you seen the news on TV?"

"No, what's going on?"

"There've been two murders at the Renaissance Institute. Two bodies discovered down at the lake."

"What … two bodies? When were they found?"

"Last night. Meg, it's not good."

"What do you mean? What happened?"

"Meghan, listen to me. I didn't want to be the one to tell you this, but …"

"Emily, what are you saying?" Meghan's breathing grew shallow. She felt her heart pounding. Not even when she ran hard did her chest ache like it did now.

Meghan's thoughts flashed through her mind. Where was Dan? Why did he not call her?

Meghan now feared the worst.

"Dan was one of the victims. Meg … Dan Rafferty was found murdered near the lake."

Oh God, it can't be. Please don't let it be true, pleaded Meghan.

"The other victim was Farraday," blurted Emily.

"It can't be Dan. We were supposed to go out last night. He told me he would probably be at home waiting for my call. I had to first meet someone last night at the institute ..." Meghan Cahill caught herself. Emily DeHaven was a good friend, but she wasn't sure if she should burden Emily with her knowledge about Jonathan's work.

"I'm so sorry to be the one to tell you about this but I just saw the TV news report. Meghan, are you okay?" Emily heard the muffled cries from her friend.

"How ... did it happen?"

"The police don't know yet. They say they have some leads though."

"I don't know ... what to say. Dan was not supposed to be at the institute last night. And why Farraday? I don't understand."

"There's more, Meghan."

"What?"

"It's about you. One of the leads concerns you. Meghan, the police are looking for you. There was this detective, I think his name was McManus, who—"

"What did you say? The police mentioned my name? For what reason?" Meghan's voice cracked. Her knees had withstood the initial shock about Dan but now buckled as she heard that she was somehow involved in the police investigation. Involved in the murders. Meghan lowered herself onto the thick, cushioned ottoman.

"I don't know any more details, but the Valley Creek Police are trying to locate you. What's this all about, Meghan?"

"Listen, I don't know. I've just been told that my lab associate for the past two years was found murdered last night at the Renaissance Institute along with the Institute's CEO. You tell me what's going on," Meghan insisted.

"You said you were supposed to meet Dan. Where—at the institute?"

"No."

"But you told me that you were at the institute last night."

Meghan hesitated. Emily was right. She did admit she was at the institute. Should she tell her now the whole story?

Her meeting with Jeffrey Manion?

Jonathan's secret research work in the subterranean lab?

It was true. Emily DeHaven was a good friend. In the beginning of her relationship with Jonathan, Emily had tried to convince her that Jonathan was someone not to trust. As a researcher working in Jonathan's lab, Emily knew what type of person he was. She also didn't care much for Jonathan's assistant, Jeffrey Manion, whom she referred to as Jonathan's inept gofer.

After several months into Meghan's relationship with Jonathan, Emily had finally told her she was on her own with him. She was tired of trying to convince her that Jonathan Ashbridge loved only one person. Himself.

Meghan now knew what she had to do.

"Emily, I know I can trust you. There's something I have to tell you. Something that I've waited to tell Dan since last night."

"What is it?" Emily asked.

"You're right. I was at the institute last night, but I wasn't at the lake. You've got to believe me. I met Jeffrey. Jeffrey Manion. He wanted to show me something in Jonathan's secret basement lab. You know, the lab that was off-limits to everyone."

"Yes, I know about that lab. I mean, I knew they were supposedly working on some kind of secret NIH experiment."

"Right. But Jeffrey contacted me on Friday. He insisted that he meet with me Saturday night. He claimed he had to report Jonathan's secret work to someone. He said he trusted me."

"Did he really? Well, let me tell you something about Jeffrey Manion. Luis Sanchez and I don't trust him, and we never trusted his 'special' work with Jonathan in that lab."

"Let me finish," Meghan insisted.

"I'm sorry, go ahead," replied Emily.

"Jeffrey brought me down to their basement lab last night. What he showed me was horrible. At first, too horrible to believe that anyone would conduct such experiments."

"Tell me what you saw down there," Emily insisted.

Meghan tightened her grip on her phone, stood up from her ottoman, and slowly walked across the living room toward the front windows.

Gusts of autumn wind struggled with the trees to loosen their hold on the salmon-colored leaves. Soon each tree seemed to admit defeat and finally released their autumn foliage. Groups of leaves fluttered away now, some pulled in flight, some across the cobblestone sidewalks, while others, less fortunate, firmly matted against the Williamsburg brick buildings.

Meghan told Emily only certain details of what Jeffrey had shown her.

"Meghan ... Jeffrey actually showed you their experiments last night?"

"Yes. Afterwards, I ran from the institute to my car and quickly drove here to West Chester."

"Did you see or hear anything down at the lake?"

"No. I don't even remember looking down there. I was too preoccupied with getting to the institute and meeting with Jeffrey. Later when I left the lab, I don't remember seeing anything except my car as I ran from the building. I just wanted to get far away from that place."

"Try to tell me what you saw down there in their basement lab," Emily asked.

"The lab smelled horrible. The air down there was filled with stench—decaying flesh. Animal flesh. I could hardly breathe."

"Wait a minute. Are you saying there were dead bodies in the lab?"

"Yes. They were laying all over the place. Dogs. I think they were all dogs. I don't know." Meghan struggled to breathe. The odor. Clumps of blood mixed with sawdust. She was there now. Back inside the lab.

"This is crazy." Emily DeHaven didn't know what else to say.

"Body parts torn apart. Dead animals in wired crates. Some I couldn't tell what they were. Pieces of flesh stuck between wire gates. It was horrible," Meghan cried out.

"What was Jeffrey doing?" Emily asked.

"At first nothing. He just stood there ... shaking his head."

"Did he tell you what they were doing down there?"

"Not at first. I never said a word either. I couldn't. Then finally, he just looked at me and knew that I had seen enough. That I needed some kind of explanation."

"My God, what did he say?"

"He told me that Jonathan was out of control. Insane, he thought. His animal experiments were supposed to find a cure for aggressive behavior in humans. Uncontrollable, pathological behavior."

"I don't understand. You mean Jonathan gave drugs to aggressive dogs to change their behavior? Make them calmer?"

"No. Jeffrey told me they developed a drug that could turn a docile animal like a beagle into an aggressive beast. So aggressive that it could actually make the beagle become a killer. Attack and ravage not only just other dogs but destroy an extremely aggressive breed. Like pit bulls. Emily, they made beagles attack and destroy pit bulls. I know it sounds crazy ..."

"This is unbelievable. Beagles drugged to attack and kill pit bulls?"

"Believe it. That's what they've been doing for the past few weeks."

"Why did Jeffrey want to tell you about this now?"

"He's afraid of Jonathan. Afraid of what he may do next."

"Next? What are you saying, Jeffrey thinks Jonathan has some sort of perverse plan for his drug?"

"I don't know. Jeffrey doesn't know either. He's just scared. I truly saw fear in his eyes. He's especially afraid that Jonathan will somehow find out that I've been told about these animal experiments. He's afraid of what Jonathan will do to him."

"You've got to report him. Now that Farraday is dead, you have to notify the institute's board of directors. They'll report him to the police," Emily directed.

"Damn it, Emily. I don't know if it's that simple."

"What do you mean?"

"Jeffrey's not the only one who's afraid of Jonathan. I'm afraid he'll come after me. He already has it in for me."

"What are you talking about?"

"It's a long story. Simply put, Farraday planned to get rid of Jonathan. Fire him. And then give all of his research money and lab space to me. In fact, Farraday planned to make me the new vice president and director of research."

"Christ—this *is* bizarre. Farraday and Dan are both dead. Killed at the same place on institute property—and don't forget, the police are still looking for you."

"I'm scared, Emily. I didn't do anything wrong. If the police think I killed Dan and Farraday, that's just crazy."

Emily heard Meghan's voice grow louder. More than just scared. Emily also knew what Jonathan was capable of doing to her friend.

Who killed those men? She didn't know. She did believe one thing.

Meghan Cahill could never harm a living soul.

"Meghan, I believe you. But you've got to get a hold of yourself. Remember, you have nothing to hide. Even though you were at the institute Saturday night, the same night they were killed, you were with Jeffrey. And then there is his disclosure about Jonathan's perverse experiments."

"I know. You're right. It's just that ... I can't accept that Dan is dead."

Meghan sighed deeply. "Dan was more than my associate. When we met at the lake last Friday, he spoke about his feelings for me. And now he's gone. It's just not fair. Someone has to pay for this," Meghan insisted.

"What are you going to do?"

"Tomorrow morning, I'll get up for work and walk into the institute. I'm not sure how I'll be able to do it, but I will. If the police want to talk to me, I'll be ready for them." Emily no longer heard fear in her friend's voice. Meghan was angry.

"I have many questions for the police about Dan's death. They may want their questions answered, but not before they answer mine," vowed Meghan.

Chapter Thirty-Two

MEGHAN CAHILL HAD NO TRAFFIC to fight on Route 202 north out of West Chester. It was 5:30 a.m., and the highway was desolate except for several deer that stood paralyzed along the grassy slopes that bordered the road. There were many times, Meghan thought, when she also felt paralyzed in her relationship with Jonathan.

Meghan kept her speed below the posted 55 mph speed limit and reviewed her strategy for when she arrived at the institute. She would enter the building and go directly to her lab. She would check her computer for recent e-mails and then contact Jeffrey. He needed to be with her when she reported Jonathan to the board of directors.

As Meghan approached the Route 30 exit, she felt her heart race. Her fingers tore into the leather steering wheel as she realized the institute was only a few minutes away.

Driving past the acres of cornfields owned by the Renaissance Institute, Meghan's focus went immediately to that area beyond the fields, toward the dense cluster of trees that encased the lake.

At one time, her lake. But not anymore.

Meghan now despised her secret haven. For Meghan, her special place had been violated.

Dan had been killed at this lake.

Meghan slowed her BMW as she turned onto Possum Hollow Road, which led to the pharmaceutical research building. A dense white mist hung low across the road and slowly flowed around the distant institute building as if some special force was trying to hide secrets that Meghan knew had to be revealed.

Meghan entered the institute's west wing and noticed the pewter clock that hung against the gray stone wall. It was 5:50 a.m. Even though the building only had three floors, an elevator existed for those who chose not to experience the open-air, Italian marble, serpentine stairway. The temporary confinement in a 6'x8' vertical, moving room somehow did not alarm most employees.

Meghan Cahill, however, was not one of those employees. She always climbed the stairs effortlessly, usually taking two steps at a time, arriving on the third floor where her lab was located, full of breath and prepared to make a difference in the world with her pediatric oncology research.

Why did she always choose to avoid the elevators? At first, she didn't care to analyze her motives. But Meghan knew why.

Confinement.

Closed space.

No control.

Meghan hated confinement, feared it, which was the reason why she had chosen to always take the stairs at work. And there were other situations in her life where she had felt confined, trapped, and unable to function as a normal human being: standing in long lines at the grocery store, sitting in her car stuck in traffic on a bridge, taking commercial airline flights. Meghan realized she had a problem and finally sought professional help. She remembered the many hours of therapy when her therapist had tried to gently guide her to identify the cause of her anxiety and thus work toward a solution, a cure for her anxiety attacks.

The therapist had shown her that the common element in each of her attacks was control. Whenever she lacked control, she lost it. Her therapist had told her the etiology for her fear of not being in control could be many things: the recent death of a loved one, the controlling personality of a partner in a relationship, unreasonable stress in one's life.

During her relationship with Jonathan, she had tried to make every scheduled session. She had felt these counseling sessions were very helpful. But Jonathan had a different opinion. He had considered her therapy a waste of time and had never hesitated to tell her so.

Meghan remembered that her last session was just after Jonathan had returned from a South Carolina research meeting.

Meghan rarely arrived at work before 6:00 a.m., but today was different. She hastened down the dimly lit corridor as she approached her lab. Soon, thoughts of Dan and what had happened to him less than forty-eight hours ago weakened her steps. Waves of nausea suddenly overtook her already empty stomach.

Her throat became dry.

Impossible to swallow.

Meghan needed a drink. The nearby water fountain outside her lab, she remembered, wasn't working. She would get a drink inside her lab. She opened her lab door and entered the dark room. Meghan instinctively reached for the wall switch that turned on the nearby desk lamp. For a second, Meghan expected Dan to appear and give his typical, cheerful "good morning."

How foolish she felt. He was dead. Murdered.

She would never hear his voice again; see his reassuring smile.

God, she needed a drink. Not water. Something stronger, but she knew this morning she would have to settle for less. Meghan grabbed a mug and turned on the faucet. She waited a full minute. No cold water.

One of the many problems at the institute, she thought. She filled the mug with lukewarm water. What she needed now was some ice from the lab's ice machine. The ice was often used to keep lab specimens chilled before they could be analyzed later.

Meghan walked toward the ice machine and lifted the cold steel cover, exposing a full bin of solid ice. Meghan reached in and searched for the ice pick that was kept inside to break apart the blocks of ice. After several seconds of searching through the mini-glaciers, Meghan's fingers stung as if tiny needles were probing her flesh.

She found no ice pick. She remembered using it just last Friday to make ice chips, which she used to pack plastic bags to preserve some specimens. She was certain she had placed it back inside the ice machine when she was finished. At least she thought she had.

Whatever, she thought. Meghan decided instead to have some hot tea.

Meghan sat down in front of her computer and pulled up her e-mails. The warm mint tea was a good choice after all. Even though Meghan had turned up the lab's thermostat when she arrived, the early morning chill still flowed throughout the room, across the steel-topped work tables and across her computer keyboard.

Would there be any news yet on the institute's Intranet? she wondered.

Meghan was surprised to find only one e-mail for her. What also surprised her was that it came from Farraday and was sent to her at 11:15 p.m. Friday evening.

It had been sent to her less than twenty-four hours before he was killed, and only several hours after she had met with him to discuss her promotion. At that meeting, Farraday had assured Meghan that as of October 1, Jonathan would no longer have anything to do with the institute. Just two more weeks, and she wouldn't have to see Jonathan ever again.

But that was before Jeffrey had shown her Jonathan's covert

experiments. She couldn't remain silent for two more weeks and allow him to escape.

Jonathan had to be stopped.

Meghan opened Farraday's e-mail and slowly read each word. It was her way to show respect to this man who had challenged Jonathan's motives and then demonstrated the courage to get rid of him.

As Meghan read through Farraday's message, she became confused.

What is he talking about? she thought. The more she read, the more her confusion became fear.

Fear of the message.

Fear of the sender.

This couldn't be Farraday. It had to be someone else.

The e-mail was quite explicit. She was being informed, supposedly by Farraday, that her research protocols had raised many suspicions among the board of directors. In addition, Farraday claimed her associate, Dan Rafferty, had reported to him that intentional errors were made on FDA reports to the government. Rafferty had accused her of falsifying lab experiments to give the appearance of successful outcomes, thereby justifying more government funds.

Farraday ended the e-mail by telling her that he wanted her immediate resignation first thing Monday morning. If not, he would fire her Monday and have security remove her from the institute.

Meghan fell back against her chair. Her hands gripped her leather armchair, creating finger impressions as if the armrests had been made of clay.

This couldn't be happening. Her meeting with Farraday Friday afternoon was anything but confrontational. He was supportive of her work and was pleased that she had accepted the promotion.

And what was this nonsense about Dan? He never reported her. And, not only would he never do such a thing, there wasn't anything to report.

Meghan closed her eyes, no longer able to stare at the accusation on her computer screen. *This e-mail was a lie—every word of it.*

What wasn't a lie, however, was the fact that Farraday and Dan were killed within twenty-four hours of when this e-mail was sent to her.

But who sent it to her?

And why?

A sudden knock on the partially opened, frosted-glass lab door forced Meghan out of her chair. She quickly turned and saw a man poised at the doorway, mid-fifties, wearing a gray tweed sport coat that partially covered a light blue tie-less shirt.

"Dr. Cahill? ... Dr. Meghan Cahill?"

"Yes," Meghan answered, slightly out of breath.

"I'm Detective McManus. I need to ask you a few questions."

Chapter Thirty-Three

MEGHAN FROZE. SHE REMEMBERED EMILY telling her that the police wanted to speak with her. She didn't think that meant this early in the morning. My God, it was 7:00 a.m. What information could she possibly have that was so important to their investigation?

"I'm sorry if I startled you. The security office did say it was okay to come up here."

"No, it's okay. It's just so early, and I didn't expect to see anyone."

"You said you didn't expect to see anyone?" questioned McManus.

Why did I say that? Meghan thought. It sounded like she wasn't even expecting to see Dan. Of course the officer must know Dan had worked with her. But Emily did tell her it was already on the TV news. Dan Rafferty was killed. It was understandable then for her to know this fact; she would never see Dan again.

"Listen. I think I know why you're here," Meghan asserted.

"You do?"

"Yes. It's about my lab associate ... Dan Rafferty."

"That's right, Dr. Cahill. Your associate was murdered. Saturday night. Along with Mr. Farraday."

"Yes, I know. What happened?" Meghan asked.

"Too early to tell. It's still under investigation."

"I still can't believe what happened. How can I help?"

"I need to ask you some questions."

"Okay."

"How long have you worked at the Renaissance Institute?"

"About two years."

"You do research?"

"Yes. I have several projects that I'm working on. Each one deals with finding cures for specific cancers in children."

"Are you a medical doctor?"

"No. I have two PhD degrees. One in pathology, the other in pharmacology."

"How long have you known Mr. Rafferty?" His questioning hastened.

"Almost two years. Since I started at the institute, Dan and I have worked together in this lab."

"When was the last time you saw him?"

"Friday. It was Friday afternoon."

"Were you supposed to work together over the weekend?"

"No." Part of Meghan wanted to tell him that Dan was more than just a coworker. He was a good friend. She also thought about telling him of their meeting Friday afternoon at the lake. Meghan's heart was beating hard. She had a feeling Detective McManus knew something he was not yet willing to disclose to her.

Meghan decided to just answer his questions.

Don't volunteer information, she thought.

"Now let me ask you about Mr. Farraday," Detective McManus pressed on.

"You said he was also killed the same night," Meghan replied.

"Mr. Farraday was found murdered down at the lake. In fact, not too far from where Rafferty's body was found."

Meghan sensed McManus was interested in her reaction, as he never looked away from her.

"How would you describe your relationship with Mr. Farraday?"

Meghan wasn't sure where he was heading with that question. She remained standing in front of her computer screen, which still showed Farraday's e-mail, or an e-mail that supposedly had come from him. She wasn't sure if she should take a chance of moving and leading McManus away from her computer. The last thing she wanted was to have this eager detective read the message that certainly didn't describe a positive relationship between them.

"We had a very good working relationship," Meghan asserted.

"I see. Were you planning to meet Mr. Farraday last Saturday evening?"

"No, of course not."

"Well, let me share something with you that we found on Farraday's cell phone. You know it stores text messages?"

"I don't understand what you're saying."

"Text messages. If you don't get someone on the phone, you can send a text message. You know, leave a printed message."

"Listen, I know what a text message is. What I don't understand is why you're telling me this."

"I'm informing you that we found Farraday's cell phone with a text message from you asking him to meet you Saturday night at the institute lake."

Meghan couldn't believe it. What was he saying? That she arranged some kind of meeting with Farraday at the lake and then killed him?

"That's ridiculous. I never sent that message. We did meet in his office Friday afternoon and discussed my promotion and work at the institute."

"If you weren't planning to meet him Saturday evening, then where were you that night?"

Meghan hesitated. Should she tell McManus about her meeting with Jeffrey Manion and about the animal experiments? She planned to tell the board of directors about Jonathan's covert work, but it was still too early for any of them to be here at work.

Meghan decided she had to be honest with Detective McManus.

"I was here Saturday night."

"Here in your lab?"

"No. I was with Jeffrey Manion. He wanted to meet with me because he said he had something very important to show me."

"What time was this?"

"He told me to meet him at 8:00 p.m., and I was on time."

"What did he show you?"

"Animal experiments. Horrible and cruel experiments."

"Where was this?"

"Jeffrey brought me to a lab located in the institute's basement. He's Jonathan's lab assistant."

"Tell me about those experiments." Detective McManus took out a notebook from his jacket and for the first time since he arrived, looked away from Meghan and now focused on finding a pen buried somewhere in one of his jacket pockets.

"Jonathan conducted animal studies in his subterranean lab. The only other person who knew about his work was Jeffrey Manion."

"Who is Jonathan?"

"I'm sorry ... Dr. Jonathan Ashbridge. He's the vice president of Research and Development. Actually, that's not true. He used to be the VP. Mr. Farraday essentially fired him and gave me his job. That's why Mr. Farraday and I met Friday afternoon. To plan my new job." Meghan sighed. She knew she would feel better telling McManus everything.

"Go on," McManus urged.

"According to Jeffrey, Jonathan gave a drug to dogs that made them aggressive. It turned normally affectionate dogs into killers. I saw mutilated dogs, their flesh torn off and scattered throughout the lab.

The smell ... the smell of decaying flesh was everywhere. I could hardly breathe."

"Why did this guy ... Jeffrey ... show you all this?"

"He was scared ... of the experiments and what their new drug was capable of doing to living things. Innocent dogs." Meghan paused. She had to tell McManus the entire truth.

"The real reason Jeffrey showed me their work was because he feared Jonathan. He told me he thought Jonathan was insane. Capable of doing anything to anyone who obstructed his research with this new drug."

"What were you planning to do with this information?"

"This morning, I was going to report all this to Mr. Farraday. That was before I heard about his death."

"And now?"

"I plan to report it to the institute's board of directors."

"Do you intend to first meet with Dr. Ashbridge, you know, before you go to the board?"

"No ... I will not." Meghan turned from McManus, walked over to the wall temperature gauge, and was surprised to see that the temperature was only 68 degrees—it felt more like 90 degrees.

A sauna. Her face felt flushed, and her cotton blouse clung to her chest.

It was difficult to swallow. Her throat ached for something cool to drink. Her fingertips and lips developed paresthesias—these tingling sensations slowly moved into her fingers and across her face. Meghan leaned back against the windowsill. It was hard for her to focus.

"Dr. Cahill, are you all right?" McManus asked.

Meghan knew what was happening. She understood the physiologic effects of hyperventilation. To know she was having an anxiety attack didn't help her control the cause.

Jonathan Ashbridge.

He was the cause, and no one could control him. Not Jeffrey Manion. And certainly not her. Fear of Jonathan grew each day since Farraday had given his position to her. Jonathan was capable of doing anything to anyone in order to protect his work and reputation.

McManus now stood in front of her, both of his hands supporting her shoulders.

"Are you okay?"

"Yes. I think so. I'm sorry about this. I haven't had breakfast," Meghan whispered.

"You should sit down … over here," McManus offered, motioning to the chair in front of Meghan's computer.

"No … no, I'm fine. Let me just rest here for a few minutes. Then I'll go down to our cafeteria."

"Okay, you're the doctor. Just tell me where I can find this guy Ashbridge. I need to talk to him."

Chapter Thirty-Four

"WHAT ARE YOU DOING IN there?" McManus said.

Jonathan Ashbridge quickly turned around and saw an unfamiliar figure standing in the doorway of CEO Farraday's office.

"Who the hell are you?" Jonathan demanded.

"I'm Detective McManus with the Valley Creek Police Department, and this office is a police-secured area under investigation. Didn't you see the yellow police tape across the doorway?" McManus said as he approached Jonathan, who was standing behind Farraday's desk.

"Yes, Detective, I did see the tape, but I'm Dr. Ashbridge, Mr. Farraday's vice president of Research and Development. We had a meeting here in this office last Friday evening, and I thought I may have left my computer notebook here. It's very important that I find it ... a lot of important information is stored on it."

"I don't care what your title is or whether you left something here ... this office is off limits to you."

After leaving Meghan Cahill, McManus chose to visit Farraday's office before looking for Dr. Ashbridge. Was this just a coincidence that he found Ashbridge here? He didn't think so. After speaking with Meghan Cahill, he felt Ashbridge was the type of person who could easily intimidate others. But not him. As for Ashbridge's lab assistant, Jeffrey Manion, Detective McManus thought he was one of those people whom Jonathan easily intimidated and controlled.

Meghan Cahill was another. McManus didn't believe her reason for almost fainting in her lab. Not having had breakfast didn't make sense; it was still early in the morning. Instead, McManus saw a woman who reacted with fear when faced with the possibility that she might have to confront Jonathan with his animal experiments.

"I'm sorry, Detective. I didn't think I would harm anything in here."

McManus didn't believe Ashbridge's passive tone. "Well, you're wrong. I could arrest you for tampering with a crime scene."

McManus enjoyed the worried expression on Ashbridge's face. "Are you aware, Dr. Ashbridge, that Mr. Farraday and another man named Dan Rafferty were found murdered down at the institute's lake?"

"Yes. I heard about it Sunday afternoon on the news. I don't know what to say. I'm still shocked about it."

"You said you had a meeting with Farraday last Friday evening?" McManus questioned.

"Yes."

"What was it about?"

"We talked about the future of the institute, what would keep our company viable and competitive in the pharmaceutical industry. As VP in charge of all research activity, I presented the risks and benefits of each research project currently under development at the institute." Jonathan paused as the early morning sun's rays began to peer through the wooden blinds covering the massive floor-to-ceiling window that formed the east wall of Farraday's office.

"Go on," McManus prompted.

"There are separate labs at the institute, each of which is run by a different director. I have my own lab where I conduct my research projects. Dr. Cahill, for instance, is another director who has a lab for her own projects, and there are several other directors, all of whom report to me weekly with updates on their individual research work. I need to know if they are meeting their research goals within the set timetable. You see, Detective, in the pharmaceutical research world, time is money. My responsibility to the institute and to Mr. Farraday is to assess the worthiness of each director's project."

"And were any decisions made during your meeting with Mr. Farraday?"

"Yes. A very difficult one."

"What do you mean?"

"It concerned Dr. Cahill's projects. Her work was always ahead of schedule. Her lab data that was routinely sent to the Food and Drug Administration in Washington DC had always been flawless."

"Then why was there any concern?" McManus asked.

"You obviously don't understand drug research," Jonathan mused.

"I never claimed to have such expertise," McManus snapped.

"Fine. When a drug is under development, it must be investigated with a certain protocol or process of investigation. Sometimes, a protocol or design to test a drug must be changed because the results are contrary to expectations. In other words, the actual drug effects produced in our animal trials or experiments may actually be harmful rather than helpful or curative to the animal's disease and would eventually become harmful to humans."

"I see. Go on."

"Well, in Dr. Cahill's case, her protocols never had to be changed or even altered in the smallest way. Her results always met her expectations for her drugs. Detective, this just never seemed right to me."

"Okay. So then what?"

"I spoke with her lab associate, Dan Rafferty. I have to admit, only after some aggressive questioning on my part did Rafferty finally talk."

"About what?"

"He confirmed what I had suspected."

"And that was?"

"Dr. Cahill altered her results to meet FDA requirements and thereby always received glowing approval for her research. As a result, she would continue to receive substantial government funding for all of her projects."

As Jonathan walked from behind Farraday's desk, he noticed McManus scribbling notes on a pad. McManus's focus was finally off him, and Jonathan realized he had only a few more seconds to scan the thick carpet for his possession.

The computer flash drive that he had used last Friday night to gain access to Farraday's computer and send incriminating e-mails to Cahill. He knew he must have left it here that night. As Jonathan scanned the carpet area around the desk, the sun's rays broke through the cloud cover that hung along the eastern skyline.

Now he saw it. The metallic disk reflected the morning sun's glare and guided Jonathan to his goal.

The small metallic flash drive lay nestled on the thick plum carpet just a few feet away from where McManus stood. Jonathan knew he could reach it before McManus stopped his note-taking.

"One more thing, Dr. Ashbridge. What were you and Mr. Farraday prepared to do about Dr. Cahill?" McManus questioned as he suddenly looked up from his notepad.

Jonathan stopped moving. He finally had it—the flash drive was now beneath his shoe.

Jonathan stood his ground and answered.

"There was no doubt about it ... Mr. Farraday was angry. He considered her behavior as a personal affront to his integrity. He told me he would report Dr. Cahill first thing Monday morning to our board of directors, who would then file a corporate disclosure statement to the FDA acknowledging her illegal and unethical conduct."

"One more question, Dr. Ashbridge."

"Yes."

"Where were you last Saturday evening?"

"I met Mr. Farraday for a drink at Ship Inn. You know, the one right here in Valley Creek. He wanted to discuss our strategy for dealing with Dr. Cahill."

"What time were you with him?"

"It was about 7:30 p.m. I was only there for about thirty minutes. Shortly afterwards, around 8:00, I met my lab assistant, Jeffrey Manion, in the Ship Inn parking lot. We had arranged to meet there. Then we drove our cars to my house for one of our research strategy dinner meetings. We were there until about 1:00 a.m."

"That's interesting. I just spoke with Dr. Cahill in her lab. She claims she was with your lab assistant, Mr. Manion, Saturday evening in some basement lab. She also claims you and your assistant have been engaged in questionable drug studies down there. Any comment?" McManus never looked away.

"Let me say this. I also find it interesting. I'm a medical doctor, not some PhD like Dr. Cahill. In my opinion, I think she's either delusional or has something to hide. Detective, I think you might want to hear this. I met Dr. Cahill for the first time right after her grandmother's death, and we dated for about two years. I assure you, she was never quite right after her grandmother's death."

"What do you mean?" probed McManus.

"She was delusional—quick to fall apart, and at times fabricated reasons for getting upset. Her strange behavior was actually the reason I stopped seeing her just a few weeks ago."

Detective McManus had heard enough. "Thanks for your time, Dr. Ashbridge. I need to see what's in Farraday's computer. I'll have security download his computer files. I want to see if he sent any e-mails to Dr. Cahill concerning Mr. Rafferty's allegations."

As McManus turned to leave, Jonathan quickly lifted his foot and grabbed the computer device.

"Are you coming?" McManus asked, turning around to face Jonathan.

"Yes, sir." Jonathan smiled. He loved the feel of the metal device safely secured in his clenched hand.

His plan would be a success. The police should know soon about the 911 text message Stefan had sent on Farraday's cell phone to the Security Department implicating Meghan in Farraday's death. The police should also soon discover the computer trail of fictitious e-mails between Meghan and Farraday.

But why wasn't the ice pick found yet? Jonathan thought. Stefan had left it in the mud next to Rafferty's body—covered with Meghan's DNA.

Stefan had told him so.

Meghan Cahill will regret she ever met him, Jonathan thought.

He liked it that way.

—∽—

Meghan had seen enough. She must have read Farraday's e-mail over a dozen times and still could not believe it. Why would someone send her this message? It certainly wasn't Farraday.

Meghan needed space to think. She needed to get to her car and drive far away from the institute. Drive to her beach house in Ocean City. She would be able to think more clearly there.

Too much had already happened.

Farraday was murdered only hours after she had met with him. And then there was Dan's death.

My God, Dan dead. Killed by someone. But who would do such a thing?

And why was Dan at the lake Saturday evening? Why did he have to be there?

As Meghan swiped her ID badge across the security checkpoint, she noticed two security guards who had their backs to her; they didn't notice her leave. They were engrossed in a discussion about a *Philadelphia Inquirer* newspaper article that reported a homicide over the weekend.

At first, Meghan thought they were reading about what had happened at the institute. About Dan and Farraday. She was wrong.

A priest ... a Capuchin friar ... was the victim. Killed sometime early Sunday morning, the one guard read aloud. As he read further, Meghan overheard that the priest was the defendant in the high-profile Philadelphia Archdiocesan abuse case.

She had heard of the trial but hadn't followed it closely. What she did know of the case allowed her to easily form an opinion.

The Catholic priest was guilty. She was sure of it.

And based on some of the controversial evidence she had read, she also believed there was a cover-up.

The Philadelphia Archdiocese had moved the priest from parish to parish to hide his abusive history and prevent a Church scandal.

Meghan believed he was guilty of child abuse.

She also believed the enablers—clerics in the archdiocesan hierarchy—were equally if not more guilty of these crimes against innocent children. They were the ones who knew about the priest's behavior and did nothing to protect the children.

They, in fact, enabled the priest to perpetuate his cruelty.

Meghan also believed in the Philadelphia DA's claim that crimes of child abuse did not end with this one priest.

There were others. Many others.

Meghan felt certain that legal and moral justice were served with the vicar's death early Sunday morning.

Chapter Thirty-Five

SEPTEMBER 19
MONDAY, 6:00 A.M.

"GOOD MORNING, PAT. IT TRULY is a good morning, isn't it?" Bishop Torrey announced.

Monsignor Pat Brannigan walked into the bishop's seminary office and was immediately met by Bishop Torrey, who suddenly jumped out of his desk chair and hurried over to his trusted friend.

"Have you heard?" Bishop Torrey's breath hastened.

"About the vicar? Yes ... I have heard," Monsignor Brannigan replied softly, his eyes fixed on the plush crimson carpet.

Bishop Torrey continued. "I understand he was found murdered early Sunday morning near Philadelphia's waterfront. I still can't believe it. I guess it's a blessing. Now we can forget about that damn abuse trial and focus instead on the upcoming Bishop's Synod in Rome. We still have a lot of preparation to do for that meeting." Bishop Torrey patted Monsignor Brannigan's arm and walked back to his desk chair.

Monsignor Brannigan did not share the bishop's surprise. He knew what had happened to the vicar. He also knew he was responsible for his death. His friend in the Vatican, Monsignor Reuss, had been true to his word.

It just didn't matter to him anymore that the vicar posed no threat to them. Even though they were now protected from the vicar's accusations, Monsignor Brannigan felt exposed. Vulnerable.

Yes, the bishop and he were finally safe from any possible criminal or archdiocesan repercussions arising out of the vicar's trial.

They were saved, Monsignor Brannigan at first believed.

Or were they? For the first time, Brannigan's chest burned with resentment toward his bishop. But why should he blame Bishop Torrey?

He wasn't the one to contact Monsignor Reuss in Rome.

And he shouldn't blame the bishop for his own sense of misdirected duty. Duty to serve Bishop Torrey. His future pope.

But was it misdirected? Monsignor Brannigan questioned.

He must faithfully serve him. There was no one else the bishop could trust to successfully carry out their plan for Bishop Torrey to fill the cardinal seat now left vacant with the recent death of Philadelphia's beloved seventy-five-year-old cardinal.

During Cardinal Thomas Quindlen's brief ten-year tenure as Philadelphia's cardinal, Bishop Torrey had refused to accept him as his church leader. He viewed the aging cardinal as a weak man who was without vision. Without ambition for his Church and certainly without ambition for himself. The cardinal was like a parochial grandfather who only saw the good qualities in people.

As the cardinal's chancellor, Bishop Torrey was placed in charge of all internal Church investigations of child abuse claims against diocesan priests.

Cardinal Thomas Quindlen had been a fool. Trusting him to

faithfully investigate the several hundred accusations from adult men who now accused over a hundred Philadelphia Diocesan priests of child abuse—claims that hard-working and spiritually dedicated priests had committed perverse sexual acts on them when they were children living in their abusers' parishes.

How fortunate his fellow priests were to have Bishop Torrey and Monsignor Brannigan monitor their alleged abuse cases. Of course they would look into each case *de novo* and follow Church Canon Law when they evaluated the merits of each claim.

Officially, the bishop had found no credible evidence for any accusation and thereby had dismissed the claims as meritless attempts to tarnish the Catholic Church. However, he had moved the accused priests from parish to parish to avoid a public scandal against the Church. However, the bishop knew for certain the abuses were real. The accused priests did in fact commit sexual abuses against many young children.

Young, innocent children who not only suffered heinous physical harm, but also suffered intense mental anguish as they relived for years the harm done to them.

Bishop Torrey grew tired of hearing this same litany, case after case, that described each priest's abuses and their effects on the parish children. The children were abused. So what? Priests must not be judged as normal men. They were agents of God and deserved special treatment. Bishop Torrey's own sexual acts committed against the children should not be judged either.

In truth, his acts would never be revealed.

He was confident of that.

Amnestic drugs. What a blessing they were for him and his children.

Bishop Torrey's own perverse actions would forever remain hidden in the subconscious webs of confusion that clouded the minds of his victims.

Shrouded their innocence with cloaks of guilt.

"The Bishop's Synod. You haven't forgotten, have you?" Bishop Torrey questioned.

Monsignor Brannigan stared out the stained-glass window overlooking a wooded section of seminary property where he had taken many private walks years ago as a seminarian. His life had drastically changed since he had first met the bishop shortly after graduation from the seminary. His history with the bishop was still a mystery to him. How could he have done those things? Just as his view of the woods through the tinted glass was blurred, so too was his vision of the future.

"Monsignor Brannigan, are you listening?"

"Yes ... I'm sorry. I was just thinking ... about the synod, about our preparations."

"Good. Let's go over them now. Today's Monday, September 19. Our Mass of Celebration and Renewal will be this Wednesday evening, September 21, at St. John the Evangelist over on 13th Street in Philadelphia. I've changed the location for the Mass. It won't be at the basilica as we had planned. Instead, I decided St. John's would be a perfect location to celebrate our special Mass since our dearly departed vicar, the Franciscan friar, was stationed at St. John's and was also kind enough to die before he could accuse us of being child abusers. Our friends in Rome, our Imago Dei brethren, will see that our plan has a renewed spirit. We have nothing to worry about. Don't you agree, Monsignor?"

Monsignor Brannigan's body ached. His legs grew weak as if finally his body refused to support his spiritless human form. Monsignor Brannigan slowly shuffled across the thick carpet to a nearby handcrafted Amish, wooden armchair.

Bishop Torrey never noticed his associate's distress. He walked back to his desk and continued his discourse.

"The day after our Mass of Celebration, we shall leave for my meeting in Rome with Pope Luke. God, I can't believe he's still alive."

"Have you heard any more news about His Holiness's health?" Monsignor Brannigan whispered.

"My friends at the Vatican phoned me late last night. He's still in control. He insists on saying Mass each day and continues to manage all official Vatican matters."

"Where does he find the strength? I mean, his disease has metastasized throughout his body, right?"

"I guess he receives some kind of special healing through his namesake ... St. Luke, the apostle and physician."

"It's just that he's been suffering for such a long time. I feel sorry for him," Monsignor Brannigan offered.

"Don't waste your energy. Remember, Pat, during the synod, I will receive His Holiness's blessing and become the new cardinal for Philadelphia. Once this happens, my Imago Dei associates in the Vatican assure me that I have enough votes among the College of Cardinals to become the next pope. They tell me that I may not get enough votes on the first ballot but will definitely receive the necessary votes on the second ballot. Of course, our good Pope Luke must die first."

Chapter Thirty-Six

"I'M GONNA SQUEEZE YOUR FUCKIN' neck till you take your last breath. Do you feel it? Do you feel it leaving you?" shouted the frail, elderly assailant, covered with torn and soiled clothes, as he squeezed his clenched and twisted fingers around the muscular neck of the six foot three bartender.

The homeless man's body shook with uncontrollable tremors, and his matted greasy hair flew around his contorted face as his jagged fingernails tore deeper into his victim's neck. The old man then pushed his unsuspecting victim down into the garbage-filled macadam street and repeatedly forced the young man's head against the cement curb. The muscular bartender struggled helplessly for air. Muffled moans of anguish vibrated through his torn larynx and escaped through pools of splattered blood that pulsated from the open neck wounds.

One final anguished breath signaled the victim's demise.

That will be the last time you throw me out into the street, the old man swore as he wiped his bruised and bloody fingers across his shirt. He gave one quick look up and down the silent street and then staggered back toward the deserted bar.

Stefan walked out from the dark alley and watched the old man shuffle down the street, through the many pieces of broken glass and garbage that comprised his worthless world. Stefan liked what he saw. He had chosen the homeless man, his clinical subject, not at random, but with the plan that he must be weaker than his victim.

The helpless old man had received the project's drug, which demonstrated to Stefan its effectiveness against the much stronger bartender. Just as the drug had worked earlier when given to the docile beagle. The pit-bull never had a chance. And neither did the bartender.

Stefan knew he had to demonstrate that the drug's potency was strong enough to cause the desired physiological changes inside his clinical subjects. If the drug worked well inside the bodies of weak individuals, it was certain to be effective inside the project's targets. So far, the bishop and monsignor did not stand a chance.

Even though the homeless man had performed well for Stefan, he didn't care what happened to him after tonight.

The police would easily trace the homeless man to the victim. The trail of bloodstains that his sneakers had smeared across the street toward the bar where he had sought liquid nourishment would certainly lead the police to an easy conviction.

The homeless itinerant had no one who would miss him. No real family. No real friends. Why else was he living in the streets? Only his fellow street "family" might notice him missing tonight from his cardboard home. However, they would have no true concern for his disappearance. Only a desire to seize their neighbor's meager possessions—a wardrobe of ill-fitting shirts and pants stolen from backyard clotheslines, valuable empty bottles that he had planned to redeem at the city's recycle center, votive candles and matches stolen from St. John the Evangelist's basement church that would be useful during a chilled autumn night, and a grocery store cart used to gather more possessions.

Jonathan was right about one thing, Stefan admitted. His chosen subject was perfect. These people who roamed the streets of Philadelphia, homeless and destitute, were easy prey for their clinical trials. Stefan found it easy to get physically close to the old man. Close enough for the street person to inhale the study drug. Just offer any cheap alcohol, and Stefan instantly became his long-lost friend.

Stefan agreed with Jonathan that these street people were no longer worthy human beings. They had lost their identity, their self-worth, long ago when they crossed that fragile line that separates society's valuable and worthy members from those human bodies that merely function as society's parasites.

Even though the homeless man had become a parasite, tonight he had served a noble purpose.

Stefan had chosen him to serve society.

The child abuse victims will have their justice soon.

The sins of the priests shall never be forgiven.

Stefan now had to choose his next victim.

Chapter Thirty-Seven

"I S HE IN?" DETECTIVE MCMANUS's receptionist nodded as the rookie Valley Creek police officer pushed his way through the wooden swing gate that separated her domain from the several temporarily constructed cubicles occupied by Valley Creek Township employees.

Normally located on the township's second floor, the township employees were temporarily relocated, due to construction needs, to the first floor where they shared space with the police department. McManus and his fellow officers were not happy since they already felt cramped for space. McManus had told his officers that the township administration had promised him it would only be for a few weeks until the second floor could be repaired and made safe for use again.

His officers, however, knew better. The township administration had only two speeds when it came to getting things done. Slow and slower. They didn't believe him, McManus realized. Come to think of it, McManus didn't believe it either.

Just before the young officer reached McManus's office door, the receptionist interrupted her phone conversation; the young officer could tell it was a social call based on the whispered words he had overheard.

"You'll have to wait. He's on the phone," the receptionist called out.

"Not to worry … he'll want to see me now," the officer rebuked, waving his hand at her as he opened the detective's office door.

"What do you want?" McManus questioned as he covered his phone's mouthpiece.

"I just got off the phone with the Renaissance Institute's Security Department. They finished downloading the Farraday and Cahill computers for us, and they just faxed all of their e-mails to us. You've got to read this stuff. Cahill's story doesn't hold up … she's been lying to us." The rookie grinned as he held up sheets of printouts.

"Can we talk later? Okay, sometime this afternoon. Thanks." McManus hung up the phone and leaned back in his wooden, swivel desk chair.

"Let me see what you have."

It didn't take long for McManus to read through the e-mails sent between Farraday and Meghan Cahill days before Farraday was killed; the young officer had highlighted the relevant passages.

McManus agreed. The e-mails didn't support Cahill's story. After reading them, it was clear Farraday was upset with Cahill over the allegations brought forth by Dan Rafferty. In several e-mails, Farraday asked to meet with Cahill to discuss her research and the falsified FDA reports. Cahill's replies were always evasive at best. She made numerous excuses for her inability to meet with him.

Interestingly, McManus noted, Cahill also wrote that she didn't trust Rafferty and knew his allegations were contrived to discredit her reputation. One e-mail went on to describe her suspicion that Rafferty was secretly working with Jonathan Ashbridge to ruin her and thereby prevent her from assuming Ashbridge's position as vice president of Research and Development.

One particular e-mail deserved close attention, McManus thought. It was highly probative as to a possible motive for Farraday's murder.

It was Farraday's final message to Cahill. He had claimed he had enough of her. Her refusal to meet with him and her refusal to explain the alleged discrepancies in her government reports were grounds for her immediate dismissal. Farraday had warned Cahill he intended to report her fraudulent activities to the US Department of Justice.

McManus finally looked up at the young officer who was pacing across the floor.

"You're right. It appears Dr. Cahill did not have the wonderful relationship with Farraday that she had led us to believe she had. For that matter, the same goes for her relationship with Rafferty," McManus concluded.

The officer finally came to rest in front of McManus's desk and pointed to the e-mail printouts strewn across the desk top. "We've got proof of Cahill's motive for each murder," the officer charged.

"We may also have proof of Cahill's opportunity to kill Farraday. Remember, we have Dr. Cahill's text message on Farraday's cell phone Saturday night setting up her meeting with him at the lake," McManus replied.

"I guess we now need to talk to this guy Jeffrey Manion," the officer said. "Remember, she claims to have been with him Saturday evening in that basement lab."

"Right ... let's drive over to the institute and see if he's around. Anything yet on the DNA samples?" McManus asked.

"The lab guys tell me they might have something for us soon. They said the skin and hair samples taken from Farraday and Rafferty require more analysis."

"Good. Just don't rush them. Those guys do good work, and we need them to do it right the first time. We can't have those samples challenged and then thrown out by the court," directed McManus.

McManus followed the young officer out of his office and stopped at his receptionist's desk.

"If Dr. Hawthorne from the Philadelphia medical examiner's office calls back, tell him to reach me on my cell phone. It may be some time before I get back to the office."

McManus knew he had to check on Cahill's alibi for Saturday night. He also knew that without a solid alibi, Dr. Cahill was in serious trouble.

As they drove the few miles back to the pharmaceutical complex, McManus remembered he also had to check with the Renaissance Institute's Security Department on another matter—Farraday's text message sent to the security department immediately after he was attacked.

Chapter Thirty-Eight

SEPTEMBER 20

9:30 A.M.

MEGHAN STOOD ON HER DECK overlooking the ocean's rough surf that had grown more intense through the night. Her gaze followed each wave's quest for land, a journey hastened by gusts of cool, moist wind that ripped across the sea's gray surface, creating wisps of whitecaps that crashed against her beach.

Each new wave pounded the wet sand closer and closer to her. She felt herself stepping away from her second-floor balcony, as if she feared the next wave's crescendo would come crashing down on her.

Why do I suddenly feel threatened here? she thought. Her home, Nana's home, had always been her haven. A place where she could go and maintain her privacy. And escape from anything or anyone that threatened her safety. That was the main reason she had chosen not to disclose her Ocean City address to the institute. She wanted to protect her privacy. She had listed her West Chester townhouse as her official home, and only a few people at work knew about her beach house. One such person was Emily DeHaven. She would visit her sometimes for the day or spend an entire weekend. Her visits had stopped abruptly after she had begun her relationship with Jonathan; Emily despised him. At the time, Meghan couldn't understand her friend's strong resentment toward him. But now she did.

Much had happened since last weekend. She was glad she had taken these past couple days off from work. She couldn't remain at the lab. It would have been a waste of time trying to get any work done there.

Tomorrow would be different. Tomorrow was the two-year anniversary of Nana's death. Nana would give her the strength to return to work, back to her lab where she knew she made a difference. Her work was important to her. Meghan's research had already discovered effective, life-saving drugs for pediatric oncology patients. They were her favorite clinical study group. The children were innocent and unsuspecting victims of life-threatening diseases that preyed on their delicate bodies. Somehow reminding herself that her work greatly benefited gravely ill children gave her renewed purpose to return to work.

But Meghan recognized her work was not accomplished alone. It was Dan Rafferty's work ethic and intuitive skills as a researcher that directly led to their many discoveries. But Meghan was alone now. She would return to the institute tomorrow morning and face her work alone. But she would not miss Dan because of his skills. She would miss *him*. The person.

She would grieve the loss of their friendship.

Chapter Thirty-Nine

"JEFFREY MANION? THE SECURITY OFFICE told us we would find you here. I'm Detective McManus, and this is Officer Greer. We're from Valley Creek Police Department." McManus saw three people, two men and a woman, working in the lab. He directed his conversation to the younger man based on a description given to him by the security guard.

"Yes, I'm Jeffrey Manion. And I don't appreciate this unannounced visit. We have important work to do here." Jeffrey returned his attention to the tissue specimen underneath the microscope.

"Right ... sorry for the interruption. We have some questions for you that concern the murders that took place here over the weekend. I'm sure you can spare a few minutes to help us with our investigation."

Jeffrey paused a few seconds, scribbled a few words in his notepad beside his microscope, and then slowly pushed away from the lab counter.

"Of course, Detective, I would be glad to assist you in any way possible. Let's take a walk."

Louis Sanchez caught Emily DeHaven's stare. He knew exactly what she was thinking. Why would the police want to speak with Jeffrey?

"What can I do for the Valley Creek Police?" Jeffrey asked as he led the two officers away from the lab and down the deserted corridor toward the elevators.

"We're investigating the deaths of Mr. Farraday and Mr. Rafferty. They were both killed Saturday evening down at the lake. But I'm sure you're already aware of their deaths," McManus stated.

"Yes, I am. I was shocked when I heard the news reports on Sunday. Do you know who killed them?" Manion asked as he walked closer to the elevator doors.

"We have several leads we're following. That's why we want to talk with you," McManus replied.

"Sure, go ahead."

"Where were you Saturday night?" Officer Greer asked.

"This past Saturday? Why, do you think I had something to do with their deaths?" Manion said sarcastically as he stood in front of the double elevator doors.

"You tell us. Were you at the lake Saturday evening?" Officer Greer retorted.

Manion turned to face the young officer who now stood only a few feet in front of him, both hands gripping his leather gun belt.

"No, I was not anywhere near the lake. In fact, I was with Dr. Ashbridge. We were working at his home all night."

"What time did you meet him?"

Jeffrey paused a few seconds. He ran his fingers through his hair and then resumed his rehearsed script.

"I think it was around 7:45 p.m. No, wait a minute, it was 8:00. I remember now because as I drove into Ship Inn's parking lot, I heard eight bell chimes coming from St. Mary's Chapel across the street from the Inn."

"I thought you said you were with Dr. Ashbridge at his home," Officer Greer questioned.

"I was. But first we met at the Inn and then drove our cars to his house. Dr. Ashbridge told me to meet him there because he already had to meet with someone else at the Inn … I think it was some kind of important meeting about his work at the institute." Jeffrey took his time with each word, careful to make his responses sound unrehearsed.

"Who did he meet with?" McManus asked, taking over the questioning.

"I don't know. He didn't tell me. He just came outside, walked over to my car, and told me to follow him. We had one of our working dinners … we got a lot done that night."

"What time did you leave his house?"

"I think it was around 1:30 in the morning."

"One more thing, Mr. Manion. We'd like you to show us Dr. Ashbridge's lab in the basement. I understand you and Dr. Ashbridge use that area for your research at times." McManus knew he could have asked Renaissance Security to show him the lab. Instead, he wanted to see Manion's reaction. Would he object or at least show some evidence that he was uncertain or nervous about taking them to their subterranean lab?

Manion reached out and pressed the down button on the elevator panel. "Of course. I'm sure it would be okay with Dr. Ashbridge."

Manion turned and met Officer Greer's glare. Within seconds, the elevator door opened.

"After you, gentlemen." Manion grinned as he followed his police escort into the elevator.

Chapter Forty

JEFFREY FIRMLY PRESSED HIS LEFT thumb print against the silicone-covered identification pad, which immediately produced a series of pulsating horizontal red lights that scanned across his thumb print. Within seconds, the heavy cement door slowly opened.

"This is the lab you wanted to see," Manion said as he led the two men into the fluorescent-lit room.

McManus paused at the doorway to give his eyes enough time to focus on his new surroundings.

"When was the last time you were in here?" McManus asked as he walked into the vacant room. The strong smell of a disinfectant filled his nostrils and soon coated his tongue with a bitter paste of chemicals and stagnant air.

"About two weeks ago. After we finished our recent work. We removed everything and had the entire lab cleaned. It's what we usually do after we finish a research project down here. Dr. Ashbridge insists on it."

"So, you weren't here last Saturday night?" McManus asked.

"No."

"Did you meet Dr. Cahill at any time last Saturday night?"

"No, of course not. I already said I was with Dr. Ashbridge all night."

"Well, Dr. Cahill told us a different story. She claims you wanted to meet her Saturday night in this exact location. In fact, she said you insisted on the meeting," McManus declared.

"That's ridiculous ... I never—"

"Let me finish. Dr. Cahill said you showed her some bizarre experiments that you and Dr. Ashbridge had conducted down here. Specifically, animal experiments that involved the use of a drug that changed normally calm dogs into aggressive and psychotic beasts."

"Let me just say this about her claims. The only bizarre and perhaps psychotic behavior around here has to do with Dr. Cahill's beliefs. I don't know why she thinks she met me here, but I can tell you this much. She's not the most stable person."

"What do you mean?" McManus questioned.

"I saw her recently upstairs in her lab, alone with Dan Rafferty, sobbing uncontrollably in the middle of the afternoon. It appeared as if Dan had just told her something that suddenly set her off. He tried to console her, but she pushed him away. Like I said, I don't know why she told you that bizarre story, but I wouldn't believe it for a second. If you want my opinion, she's not only emotionally labile, but she's also a liar."

"You think so?"

"Yes, I do. And I wouldn't be surprised if she knew something about these murders."

"Why do you say that?"

"I overheard a conversation between Mr. Farraday and Rafferty. I was standing outside Mr. Farraday's office Friday afternoon when I heard Mr. Farraday shout out something like ... *Cahill will ruin our reputation. She must be stopped.* I didn't understand what he meant at the time, but now I think it has something to do with his murder."

"Thank you, Mr. Manion. We'll be in touch." McManus and Officer Greer turned and left Jeffrey Manion standing alone in the lab.

As the two men exited the elevator on the second floor, they walked toward the end of the hallway where Dr. Cahill's lab was located.

"Cahill's in trouble. We've got motive, and now we've got opportunity. Her alibi sucks. Now, let's see if the doctor is in," Officer Greer announced as he opened Meghan Cahill's laboratory door.

Chapter Forty-One

"HELLO. IS DR. CAHILL HERE?" Officer Greer shouted as he strode through the doorway first.

A woman with pale blue eyes set above ruddy, wrinkled cheeks and dressed in blue scrubs quickly stepped out from behind a wide pillar located at the far end of the lab.

"I beg your pardon?" the startled woman who appeared to be in her mid-sixties asked.

Detective McManus then entered, quickly scanned the room, and realized the woman was alone in the lab. "I'm sorry if we frightened you, ma'am. We're with the Valley Creek Police. Is Dr. Cahill in her office?"

"No. Dr. Cahill is not here today. I heard she called in sick," the woman announced in a somewhat perturbed Irish brogue. She moved away from the ice dispenser next to the doorway, reached for a pair of vinyl gloves that protruded from a small box atop her cleaning cart, and then resumed her work.

McManus noticed several magnetic stickers on the cart's front metal trash bin, some with photographs of young children and infants, while others were holding holy cards. He was amused as he looked closer at the magnets and read some of their messages.

SPCA cares about animal rights, do you?
Animals are God's creatures, too!

Clearly, the woman was devoted to her family. The pictures were probably of her grandchildren, McManus thought. He also admired her confidence in her convictions. Working in a pharmaceutical research company that studied drug effects on animals certainly didn't deter her from expressing her beliefs.

"Will Dr. Cahill be here tomorrow?" McManus asked.

The cleaning lady never looked up. Strands of gray hair that were once tightly wrapped in a bun now swept freely against her exposed neck as she attacked numerous stains embedded in the lab's porcelain sink basin.

"Glory be … I took two days off and returned to find no one has been in here to clean. Why would anyone with the good sense God gave them ever use porcelain in a laboratory sink?"

"Excuse me. I was wondering if you know whether Dr. Cahill will be working tomorrow." McManus repeated his question.

"Heaven's sake, good man … Dr. Cahill doesn't report to me. And, if you don't mind, I still have a lot of work to do here … work other people should have done while I was on holiday," the woman snapped.

McManus liked this woman's no-nonsense work ethic. He would have hired her in an instant to work for him in his office.

McManus considered visiting Dr. Cahill at her home in West Chester, but he decided to wait and see if she returned to work tomorrow. If she was really sick, questioning her at this time wouldn't benefit him.

The two men left the lab and walked down the corridor to the elevators. Hearing the laboratory door close, the cleaning woman raised her head and turned to confirm that the intruders had finally left her alone.

She was glad Dr. Cahill was spared the ordeal of their questions. Why did the police want to speak with her again? It was harassment, she felt. The woman remembered seeing Dr. Cahill early Monday morning after McManus had left her. She was distraught, overwhelmed with grief—and no wonder, the woman thought. Dr. Cahill's dear friend, Dan Rafferty, was murdered.

The woman walked over to the ice bin and slid open the metal door. Once again, she looked inside and confirmed her earlier discovery.

The ice pick was missing. Dr. Cahill's ice pick. She had heard the preliminary news reports on TV that had described the possible cause of death. *A sharp, stab wound to the heart made by some kind of surgical instrument or possibly an ice pick.*

The cleaning woman knew Dr. Cahill was innocent. Just to be safe, she decided she would replace the ice pick with a new one. Dr. Cahill deserved it.

While waiting for the elevator, McManus's cell phone suddenly came to life with Beethoven's "Ode to Joy."

"Hello, yes, this is Detective McManus. I understand ... you realize, this is information I need to have right away. When will you have your communications system fixed?" McManus shook his head as he stared at his young associate.

"Okay, fine, tomorrow morning. No ... I'll give you guys a call." McManus returned his cell phone to an inside jacket pocket.

"Who was that?" Officer Greer asked.

"Head of security here at the prestigious Renaissance Institute." McManus gave a sarcastic grin. "Apparently, their computer-memory system is not working. They can't retrieve Farraday's 911 call made Saturday night at the lake. The guy assured me, however, they'll have the recorded message for us first thing tomorrow morning."

"What amateurs." Officer Greer grinned. "Okay, we'll come back tomorrow morning to get whatever message Farraday sent to security when he was attacked. Then we'll pay Cahill another visit. I want to see her reaction when we confront her with Jeffrey Manion's story."

Detective McManus nodded. He agreed it was not looking good for Dr. Cahill.

Chapter Forty-Two

S TEFAN CHECKED HIS WATCH. IT was almost three hours since he had administered the spray into the homeless woman's mouth. He had time for one more drink before he checked on his subject's reaction to the drug.

After searching the usual streets in Philadelphia where the homeless had set up residence, Stefan finally had found a worthy subject. A woman, grossly cachectic, her dark sunken eyes barely visible beneath her protruding cheek bones, was ideal for the Pegasus Project's study. Her tattered, baggy clothes hung on her petite and bony frame as if they weren't covering an adult human body, but rather a child's stick-figure play toy.

Her diet probably consisted of alcohol and the street's garbage. *She is another perfect choice*, Stefan thought.

Stefan had followed her movements for hours. He had watched her roam the alleys and side streets off Walnut Street behind the Forrest Theater where *Les Miserables* was showing. Stefan thought it was ironic that this pathetic and forgotten human being who struggled to stay alive in the streets of Philadelphia shared a similar tragedy with the destitute French citizens depicted in the nineteenth-century musical.

Tonight, Stefan would elevate this forgotten woman from the dark shadows of her abyss. He would grant her a temporary noble and worthy life, an existence she probably never experienced even as a child. In a short while, on the streets that she called home, this subject would help avenge the misery of children injured and forgotten by Philadelphia's abusive Catholic priests and their hierarchy. Stefan guaranteed it.

Chapter Forty-Three

STEFAN TASTED HIS FINAL SWALLOW of St. Remy Cognac. It was now time to check on his subject. Stefan was glad he didn't have to walk far from the Lunar Eclipse Lounge located on Walnut Street across from Moriarity's Pub to witness the effects of the drug.

As he walked across Walnut Street, he noticed several young women leave the Forrest Theater through a side exit door that opened onto Quince Street, which ran between Moriarity's and the Forrest. *Probably performers from the play*, Stefan thought. At this time of night, they must have felt it was safer to walk the city's streets as a group.

Stefan paused a few seconds at the entrance to Quince Street and allowed the women to leave the narrow, cobblestone street and proceed past him across Walnut Street toward the Lunar Eclipse Lounge. When he finished with his work tonight, he would grab a nightcap back at the lounge. Maybe they would still be there.

Stefan entered Quince Street, which was dimly lit by the flicker of several gas lights along the brick wall of the Forrest Theater's front entrance. Broken pieces of glass cracked beneath Stefan's shoes as he walked farther down the narrow and now darker street where the yellow glow from distant gas lights no longer guided his steps.

Soon, the smells of decaying garbage and urine filled Stefan's nostrils, signaling that he was near the home of his subject. Suddenly, Stefan heard men's voices shout out unintelligible language. Their location came from St. James Street, an even narrower side street perpendicular to Quince Street. Stefan knew this neighborhood. It was here, only a couple of hours ago, where he had administered the vapor to the homeless woman. Her home was St. James Street. Amidst the wet cardboard boxes, garbage, and human waste. Her home, encased by broken-brick, three-story walls that secreted a thick, dark, caramel-like substance, served as Stefan's clinical laboratory.

Stefan walked down St. James Street and saw two bearded and overweight homeless men grab his subject and begin to tear off her layered, baggy clothes. The woman offered little resistance. She knew her assailants were much stronger. Their bodies towered over her small, weak frame. The men then forced her back against a brick wall where they ran their soiled hands over her half-naked body. Soon, the assailants began to fight each other for sole possession of the woman. Each man grabbed a part of her—one, a handful of gray stringy hair, the other, a bony arm. As the men continued their assault, they dragged the woman's exposed back against the wall where protruding corroded pipes tore into her flesh.

The woman finally let out a weak, anguished cry that echoed down St. James Street's cold cobblestone walkway.

When will she respond to the drug? Stefan wondered. She had no fight left in her. It appeared to Stefan as if she hoped her assailants would make this her last night of living in the streets.

He didn't want her to be the victim. He wanted to help her but hesitated to intervene.

"The drug will work. I must give it more time," Stefan said aloud.

Within seconds, the battered woman's weak cry grew stronger. It was no longer a cry of pain and submission, but rather a warning of her retaliation.

With an effortless movement, the woman broke free from her assailants' hold, forcing one man to fall backward against the street. Standing before her now was her other assailant, who struggled to regain his balance. His dazed stare revealed his disbelief.

The woman lunged at her assailant. She dug her fingers deep inside the man's jaundiced eyes. Blood-tinged yellow eye fluid quickly flowed through her trembling fingers, which remained embedded inside her assailant's eye sockets.

Loud, guttural moans of protest escaped from his blood-filled mouth. His attempts to escape her attack, however, were futile. His massive forearms, previously able to subdue her, now could not garner enough strength to overpower her.

The woman was now in control, Stefan observed. She finally released her grip from the man's face and turned her attention now to her other assailant, who had already crawled several yards away from her.

His assault on her would also be answered with a just punishment, Stefan predicted.

The emaciated woman quickly reached the man and grabbed his greasy, tangled hair between her fingers. She twisted his head around, which pulled his heavy body closer to her. She then quickly straddled the man's barrel chest and stared into the frightened man's eyes. Despite the man's many pleas for mercy, the homeless woman swiftly executed his sentence as she compressed her bony fingers against his trachea.

Stefan moved closer. He pushed away the enucleated assailant's body that staggered helplessly toward him. The woman's second victim attempted to resist her stranglehold. His meaty arms and thick legs shook as he was deprived of oxygen.

Stefan smiled as he heard the familiar sound of the victim's windpipe crack beneath the woman's forced compressions against his neck. In a few seconds, the man's once aggressive body lay still.

Stefan moved away from the woman and stood in the darkness against the jagged brick wall. Stefan liked what he had seen. His subject was a worthy choice. Tonight's experiment was another success for the project.

The drug was now ready for the Bishop and Monsignor, Stefan decided. They would inhale the drug during tomorrow night's Mass at St. John the Evangelist Catholic Church.

Chapter Forty-Four

MEGHAN CAHILL'S EYES BURNED. SHE had been at it for almost three hours but knew her efforts were futile. She tried to concentrate but found her thoughts stray from her work on an overdue research proposal.

She was alone in her office, which was next to her lab where she had struggled since early this morning to complete the required FDA application packet for her proposed research study. Why was it so difficult for her to get through this simple task? She had worked on over a hundred of these applications before without any problems.

But this one was different. She knew what distracted her. But she thought she could deal with it.

Dan Rafferty. Dan's death ... how could she ignore that?

While at the beach house yesterday, she took the time to think of him. To mourn him. To remember him. Yes, she would remember him—now, this morning, and always.

Meghan thought she could return to the institute and allow herself to become absorbed in her work. Her research would be good therapy for her, she thought, but she was a changed person ever since Emily called her last Sunday with the news about Dan's murder.

Sitting at her desk, reading through the completed sections of the research application forms was just too much for her. They were his words. Dan's handwritten notes that she had read over and over again. How could she expect herself to see his words and not feel sad?

Meghan stood up and walked over to her windows overlooking the withered and decayed cornstalks that surrounded the lake. There was no longer just one path through the stalks that led down to the lake, the path she had taken many times. Many paths had been cut recklessly through the cornfield, disorganized and obviously made in haste by the police who had responded that night with the hope of saving a life.

But no lives were saved that night. Their attempts had been futile.

And her efforts to work this morning were just as futile.

What should I do now? Meghan thought.

Suddenly, the phone rang. Meghan instinctively brought both hands up to her chest as if to shield herself from some unknown threat that was about to harm her.

After the fourth ring, Meghan reached for the phone. "Hello," she whispered as her heart pounded.

"Meghan, is that you?" Emily DeHaven's voice was frantic.

"Yes, it is. Emily, is that you?"

"Meghan, you've got to get out of there, now."

"Why? What's wrong?"

"It's the police. They're on their way to arrest you. Did you hear me ... arrest you."

"What for? I haven't done anything wrong."

"Will you just listen. There's not much time. They just left my lab and now they're heading over to your lab. They think you killed Farraday and Dan."

"What … that's ridiculous. Why would I—"

"Stop it. You can't stay there. There's a lot I need to tell you, but not now. There's no time. You've got to leave the institute, *now.*

"Where do I go?"

"Anywhere. I'll call you as soon as I can on your cell phone. Just get out of there."

Meghan heard the phone disconnect. She slammed the receiver down and grabbed her purse. She noticed several glass vials of the narcotic, Fentanyl, still sitting on the lab counter. Earlier this morning, she had taken them out from the narcotic dispenser when she had checked the inventory and their expiration dates. She now realized she had forgotten to put them back.

Meghan realized she didn't have time to return them to the drug dispenser and decided instead to put them inside her handbag. If the police were indeed after her, she didn't want them to see drugs carelessly left around the lab.

Meghan ran out into the hallway and immediately heard the elevator signal its arrival on the third floor. Her floor.

They are already here. It's too late to escape them, she thought. *Or is it?*

Meghan had a thought. The stairway. Of course. Why not? Maybe the police hadn't thought of it yet.

As Meghan closed the stairway door behind her, she could hear Detective McManus's voice getting closer from around the hallway corner.

Meghan flew down the concrete stairs, taking two and three steps at a time. When she arrived on the first floor, she scanned the lobby for any police who may have been left behind to secure the front door. She was in luck. No police. And for that matter, no guards either. She wondered if the lobby guard was temporarily pulled to assist with her arrest. Was she really that much of a threat?

As Meghan raced across the west parking lot, she had another fear. Would the police know her car and be waiting for her there? Meghan slowed down and retreated behind a group of evergreens. She separated several thick green branches and stared in the direction of her parking space.

What? It couldn't be. Her car wasn't there. The police did know her car and probably had it towed away.

Meghan felt it hard to breathe. Her mouth was dry, and it was difficult for her to swallow. What was she supposed to do now? Wait for the police to find her? Or would it be better for her if she turned herself in? She had nothing to hide. She was innocent.

Meghan walked out from behind the group of white pines and stared out at the lake. She now hated that lake. It was not her special place any more. Meghan sensed her life at the institute was over. She would be arrested soon. But why? She did nothing wrong.

Suddenly, Meghan remembered. She didn't park early this morning in her usual space. She didn't want to drive near the lake along the west end of the institute, so she had decided instead to park on the other side of the building. *That's right,* she thought. She had parked her BMW on the east side of the institute.

Meghan felt a surge of renewed energy. She sprinted around the building and saw no one near her car. She was safe, at least for now.

Chapter Forty-Five

"SHE'S NOT HERE. YOU TOLD us she would be in her lab," McManus accused as he glared at the lobby security guard who had accompanied him.

"I thought ... I mean, she should've been here. One of the other guards told me he had just seen her in her office when he was making rounds. I don't understand. I don't understand what—"

"Forget it. We'll find her. Just have your guards check the parking lot for her car. Do you think you can do that?" McManus challenged.

The security guard raced down the hallway and made the turn toward the elevators. McManus could hear him shouting orders into his walkie-talkie.

"Where do you think she is?" Officer Greer asked.

"If her car is gone, so is she. Someone tipped her off. Look around. Her office door is wide open, there are papers scattered on the floor, and her jacket is still on the back of her desk chair. She sure left in a hurry," McManus said.

"I'll call in a description of her car," the young officer announced as he started for the door.

"Also, have our guys call the West Chester Police. She might be heading to her townhouse in West Chester, so we'll need their help," McManus ordered.

McManus remained in the lab as Officer Greer hurried out to check the nearby stairway for some sign of Meghan Cahill. Soon the lab became silent. McManus looked around and wondered why Cahill, who had it all—young, attractive, great job at a prestigious pharmaceutical company—had become a killer.

A premeditated killer.

McManus reviewed the evidence so far against his prime suspect.

According to the security department's computer records of Farraday's e-mails to Cahill, she obviously knew Farraday had suspected she falsified her research results to the government and thereby feared public exposure of her illegal acts. Such acts she probably knew would result in civil and criminal repercussions. Since Dan Rafferty was the one to disclose her illegal activities to Farraday, she killed Rafferty as retribution for his disloyalty to her. This evidence clearly established Dr. Cahill's motive for the two murders, McManus thought.

As of thirty minutes ago, McManus also knew he had established opportunity for Dr. Cahill's crimes. Farraday's 911 text message sent to the institute's security department shortly before he died had been recorded and saved on the Renaissance Institute's computer system. This morning, after finally fixing a computer malfunction, the security department was now able to supply McManus with Farraday's final words before he had died.

Farraday had named Meghan Cahill as his killer.

It didn't surprise McManus that Farraday's message had been sent in text form since the stab wound to his heart muscle would immediately cause Farraday to become hypotensive, making it difficult for him to speak.

McManus was lost in thought. The dead silence that pervaded the lab nurtured his deep thoughts as he continued to develop his theory.

Lying on the ground, in the mud, Farraday probably had just enough strength to press his cell phone key pad and send the incriminating message, McManus thought.

McManus's thoughts continued in the stillness of Meghan Cahill's laboratory. McManus realized he lacked the murder weapon. Even though finding the weapon wasn't absolutely necessary to convict Cahill, having it would certainly seal her fate. He was glad that his friend, Dr. Evan Hawthorne, the Philadelphia medical examiner, had called him late Monday night and had given him the probable identity of the murder weapon. Based on the photographs taken of the victims' wounds and the meticulous description of the autopsy given to his friend by the Chester County's M.E., Dr. Hawthorne was able to narrow down the type of instrument that probably had caused such injuries.

A long, slender, single-steel blade.

An ice pick.

Suddenly, McManus became aware of a faint, humming sound. He hastened across the room and peered around the wide floor-to-ceiling pillar that obscured the source of the persistent hum. *The laboratory's ice machine.* As he slid the steel door open, it screeched against its rubber track. This sound was familiar, but he couldn't remember when or where he had last heard it.

He lowered his head and peered inside. A cloud of cold mist flowed across his face, stinging his skin as if he were walking into a winter's storm. McManus saw thick blocks of crushed ice spread inside the ice machine bin. He remembered when Cahill had explained her work to him two days ago. At times, she needed the crushed ice to store her animal blood and tissue samples, thereby preventing any chemical breakdown in them. Even though the machine produced crushed ice, over time McManus knew the pieces of ice would solidify and become like a glacier. Unless, of course, the glacier was periodically broken apart.

McManus didn't have to look far. The long, slender steel blade of an ice pick with its wooden handle lay frozen, partially embedded in ice against the machine's inside steel wall. McManus reached inside his jacket and pulled out a plastic bag and a pair of vinyl gloves, which he put on before retrieving the possible murder weapon. He then gently placed the ice pick inside his large, thick evidence bag. If there had been any incriminating evidence on it, he thought, the cold temperature would have preserved the evidence, such as traces of DNA. It was ironic, McManus thought, that Cahill's ice machine might actually be responsible for solidifying his case against her.

McManus left the lab and walked down the hallway. As he turned the corner, he noticed Emily DeHaven hurrying to one of the elevators. She appeared preoccupied with her cell phone conversation since she never looked back at Jonathan Ashbridge, who stood outside their lab calling out for her to stop.

Detective McManus had to get his evidence to the crime lab right away. He also had to find Dr. Cahill. Even though he tried not to convict a suspect before all of the evidence was in, McManus felt that Dr. Cahill was more than a suspect—more than a person under suspicion.

She was not the innocent, dedicated researcher that she would have everyone believe she was.

Why else did she run?

And where could she possibly run to now and hide? McManus pondered.

Chapter Forty-Six

"MEGHAN, WHY AREN'T YOU ANSWERING your phone?" Emily called out as she drove her car out of the institute parking lot.

Emily wasn't sure where to go. She wanted to find her friend right away and tell her about the new evidence. Farraday's text message. It still didn't make sense ... Meghan Cahill responsible for two murders.

Meghan Cahill ... a killer.

Emily refused to believe the evidence when Jonathan had given her the news. He had claimed there was solid DNA evidence that clearly identified Meghan as the killer. The police had told him so this morning, Jonathan had said to her. Still, Emily would never believe it. She knew Meghan was not capable of hurting anyone. Emily vowed to help her friend.

—◆◆◆—

Almost an hour had gone by since she had received the call from Emily back at the lab. Why hadn't she called her back? Meghan wondered. She reached over on the passenger seat, picked up her cell phone, and stared down at the blank, glass face.

My God, her phone was dead. She must have forgotten to charge it. Meghan opened her console and pulled out the charger. It didn't take long before her cell phone chirped new life.

Suddenly, Meghan's phone rang. "Emily?"

"Meghan, where have you been? I've been trying to reach you."

"My phone went dead. What's going on?" pleaded Meghan.

"Where are you now?"

"I'm on the Atlantic City Expressway. I'm going to Ocean City."

"Good. The last place you want to be is at your townhouse in West Chester. I'm sure the police are there by now."

"Why are the police after me? I haven't done anything wrong," Meghan said.

"I know. I believe you. You've got to remember that. What I have to tell you … I know sounds crazy … but the police have e-mails sent by Farraday to you, implicating you in some illegal research activity."

"Wait a minute. I read those e-mails Monday morning, and I didn't understand them."

"Well that's only half of it. The police have a recorded message sent by Farraday only minutes before he died, telling our security department that you attacked him … stabbed him. And the police have found physical evidence on the bodies that matches your DNA on file at the institute."

"That's not true … it's a lie!" Meghan screamed. She felt her hand that gripped the steering wheel suddenly grow weak. Her chest felt heavy … it was hard to breathe.

"Listen, Meghan, calm down. I will help, but you've got to listen to me." Emily paused, giving her friend time to take several deep breaths.

"I'm sorry, Emily. What should I do?" Meghan whispered.

"Go to your beach house and wait there. I don't think the police know about your house in Ocean City. I'll meet you there, and we'll go over this whole thing."

"Okay ... I will ... thanks, Em." Meghan breathed deeply.

Emily waited to hear Meghan hang up. She knew her friend was in trouble. Right now, she had no idea how to help her.

She only hoped she would have something for Meghan when she arrived at her beach house.

Chapter Forty-Seven

DETECTIVE McMANUS DROVE HIS UNMARKED police sedan down High Street, crossed over Gay Street, and then came to a stop at the Market Street traffic light. From that intersection, he was able to look ahead down High Street and see that there were already four West Chester police vehicles. Three were positioned in front of Meghan Cahill's townhouse, with the fourth squad car angled before him at the Market Street intersection, where it prevented all traffic from proceeding in the direction of the townhouse. Two additional police cars from his Valley Creek Department were strategically positioned at the entrance to an alley that ran alongside Cahill's home.

At first, McManus thought the police response was overkill, with all of their red and blue lights pulsating against the Williamsburg brick townhouse. But then he reminded himself that Cahill was not to be trusted. She had been a convincing liar. Meghan Cahill was capable of doing anything, especially if she felt trapped with nowhere to go. The police response was appropriate, he concluded.

The light turned green, and McManus drove ahead past the police car sentry after he showed his detective's gold shield pass. McManus parked his car on the street behind the array of police cars and noticed several police officers standing in position on either side of Cahill's front door and along the adjacent alley that led to the townhouse's back door.

"Detective McManus, how nice of you to finally show up," the West Chester official grinned. "We've been ready to go in, but Officer Greer assured me that you would be here soon. Trust me, I didn't wait because of your rookie's assurances. You and I go way back ... just call it professional courtesy."

The West Chester detective brought an immediate smile to McManus's face. It had been several years since McManus last saw him. At that time, the detective was still with the Philadelphia Police Department and had met with McManus to get his recommendation for a detective position that had opened up in the West Chester Police Department. McManus knew he didn't need his recommendation for the job. He had one of the best credentials of any Philadelphia detective McManus had worked with.

"Thanks, Detective Barrett. You always did look after me," McManus said as the two men shook hands.

"Your rookie filled me in on this case. Do you think she killed those guys last weekend?" Barrett asked.

"If you asked me yesterday, I'd have to say I wasn't sure. However, this morning we got some convincing evidence that proves she's guilty."

"You mean the victim's text message? Officer Greer over there filled me in."

"More than that. While driving over to the institute this morning, I got a call from a private lab in Harrisburg. We gave them some fingernail scrapings of skin and saliva and also hair samples that we collected from the two victims. Fortunate for us, the Renaissance Institute requires each employee to submit their DNA sample in order to work there. Some kind of background clearance check is needed because at times, the institute does classified research work for the government. The crime lab compared our preliminary DNA analysis to each employee's DNA that's on file at the institute."

"Did they find a match?" Barrett asked.

"They sure did. The crime lab's analysis and their findings are not complete, but all the evidence we have so far still points to Cahill as our killer. It was her skin and saliva that we found under Farraday's fingernails. Strands of her hair were also found on his body. In fact, the same incriminating evidence was also found on Rafferty's body. So, the only thing left to do is make the arrest. Are you ready to go in?" McManus urged.

"Let me make sure our guys are ready in the back."

McManus walked toward the front door of the three-story townhouse. Suddenly, the distant sound of church bells chimed a series of notes that were immediately familiar to McManus. He remembered hearing that same melody just a few days ago.

It was Sunday morning.

The church bells played "Ave Maria."

He had heard it when he answered Dan Rafferty's cell phone. At the time, he didn't know the identity of the caller. Only that the caller ID was a Jeffrey Perseus; no one with that name was listed in the Renaissance Institute's employee records.

The church bells finished their rendition of "Ave Maria" and began to toll the hour of the day.

From within St. Agnes Catholic Church's gray stone bell tower chimed the final eleventh tone. Even though the church was almost five blocks away, each tone seemed to resonate inside McManus's head, as if he were standing directly beneath the bell tower.

He now knew who the caller was.

Cahill.

The unknown caller on Dan Rafferty's cell phone was Meghan Cahill. It had to be her. This would be too much of a coincidence otherwise.

But why would she call Rafferty's cell on the day after she killed him? McManus thought.

"We're ready," Detective Barrett shouted.

McManus nodded.

"Break it down," Barrett commanded to his eager assault team.

For some reason, McManus had a strong feeling Cahill would not be inside her townhouse.

"You searched everywhere?" McManus questioned.

"We did. It doesn't look like she's been here recently. The soap dish is dry, and so is her toothbrush. The shower stall doesn't have a single drop anywhere," Barrett replied.

"What do you think? Empty for two or three days?"

"I'd say so. Which means, where has she been living for the past few days?" Barrett asked.

"I think I should have a talk with Dr. Ashbridge. He dated Cahill for a couple of years. Maybe he knows something that will help us find her," McManus said.

Chapter Forty-Eight

THE STATIC MESSAGE FROM EMILY DeHaven's car radio did not predict good news. The weather report warned of heavy rains with winds gusting up to eighty miles an hour. Emily didn't need this weather confirmation. She knew what a Nor'easter was and feared she was already in the storm's clutches, experiencing the torrential rains and blinding crosswinds that tried to lift and force her over the guard rail and off the 34th Street bridge. Emily prayed her car would soon lead her to safety and into Ocean City where Meghan was waiting.

Emily's grip tightened around her steering wheel as she felt her car move sideways across the two-lane bridge. Suddenly, a jagged streak of lightning lit up the road ahead of her. Thank God, she had finally made it to the top of the bridge. She was almost in Ocean City. Halfway there, she reminded herself.

But the flash of light never burned out. It shined bright against her mirrors, blinding her vision as it reflected into her eyes. Emily stared down at her feet. But it didn't help. She couldn't escape the glaring light that flooded the inside of her car.

Without warning, her car was hit from behind ... then again. The force drove her against the steel side rail. The shrill grinding sound of her car's metal body ripping apart deafened her ears as she tried frantically to turn her car away from the railing.

It was no use. She was hit again. This time, however, much harder and now against her driver's side door. She was trapped. The force that had been hitting her from behind was now against the side of her, pushing her farther along the railing. Emily no longer controlled her vehicle as it continued to grind against the metal rail, engulfing her car in yellow and orange sparks.

Emily tried to brake but felt her vehicle's tires flow across the deep puddles. She was hydroplaning, she quickly realized. *Don't slam on the brakes. Try to pump them gently.*

Her car would not slow down. Instead, another blow rammed into the rear of her car. Emily's fingers throbbed, and her knuckles grew whiter as her death-grip tightened around her leather steering wheel. Emily realized this new force behind her was working in partnership with the force that remained along her side. Two cars pushing her harder and faster against the edge of the bridge and toward the empty darkness that lay below in the surging bay.

The last sound Emily heard was her own scream as her car plunged into the cold, dark bay water.

Meghan paced across the kitchen floor. She needed one more drink. This would be her fourth glass of wine. It would be her last, she promised herself, at least until Emily got here.

Thank God for her. Meghan sighed. If Emily had not warned her back at the lab, she would have been arrested immediately. And for what crime? She didn't kill anyone. But why all the mounting evidence against her? Farraday's e-mails and supposedly a text message sent by her to Farraday asking him to meet her at the lake Saturday night.

All lies. But the police didn't think so. They obviously felt they had enough evidence to justify her arrest.

At least Emily believed her. She needed her help more than ever right now. She would know what to do. Like her grandmother, Emily would calm her with her strong, loving guidance. She was sure to have a plan.

What was happening to her life now?

Who was doing this to her? Maybe she should call Jeffrey Manion. Maybe he was also in trouble.

Stop it.

What was she doing?

Why was she afraid to admit it to herself?

She knew who must be responsible for her problem with the police.

Jonathan Ashbridge. It had to be him. But Meghan still had many unanswered questions.

What did she do to him that deserved such retribution? And why was Jonathan tormenting her?

It couldn't be because Jeffrey had revealed their covert experiments to her. He had shown their work to her Saturday night, probably around the same time the killings had taken place. It was impossible for Jonathan to know that soon about Jeffrey's disclosure to her.

She and Jeffrey were alone that night in the subterranean lab. No one else was around. No one. Nothing, except for the ravaged animals.

Meghan grew nauseous. Her memory of Saturday night sickened her. She forced herself to forget that evening. Focus instead on Emily's arrival.

She would be here soon.

She has to be, Meghan prayed.

Chapter Forty-Nine

I T WAS THE STORM. IT had to be the storm. That's why Emily was late, Meghan insisted. She tried to give her friend that excuse, but it wasn't working because why hadn't Emily called her?

A sudden flash of lightning followed by an immediate explosion of thunder shook Meghan from her thoughts. The storm had intensified, forcing its torrential rain against her windows as if demanding immediate entry into her safe haven.

Meghan turned on the TV, looking for some distraction from the storm's relentless wind that howled against the walls of her Victorian beach house.

Breaking news. According to two eyewitness accounts, a white Volkswagen Jetta heading into Ocean City lost control and crashed into the guardrail at the top of the 34th Street bridge. Upon impact, the car then flipped over the side of the bridge and plunged into the bay. Rescue teams are on the scene and have located the wreckage. The identity of the young female driver is being withheld pending the notification of her family.

"No … no … it can't be true. It just can't be!" Meghan screamed as she covered both ears with her trembling hands. Her petite body grew limp, and slowly, Meghan slumped to her knees. She rocked back and forth.

"Please, God … please, don't let it be Emily," Meghan moaned. But she knew even God could not change the facts that she had just heard.

Emily drove a white Volkswagen Jetta.

Emily always took the 34th Street bridge whenever she visited her in Ocean City.

And, Emily was late.

Even if the storm had made her late, she would have called. Emily knew Meghan was waiting for her, worried about the police, unsure of what was happening to her.

Meghan Cahill feared that her freedom and her life were now threatened more than ever. There was no one alive who believed in her—no one she could trust. Everyone who had touched her life was either dead or had manipulated and deceived her.

Nana … Dan … Jonathan. And now, *Emily.* She was gone forever.

There was no hope remaining for Meghan to hold onto. She couldn't even feel Nana's presence anymore. Today was September 21, the two-year anniversary of Nana's death, and Meghan could not feel her grandmother's spirit.

The relentless sound of pounding water against the windowpanes of her beach house filled the living room and her troubled mind. Meghan's body shivered. She was numb with fear. Her ears ached from the piercing, drowning rain. Meghan's breathing increased. She felt it harder to reach inside for her next breath. The storm was not just outside but all around her, inside her beach house.

Meghan stood up. She had to find a way to escape the storm's reach. She needed someplace where she could breathe.

Meghan raced from room to room. First, the kitchen. Then into her haven, her special room used for self-renewal where she would paint, think of Nana, and become one with her spirit. The room was now humid and air-less. Even Nana's oil painting that hung over the mahogany piano—the one depicting the sailboat coursing through an ocean storm—no longer nourished her weakening spirit. The many black and white photographs of her grandmother no longer brought her comfort; they only intensified her loneliness.

Meghan was alone. Her life had nothing to offer her but criminal prosecution for crimes she did not commit.

Meghan sighed. She turned and walked back through the double atrium doors that led from her haven into her kitchen. She walked over to the granite countertop and reached inside her purse. She carefully retrieved the five vials of the narcotic, fentanyl, which she had grabbed from her lab counter as she ran out after Emily's warning phone call.

Meghan stared down at the five glass ampules. She had been distracted with Dan's murder and hadn't finished with her inventory of narcotics back at her lab that she routinely performed daily and which was now several days overdue. And to think, she was worried about leaving them out on her lab table to be discovered by McManus.

Concerned with what he might think of her.

Reckless with her drugs.

Reckless with her research.

Reckless. Unpredictable. Capable of doing anything.

Even murder.

Meghan no longer cared. About McManus ... Jonathan ... or the Renaissance Institute.

She needed something else. Meghan opened the kitchen drawer and removed a box filled with syringes and needles. Nana's syringes used for her daily insulin injections. Meghan remembered the comments made to her at her grandmother's funeral; you should be grateful, she was told, your grandmother lived as long as she did, especially having diabetes. *What did they know?* Meghan thought. Her grandmother should not have died. She should not have been taken away from her. She never wanted Nana to leave her side.

Meghan walked over to the pantry where she kept her wine and liquor and grabbed a full bottle of Jameson Irish whiskey. *It was Jonathan's favorite whiskey … he won't be missing it,* she thought.

Meghan carefully chose a clean glass from the drying rack and dropped three fully formed ice cubes into it. She turned and walked down the oak wood floor of her hallway that led to her bedroom.

She was not reckless.

She also knew she could never harm another human being.

Chapter Fifty

JONATHAN DROVE HIS HUMMER INTO the wreckage plant located in Camden, New Jersey, near the Delaware River waterfront. Even though there was only minimal damage to the right bumper and side panel, he decided to stay with the plan.

Within a few minutes, a Land Cruiser pulled along next to him. Jonathan got out of the Hummer and walked over to his nearby BMW that he had parked there late this morning near the wreckage compressor unit. As he opened the driver's door, Jonathan heard a shout come from the direction of the Land Cruiser.

"That was incredible ... she didn't stand a chance!" Jeffrey Manion shouted, slamming shut the Land Cruiser door. He walked along the front of the SUV and surveyed the damage.

"Amazing. I was expecting more damage. Then again, a Volkswagen Jetta ... not a chance," Jeffrey smirked.

Jonathan never turned around. He didn't enjoy what they had just done but knew there was no other way. Emily would have been a problem. It was not his fault she was Meghan's friend. Fortunately, this morning, he had been able to reach Stefan on his cell phone and review the matter with him. What should be done about Meghan's ally?

Stefan never hesitated, Jonathan recalled. He had told Jonathan exactly what to do.

Drive to the Camden plant, pick up the two vehicles that would be waiting for them, and then return them to the wreckage plant once their assignment was completed. Stefan said he would have them destroyed in the compressor unit.

No trace of the Hummer or the Land Cruiser, Stefan had assured it.

Stefan had then warned Jonathan not to bother him anymore. He had to prepare for tonight's church services.

Chapter Fifty-One

FRIAR VINCENT WAGNER STEPPED OFF 13th Street and proceeded east along Clover Street, a narrow cobblestone footpath in desperate need of repair in Center City, Philadelphia.

The friar gazed up toward the sky; the Nor'easter's storm clouds that clung to the Jersey Shore were now moving west, cloaking their black shroud over the Philadelphia evening sky. He noticed how much darker it suddenly became since he had started down Clover Street, which was overshadowed on the one side by a ten-story, dilapidated stone rooming house, and on the other side by St. John the Evangelist Catholic Church.

Even without the storm's cloud cover, Stefan judged, these two tall structures would have blocked any trace of the sunset's brilliant rays. Still, the friar took joy in noticing another brilliant showcase. Positioned approximately twenty feet high up along the side of St. John's weathered granite stone building were seven stained-glass windows through which the soft glow of flickering candlelight flowed from within the church. The intensity of light was sufficient for the friar to make out the artistic etching on each window—the last seven of the fourteen Stations of the Cross.

As he walked beneath each stained-glass window, the friar knew he was following Christ's journey to the cross.

He was fulfilling Christ's mission.

And his own mission.

As well as the mission of Imago Dei.

The friar arrived at the rectory located directly behind the church, and as he had been directed by St. John's pastor, he walked up to the steel side door. There was a wrought iron lamp shaped in an arc above the doorway that sprayed yellow light across the entrance. The friar pulled on the tarnished chain that hung down next to the door. Immediately, a bell chimed throughout the once quiet street.

Suddenly, a group of pigeons fluttered by, flushed out from behind a city dumpster that had overflowed with garbage. They flew by the friar, close enough for him to hear their wings beating against the wind and to see remnants of their dinner still trapped in their mouths.

"Friar Vincent, I presume. Welcome to our humble home," St. John's pastor greeted as he opened the heavy steel door.

"Good evening. It was so nice of you to invite me to dinner and to your church services tonight," the friar responded.

"Well, you are a fellow Capuchin friar and visiting Philadelphia from so far away. As I told you this morning when you called, you are welcome to stay with us here at St. John's as long as you wish."

"You are very kind ... I do appreciate your offer, but I think I'll remain with my Augustinian friend at Villanova University. There's plenty of room in his house on campus since several priests are away on sabbatical."

"Well, you're always welcome here. Now do come in and tell me more about your assignment at our Capuchin Monastery in Palermo."

The pastor, a bearded man in his sixties, wearing worn sandals with no socks and a rope-belted brown robe with a hood that fell back against his neck, escorted Friar Vincent into the rectory's study. He offered his visitor the wooden chair nearest to the fireplace. The friar's chill from his early evening walk to the rectory was soon a distant memory.

The friar sensed he was being treated as an honored guest, a representative from their European Monastery Headquarters located in Palermo, Sicily. They were in the study for only a few minutes when a firm knock resounded off the study door. The pastor never took his eyes off his visitor and continued to listen intently to Friar Vincent's account of his religious studies in Palermo. Finally, after the fourth knock, the pastor rose from his seat and slowly walked to the door. He slid the heavy oak door open and nodded to the robed messenger.

"I'm being summoned by the bishop. I'm sorry to cut short our visit. I so wanted to hear more of your life in Palermo. It's been many years since I've been there. But now, my services are required elsewhere. Before I leave, I want you to know you will be con-celebrating our Mass this evening with Bishop Torrey and his assistant, Monsignor Brannigan. This is an honor for me to have you on the altar with them."

"Thank you. As you can see, though, I haven't brought my stole or any other vestments."

"Not to worry ... we have more than enough vestments to go around. As I said before, it is an honor for me to have you on the altar, especially after ... no ... I shouldn't trouble you with that information." The pastor lowered his eyes and gazed into the burning embers. He slowly shook his head as he murmured a short prayer.

"What's wrong?" the friar asked, rising from his chair and placing a hand against the pastor's back.

"It was horrible. One of our brothers who was assigned here was recently murdered along the waterfront." The pastor turned and faced his guest. The friar's cold, ice-blue eyes were wide open in disbelief.

"That's terrible ... I am so sorry for your loss. Have the police made any arrests?"

"No. They do keep me informed every day though. They tell me there's not much to go on. Except one thing ..."

"What's that?"

"The police say the murderer used a knife and engraved a mark into the vicar's chest."

"What do you mean ... a mark?" The friar's brow tightened.

"Yes ... the police actually called it a dodecagon ... a geometrical design or figure with twelve sides ... etched into his skin."

"That's horrible ... sinful," Friar Vincent replied, blessing himself.

"If that wasn't enough, the murderer engraved a cross in the center of the figure. Why would anyone do such a thing?" the pastor said.

The friar knew the reason.

The friar shook his head and embraced the pastor. "I don't know, but permit me to ask this of you. Allow me to offer a special prayer at the beginning of Mass tonight for our slain Capuchin brother."

The pastor stepped back and met the friar's gaze. "That is so thoughtful of you. God truly sent you here tonight."

The friar pursed his lips together and smiled softly. "I have a special request, though. I would like to use incense for my offering. I trust you do have some here."

Chapter Fifty-Two

MEGHAN CAHILL WAS EXHAUSTED. SHE sat on her bed, and her outstretched arms shook as they leaned against her knees. Her stare remained fixed on the shattered windowpane glass scattered across her bedroom floor. Even though Jonathan was not the one who had filled the syringe with the toxic dose of narcotic, tonight his evil power had controlled Meghan's self-destructive behavior.

She knew it.

And, she felt it.

But Meghan was saved tonight. She was given a reprieve from Jonathan's evil sentence.

Was it fate that saved her? Meghan remembered a blinding light had flashed before her eyes just as she was about to inject the poison into her vein. But she knew better. It wasn't that simple and easy to explain away. Not as cold and remote either, as fate is often described.

It was Nana.

Nana.

Only her grandmother's spirit could be strong enough to intercede for her and overpower Jonathan's hold over her. Meghan knew of no other reason why her life was saved tonight.

Nana's spirit had breathed new life into her. She now knew what she had to do. She must expose Jonathan's evil work at the institute and expose whatever his Pegasus Project was designed to do.

And, she must fight for her innocence.

Meghan quickly got dressed and grabbed her hooded rain slicker. She picked up her car keys and purse and raced to the front door. As she entered the foyer, she noticed red and blue lights flashing against her front windows. Meghan didn't have to look outside. She knew the police had come for her.

She had to act fast. Meghan turned and ran across her second-floor living room, into her kitchen, and through the atrium doors that finally led her outside onto the second-floor stone deck. The Nor'easter wind rudely greeted Meghan with its bullet-like torrential rain, stinging her face as the horizontal-driven water pelted her skin.

Meghan looked down over the waist-high wrought iron fence that separated her from the gray, saturated sand some twenty feet below. There was no other way out. In a few minutes, the police would have her house surrounded.

She had to do it.

She had to jump now.

As Meghan released her grasp on the railing, she reminded herself that the sand would not cushion her fall. The heavy rains had taken care of that for her. Landing on the beach would be like landing on cement. Hard and unforgiving.

But Meghan didn't care. She was ready to fight back.

After landing hard on the saturated sand, Meghan paused for a few seconds before subjecting her legs to her full body weight. Nothing broken. Not even a sprain. Her style of landing wasn't pretty but obviously effective. She had designed her fall to mimic the landing technique used by WWII parachutists whom she saw recently on the History Channel. *Hit the ground with both legs bent and immediately roll your body across the ground. This maneuver will decrease the stress to the lower extremities.*

The History Channel would remain her favorite TV listing, Meghan promised herself.

Racing across the beach, Meghan wondered how she could get out of Ocean City and off her island. She knew the 34th Street bridge would be closed. That only left the toll bridge located in the Gardens, the one she had used many times during her several-mile run excursions.

What was once a small wooden bridge had become a newly constructed concrete bridge that would take her off the island. She would cross over the Ocean City-Longport Bridge, located several blocks away from her beach house on Gull Road, which would then put her onto a narrow causeway and take her into the Northern Shore Islands. Meghan thought that if she could just make it to Atlantic City, she would then be able to enter the Atlantic City Expressway, which would safely take her away from the police.

The only task left for her to do now was to reach her car. When she had driven home this morning, not really knowing at the time her reason for doing so, she decided to park on Sea Spray Road, several blocks away from her beach house. Maybe it was her feeling that someone was following her. Or her fear that her accusers would see that she was at home. Whatever the reason, she knew her strategy had paid off.

This is the second time I've chosen correctly where to park my car, Meghan thought.

The driving-rain continued its assault on the Ocean City Beach island as Meghan turned off Sea Spray Road and slowly drove her BMW along the Gardens Parkway toward the toll bridge. She strained to look ahead through her flooded windshield that, despite the frantic motion of her windshield blades, only offered an obscured view of the approaching bridge's yellow flashing lights. Still, Meghan was relieved to see only yellow lights atop the toll booth and no red and blue lights from police cars waiting to thwart her escape.

The Ocean City Police were probably already spread thin with several units assigned to the 34th Street bridge accident, while a few other units were assigned to set up a checkpoint at the 9th Street bridge. That only left a couple police cars that were dispatched to arrest her tonight.

It took Meghan a couple of minutes to reach the Ocean City-Longport Bridge, which was dark and desolate. As she drove up to the booth, she couldn't tell if anyone was inside to collect the $1.00 toll. Seeing the lowered gate with its attached red light burning strong to remind the driver not to proceed until payment was made sent a shiver of fear through Meghan. If the toll booth was in fact empty, did that mean the Ocean City Police had decided, due to the storm's high winds and poor visibility, it was unsafe to cross the bridge? Had they closed it for the night?

It couldn't be. She had made it this far ... she couldn't turn back now.

Meghan's thoughts raced through her head. There was no sign saying it was closed. *The police have a duty to warn drivers when a bridge is suddenly closed*, Meghan insisted.

As she pulled alongside the rain-battered glass booth, the steel-framed window broke its seal against the wall and slowly slid open.

"What brings you out on a night like this?" the attendant yelled out as he pulled his raincoat collar up around his neck.

Meghan was relieved. She lowered her window just enough to pass through a dollar bill. Not turning her head to acknowledge that she had heard the old man's question, Meghan kept her face buried inside the pulled-up hood of her rain slicker.

Meghan sat for hours, or at least it seemed that long to her, waiting for the green light to appear and her barrier to lift, sending her far away from her pursuers.

"You be careful out there!" the old man shouted as he slammed the glass window shut. Finally, Meghan saw the light she was hoping for. As she passed under the raised gate, she remembered reading the novel *The Great Gatsby*. As she had done this evening, alone and uncertain but hoping for a chance at freedom, Jay Gatsby also had looked out one night and seen a speckle of green light painted on a distant shore across Long Island Sound, hoping that he could be with his lover and free her from her unhappy and painful life.

Driving now along the dark and deserted causeway that separated the bay from the Atlantic Ocean, Meghan searched her thoughts for some direction and a plan to clear her name. Her mind was restless, and her thoughts raced as if trying to keep up with the high-speed windshield wipers that moved like a hyperactive metronome.

She needed a plan, and it had to come from her. She was alone. And Emily was gone.

Meghan tried to remember specifically how and when her life had suddenly become threatened. She remembered standing in her lab on Monday morning—just two days ago—reading Farraday's e-mails accusing her of fraud. Falsifying research data on FDA documents. Then, she read e-mails allegedly sent by her to Farraday, which she noticed were blind-copied to herself, challenging his claim and demanding to meet with him over the weekend. And, then there was Detective McManus's visit to her lab on Monday. As she had just finished reading the e-mail lies, McManus arrived to tell her that Farraday's cell phone had a stored text message from her, asking Farraday to meet her at the lake the night he was killed.

And, there was Emily DeHaven's cryptic phone call to her this morning telling her the police were on their way to her lab to arrest her. Later, Emily had told her that they had new physical evidence found on the victims that implicated her in the murders of Farraday and Dan Rafferty. Emily had told her the police claimed that their physical evidence matched her DNA on file at the Renaissance Institute.

What was this physical evidence and how could it possibly match her DNA?

Meghan Cahill. Her DNA found on the murder victims' bodies? That's impossible. It couldn't be so.

Lies. All lies.

And what did Jeffrey want her to know last Saturday night when he had shown her Jonathan's secret animal experiments?

What did he mean when he said these experiments were part of the Pegasus Project?

Meghan remembered she had questioned Jeffrey about the Pegasus Project, but it was no use. Jeffrey was scared to death and couldn't give her any further explanation about their secret work. She saw terror in Jeffrey's eyes. He was numb with fear, she remembered.

Fear for his safety.

Fear of what Jonathan would do to him.

False e-mails and text messages.

Physical evidence that matched her DNA.

Meghan knew her remaining time of freedom was quickly diminishing. She had to find a way, something or someone to help.

Help her now. Tonight.

It was the physical evidence, the DNA evidence that she focused on.

Meghan knew something about physical evidence at a crime scene. During her PhD work in pathology and pharmacology at the University of Pennsylvania, she had taken several courses in forensic medicine. The material interested her so much, she almost pursued a career in forensic pathology. Not as a physician, but as a scientist. One particular professor at Penn had impressed her, not only with his dual background in law and medicine, but also, more importantly, with his honesty and devoted work ethic.

Dr. Evan Hawthorne. He had been her favorite. Even though he appeared on the surface to have tunnel vision for his work, Meghan had seen another side to him, as a physician-attorney with a great sense of humor. He had once told her that he often looked at himself as a kind of

Dr. Jekyll-Mr. Hyde. He attributed his former life as a criminal defense attorney to the Mr. Hyde character.

Dr. Hawthorne was Philadelphia's chief medical examiner. Even though she hadn't spoken to him for over two years, not since Nana's death, Meghan felt sure he would remember her. Meghan also believed that if there was anyone left in her life that could possibly help her, it would be him.

Tainted evidence threatened her life. And Jonathan was responsible for it. She only needed proof. Proof to clear her name and to implicate Jonathan Ashbridge. He had to be the one responsible for the murders. And her mentor, Dr. Evan Hawthorne, Meghan hoped, would be the one to help clear her name.

Meghan decided to take the chance and drive to Philadelphia. It was almost 9:30 p.m., and there was the possibility he was working late.

She prayed that he still put in long hours as Philadelphia's M.E.

Chapter Fifty-Three

"BISHOP TORREY, I WOULD LIKE to introduce you to Friar Vincent Wagner," the Capuchin pastor announced as he escorted his guest into the sacristy, a small room located directly behind the altar where the bishop and his monsignor were preparing for their 9:00 p.m. Mass of Celebration and Renewal.

Bishop Torrey chose not to turn around but remained standing in front of the seven-foot mirror, scrutinizing the monsignor's final adjustments made to his vestments. The only acknowledgment the bishop offered in response to the pastor's introduction was a slight nod as he noticed the "honored" guest's reflection in the mirror. The bishop did not share the pastor's awestruck feelings about the friar's visit to St. John's Church.

During his dinner earlier this evening with the pastor and his staff, the bishop had heard from the pastor all about the friar's visit to the Philadelphia area, where he was invited to give a series of lectures at local Catholic universities. The pastor had labored the point, almost apologetically to the bishop and monsignor, that even though his subject matter was highly controversial for the Catholic Church, the friar's message was always spoken with words of honesty and sincerity.

The friar's message, the pastor had continued, was to enlighten the hearts and souls of his fellow theologians and stir within them a solemn commitment to protect the innocence of children and to heal the abused children's abhorrent injuries suffered at the hands of abusive Catholic priests. The friar's lectures espoused further, according to the pastor, that in order to restore confidence in the faithful for their Church, theologians at all levels, priests to the pope himself, must self-police their ranks with honesty and integrity, and report to civil authorities any and all suspicions of child abuse and suspicions of any cover-up by the Church hierarchy. The friar did not end there. He also argued for state governments to temporarily suspend the statute of limitations that had prevented child abuse victims from filing lawsuits against the Catholic Church.

The bishop had heard more than enough at dinner. Now he finally met in person the "holy messenger," as the pastor had referred to him during dinner.

This Capuchin friar.

This mortal man would not be permitted to continue his anti-Catholic mission. As the current head of the Catholic Congregation for the Doctrine of the Faith, Bishop Torrey could guarantee the friar's silence. The friar's words would be censored.

As pope, the bishop could guarantee the friar's religious death—his ex-communication from the Catholic Church.

Chapter Fifty-Four

DRESSED IN A BORROWED, BROWN-BELTED robe and sandals, the friar walked over to the bishop's extended right hand and knelt to kiss the ruby-stone bishop's ring.

"Our good pastor has told me many interesting things about you, Friar Vincent. It seems ... you are entangled in much controversy with our Church." Bishop Torrey's discourse was interrupted by several congested coughs. The bishop covered his mouth with the sleeve of his alb as he placed his left hand atop the friar's closely cropped, white-blond hair. He then assisted the friar to his feet.

"It is an honor to celebrate this Mass with you, Your Excellency," the friar replied with his head still bowed.

"I understand you would like to perform a special dedication prayer on behalf of the murdered vicar. You may not know this, but the monsignor and I worked with him in the past. We both knew him very well and were shocked to hear of his horrible death. I think your prayer offering is most thoughtful and ..." The bishop pulled out a handkerchief to muffle a sneeze. "I would be most happy to assist you with your special prayer." Bishop Torrey turned to the monsignor, who handed him a glass of water.

"I'm sorry about this cold … I hope I will not contaminate anyone tonight."

The bishop's attempt to breathe through his nose was futile. He took a deep sigh through his mouth and finished his drink. He then watched the pastor guide his guest to the wooden table that held the friar's vestments.

After tonight's Mass, the friar's life will be changed forever, the bishop thought.

The next time he sees this holy messenger will be at the friar's Excommunication Inquiry in Vatican City.

Only this time, he would be pope and the friar would be kissing his papal ring, the bishop vowed.

The Vatican's Imago Dei had guaranteed it.

Chapter Fifty-Five

WAITING INSIDE ST. JOHN THE Evangelist's Church vestibule, Friar Vincent Wagner's thoughts wandered ...

> *"Two men will be out in the field; one will be taken, and one will be left. Two women will be grinding at the mill; one will be taken, and one will be left. Therefore, stay awake! For you do not know on which day your Lord will come." Matthew 24:40–42*

As the opening notes from Albinoni's Adagio in G Minor were played by St. John the Evangelist's organist and violin quartet, Friar Wagner, while firmly holding a gold incense boat, proceeded out from the vestibule and slowly walked up the church aisle behind the two young, female altar servers. One carried a bronze crucifix firmly affixed to an oak staff, while the other server carried a three-chained Cypress Byzantine gold incense burner. They advanced up the aisle and set the pace for the procession to follow.

Behind them in the procession were the monsignor and Bishop Torrey, careful to maintain their distance so as to clearly demonstrate their elite status in the Catholic Church hierarchy to the standing-room-only congregation.

The two servers soon arrived at the three marble steps that led up to the front of the altar, genuflected, and then turned and walked a few yards to the left where they stood waiting for the friar to join them. After a sustained bow before the altar, the friar slowly stood erect and gazed up into the suffering eyes of the Christ figure hanging on the Italian marble cross below the stained-glass windows behind the altar. The friar reflected for a moment.

... *For you do not know on which day your*
Lord will come.

He then walked to the side of the altar where he joined the altar servers and watched as Monsignor Brannigan and Bishop Torrey slowly advanced up the aisle.

The bishop smiled and raised his right hand as he blessed the crowded congregation, his flock, who at times spilled out onto the center aisle in order to catch a better view of their anticipated next cardinal. Since the death of Cardinal Thomas Quindlen, the Philadelphia Archdiocesan faithful yearned for a successor who would be strong enough to lead them through the recent Catholic priest-child-abuse scandal. The Catholic faithful had read the *Philadelphia Inquirer's* explicit and well-researched articles exposing certain Philadelphia clergy who were under suspicion for child abuse. At first, the faithful were shocked. Soon, their feelings turned to disbelief and anger. The same paper had also written the lead story covering Pope Luke's probable choice for the next cardinal in Philadelphia.

That man was Bishop Torrey, described as a conservative and staunch supporter of the Vatican and His Holiness.

The congregation prayed that with his demonstrated theological leadership as head of the Catholic Congregation for the Doctrine of the Faith, Bishop Torrey would be the strong and effective successor so desperately needed to restore faith and confidence in Catholic priests.

As the organist and string quartet intensified their efforts while embarking on Albonini's Crescendo Movement, the bishop and monsignor passed through the altar rail and walked the short distance to the bottom three steps that led up to the altar. There, they bowed in unison, the bishop quick to rise while his aide remained prostrate for several seconds longer.

The monsignor's prolonged act of reverence did not escape the bishop's notice. *Holier than thou? I think not,* the bishop scoffed to himself. *Your attempt to appear pious to my congregation won't work. Or is this demonstration of piety your way of atonement for your past sins against the so-called innocence of children? Whatever your motive, my friend, get over it. And, get over it quickly,* the bishop admonished in his head.

He had had enough with the monsignor's feelings of guilt. During their chauffeured limousine ride from the seminary to the church, Monsignor Brannigan had spoken of nothing else but his resolve to never harm another human being. Not another child. Not anyone. The bishop finally had to forcibly grab the back of the monsignor's neck, immediately putting an end to his lament over his prior abusive acts.

It is now time for the special prayer offering for the slain friar—the prayer offering sent with incense, Friar Wagner mused.

Now holding the incense boat and gold-chained censer, the friar walked a few steps over to where the bishop stood awaiting the ceremonial instruments. After the bishop quickly took hold of the incense holder and boat, the friar bowed and returned to the other side of the altar where the young female servers patiently remained standing.

Bishop Torrey lifted the lid of the censer, which exposed several smoldering charcoals in its base. As he had routinely done for many years, Monsignor Brannigan opened the lid of the incense boat and sprinkled several spoonfuls of incense across the hot charcoal wafers. To enhance the production of incense smoke, Monsignor Brannigan then gently used the small boat-spoon and broke apart the wafers, enabling its hot pieces to react with the incense powder. Within seconds, thick plumes of smoke arose from the broken pieces of burning wafers mixed with incense, sending the heavy but sweet odor up against the faces of the bishop and monsignor. The bishop then nodded to the monsignor and brought the incense holder's lid back down against the three chains and across the base where thick grayish-black smoke continued to flow through the censer's silver-etched pores.

The metallic sound of the chains running through the falling lid alerted the friar that his mission here tonight was almost finished. At that moment, the friar recalled one of his favorite biblical references.

> *"And another angel came and stood before the altar, having a golden censer: and there was given to him much incense that he should offer of the prayers of all saints, upon the golden altar which is before the throne of God. And the smoke of the incense of the prayers of the saints ascended up before God from the hand of the angel." Apocalypse 8:3–4*

The friar mentally counted off the many seconds the two men had stood engulfed in the incense smoke. Having used a stronger drug dose in the incense than what he had previously used with the homeless man, the friar was confident that the desired drug effect would occur much quicker tonight.

As the angels in heaven used incense to deliver the prayers of saints to God, the friar also stood here tonight and offered his own Knight's Allegiance, his loyalty to the Sovereign Military Order of the Temple of Jerusalem (S.M.O.T.J.).

As a member of the Orders Knights Templar, an ancient religious and military Order of Knighthood recognized by Pope Innocent III in AD 1118 to offer protection to pilgrims traveling to the Holy Land, Friar Wagner's commitment to the Pegasus Project was based on the ideals of Templar Chivalry. Many years ago, the friar had taken a sacred oath to defend the dignity of all mankind and to combat all evil forces that harm human rights.

The Catholic Church hierarchy, who injured, and who also chose to forget the innocent children, shall be his enemy, the friar swore. All the priests who were abusers and the hierarchy who enabled these priests to continue their heinous acts against the children by reassigning the abuser-priest from parish to parish would be hunted down and scourged by the swords of millions of members of the Knights Templar.

As a Knight Templar, Stefan had sworn his commitment to the success of the Pegasus Project.

Others did as well.

The Pegasus Project will not fail, the friar vowed.

Chapter Fifty-Six

EVEN THOUGH THE MASS OF Celebration and Renewal had finished over thirty minutes ago, several congregation members still remained in the church, either kneeling in pews to offer final prayers, or standing in small groups expressing their opinions on whether Bishop Torrey would be the pope's choice to become the next cardinal of Philadelphia.

Friar Vincent Wagner stood alone in the sacristy doorway behind the altar, watching the elderly pious women with their heads lowered in prayer and covered by lace veils, a Catholic tradition abandoned long ago by many women members of the Church.

Their petitions to God were his responsibility. His mission.

The pastor of St. John the Evangelist was right when he told the bishop that Friar Wagner was a Holy Messenger. Stefan was the Holy

Messenger sent by God to answer his followers' prayers. He believed their suffering and oppression would find healing and justice through his mission.

Stefan turned around and noticed that the monsignor was gone; he had offered to stay behind with Stefan to help put away the vestments and clean the incense holder. During the few minutes that Stefan had taken to gaze out at the church pews from the sacristy doorway near the altar, Stefan realized, the monsignor had silently walked out. Stefan needed to find the bishop and the monsignor to evaluate the drug's effect on them.

Stefan exited the sacristy through its only other doorway, which led into a dark-stained mahogany-walled hallway. He had two choices. One way down the hallway would take him back to the rectory, which was the direction taken earlier by the bishop and pastor immediately after the end of Mass. If he chose the opposite direction, it would take him down a winding, dimly lit passageway, which according to the pastor would eventually lead him to the church's bell tower stairway.

Just as Stefan was ready to head back toward the rectory, thinking the monsignor had probably wanted to join his bishop, the loud sound of a heavy door slamming shut echoed down the dark and winding hallway from the other direction.

Had the monsignor mistakenly taken the wrong way? Stefan wondered. Or, did he intentionally choose that direction to search for someone or something? Or was someone else responsible for shutting the door? Stefan had to find out.

Stefan embarked down the dark cement walkway. His stride was slow and cautious since the floor was barely made visible by the widely-spaced candles in wrought-iron holders along the walls. Within a minute, Stefan found himself standing in front of two cement steps that led up to a closed door made of wide wooden panels. Despite the weak illumination from a nearby flickering candle, Stefan was able to discern that time and climate had abused the door; its wooden planks were warped, and its hinges and doorknob were coated with rust. Stefan knew that this must be the door he had heard slam shut.

As he turned the cold metal doorknob, Stefan heard a sustained squeak come from the knob's internal locking gear, which was probably rusted as well, Stefan thought. The heavy door slowly swung open, its rusted hinges crying out to be left alone. Looking up the cement-spiraled staircase, Stefan saw a soft white glow engulf the stairway's darkness. Not a flickering light from a candle or flashlight, but a light that remained constant and motionless, and strong enough to guide Stefan up toward the bell tower.

Who was it that had walked through this door and up these stairs? Was it the Monsignor or maybe a custodian?

Stefan didn't have to wait long to find the answer. Suddenly, the sound of muffled, anguished cries filled the narrow, cement-walled stairway.

It was the monsignor. Stefan was sure of it now.

The drug was working.

Stefan started up the stairway. He hoped he would soon witness the monsignor's torment.

Chapter Fifty-Seven

LEAVING THE STAIRWAY AND STEPPING outside onto the canvas-covered wooden platform located approximately thirty feet beneath the church bell, Stefan looked up inside the silent bell tower, which was supported by four equidistant stone spires that stretched their arms up toward the full moon. Stefan acknowledged the momentary break in the dense cloud cover that gave him a moment of illumination, allowing safe navigation along the winding tower staircase.

Suddenly, anguished moans replaced the stillness of the night. Sitting in the far corner of the platform against one of the spires, a human figure rocked back and forth. Stefan walked closer. It was the monsignor curled up in a fetal position, grabbing at his own matted hair, oblivious to Stefan's presence. With both knees pulled tightly up against his chest, the monsignor stared up into the sky uttering desperate pleas for mercy.

Stefan now stood over the trembling priest and placed a hand on the back of the monsignor's neck. It was soaked with perspiration. His dark, mangled hair fell across his tearing eyes, which nervously darted from side to side. The drug was working and was having a unique effect on the cleric. Deep inside the victim's brain, the drug had caused severe despair and anguish and not the aggressive behavior exhibited earlier by the homeless subject. Stefan knew the drug would uniquely affect each subject's amygdala—the area in the brain that controls behavioral impulses. The monsignor was obviously consumed with guilt and remorse because of his involvement with child abuse.

But Imago Dei didn't want Stefan to simply murder his targets. Imago Dei wanted more than revenge. They wanted the targets to suffer pain and anguish as their punishment. Stefan's role was to administer the drug and ensure that a just retribution was successfully achieved. Imago Dei had given Stefan license to decide how to finally end each target's life.

Not expecting an answer, Stefan asked his question anyway, playing his role as the concerned Capuchin friar from Palermo.

"Are you all right, Monsignor?"

"Oh, please, please help me, Lord ... I know I have sinned and don't deserve your forgiveness ... help me ... please, oh, God, help me," the Monsignor cried out, still not aware that Stefan was standing over him.

"Forgiveness, is that what you want? Forgiveness from your God? Well, he has sent me to help you. Help you atone for your sins."

Grabbing the monsignor's hair, Stefan pulled the monsignor to his feet and drove his head back against the stone spire. Stefan heard his skull crack. Immediately, bright red blood flowed through the monsignor's hair and across Stefan's hand. Pieces of scalp tissue soaked in blood stuck to the stone spire. Stefan withdrew his bloodied hand and brought it close to his face. The heavy, stagnant odor brought a smile to Stefan's face. He then slowly dragged his blood-soaked hand across the monsignor's face and whispered into his ear.

"Smell it, Monsignor. Doesn't it smell sinful? Your blood carries all your sins against the innocent children. Prepare to offer your life and only then receive forgiveness."

Stefan looked at his watch. It was 11:30 p.m., and he knew the bell would toll early tonight. *Before midnight, the monsignor, the spiritually convicted child abuser and enabling member of the Catholic Church hierarchy, will atone for his crimes against the weak and oppressed,* Stefan vowed.

Stefan reached behind the monsignor and untied the bell rope from one of the spire's iron rungs that ran up its side like a ladder toward the top of the tower. He then wrapped the coarse rope around the neck of the monsignor, who was still dazed from the head concussion.

Should I wait until after he is dead, or do it now? Stefan thought.

The decision came quickly.

Stefan decided the monsignor must feel the Sign of the Knights Templar before he died.

Ripping open the black cleric's shirt, Stefan immediately exposed his victim's chest. Reaching inside his own pocket, Stefan pulled out a leather case. He quickly removed a silver scalpel, its handle etched with the figure of a knight kneeling in prayer. Stefan's blood-stained hand grabbed the monsignor's throat, which quickly awakened him from his traumatic stupor.

"Excellent, your senses have been restored. I want you to remember the pain that comes from my knight's lancet," Stefan announced.

Stefan brought the sharp blade closer to his victim. The monsignor's flesh easily parted beneath the scalpel's pressure against his chest. Once again, the monsignor's sins flowed from his body and across the stainless steel blade. The monsignor couldn't fight off the knife. He couldn't even scream. All of his defensive efforts were devoted to stopping Stefan's fingers from crushing his throat.

Finally, Stefan withdrew the blade from the monsignor's bloody chest. The Sign of the Knights Templar was engraved forever.

Stefan wiped the scalpel clean against the monsignor's torn shirt. He then dragged the monsignor over to the edge of the tower's stone wall that joined each of the four corner spires and lifted his weak victim to a sitting position atop the wall.

"Please, help me ... please, I've committed horrible sins against many children. I need ... forgiveness," the monsignor cried out, looking deeply into Stefan's ice-blue eyes.

"I absolve you from all your sins," Stefan replied, smiling as he pushed the monsignor over the wall.

The bell tower at St. John the Evangelist Catholic Church rang out prematurely into the starry night.

It was 11:45 p.m. Now where was the bishop? Stefan wondered.

Chapter Fifty-Eight

THE SEMINARY'S NATATORIUM WAS DARK except for the few underwater pool lights that cast their soft yellow beams through the still water. The bishop was floating on his back in the deep end, gazing up toward the fourth-story stained-glass dome overhead, glad he hadn't accepted the Capuchin pastor's offer to stay overnight in his rectory.

Whatever had become of the monsignor was not important to him then or now. The bishop had waited in the pastor's study for over thirty minutes, listening to the pastor go on and on about how wonderful it was to have had Friar Wagner visit from Europe and participate in the evening Mass. Bishop Torrey had enough. If his aide did not think it was important to join him in a timely manner, then so be it. Monsignor

Brannigan could certainly either spend a peaceful night in the Capuchin friars' rectory or find his own way back to the seminary.

Bishop Torrey loved these silent moments in the seminary's pool. The only sound he heard was the occasional rippling as the bishop slowly moved his hands through the smooth glass-like surface of water.

Suddenly, the metal double doors leading into the natatorium swung open, creating a loud, resonating echo that at any other time would have disturbed the bishop. Tonight was different, however. The bishop was expecting a guest.

"I'm so sorry, Bishop Torrey, for being late. I was studying for my Bioethics test tomorrow," the first-year seminarian announced as he hurried across the alabaster pool deck.

The bishop began treading water in the twelve-foot section and gave a slight wave as he beckoned the young student toward him.

"Yes, you are late ... quite late as a matter of fact, but don't worry about it now. The important thing is that you are here. Now, come closer."

The seminarian dropped his towel on the white-tiled bench against the far wall. Wearing a pair of over-sized baggy swim trunks that hung over his skinny thighs, the lanky student slowly walked toward the deep end. Standing along the water's edge with his arms tightly folded across his chest, the seminarian nervously peered down into the deep, dark water.

"Pardon me, Your Eminence ... but I would like to remind you ... I can't ... swim," the seminarian stammered. Even though the humidity from the warm pool water filled the room, the young student's body trembled, and his lips quivered.

"There's nothing to fear, my son. Come in the water, and I'll help you. You must trust your bishop."

The student nodded. He obediently sat down on the marble gray coping and slowly turned himself around as he eased into the water while maintaining his death-grip on the edge of the deck.

"There now, that wasn't difficult, was it?" The bishop grinned as he treaded closer to the student.

"Bishop Torrey, I have to be honest with you. I don't feel comfortable here in the deep end. Can we please move to the shallow end where I can stand? I can talk to you better there about my studies here at the seminary."

The bishop's face suddenly grew solemn.

"Who the hell do you think you are?" the bishop said as he reached out with both hands and pushed the seminarian's head firmly against the pool's edge. Again and again, he drove the young student's skull into the gray stone coping.

"How dare you disobey me. I am your spiritual leader. Your shepherd. Your future pope!" Bishop Torrey yelled, his voice unwavering.

The seminarian's bright red blood splattered into the air and fell against the pristine pool deck and across the undulating pool surface. Within seconds, a red liquid cloud slowly moved through the water claiming its territory.

After several minutes, the bishop finally let go, and the student's body slowly floated away. His young body hunched over the water's surface, his extremities hanging down like a jellyfish waiting patiently for its next strike. But the seminarian was not the predator. This evening he had been the unsuspecting prey.

You could have been someone important. Someone I could have trusted. If you only had obeyed me tonight, the bishop reflected.

Fuck it. I need to prepare for my trip tomorrow to Vatican City, Bishop Torrey decided as he pulled himself out of the crimson water.

Now where the hell is Monsignor Brannigan? questioned the bishop.

Chapter Fifty-Nine

THE MEDICAL EXAMINER'S WHITE VAN, with two stripes of yellow and blue draped across its doors, slowly backed up to the three-foot-high cement receiving dock located on the west side of Philadelphia's Spellman Medical Examiner Building at the corner of University Avenue and Curie Road, where all bodies destined for an autopsy in Philadelphia were delivered.

Two M.E. technicians climbed down from the van and walked around to the rear panel door, where they unceremoniously removed the cold, stiff body that was temporarily encased in a black leather shroud. After depositing the body on a metal transport stretcher, the two workers guided the corpse through the doorway that had already been opened by the guard seated inside near the security camera.

Dr. Evan Hawthorne was working late, making his final preparations for his appearance tomorrow morning in Philadelphia common pleas court where he was scheduled to give his testimony as the medical examiner for the prosecution in a murder trial. Even though he wasn't on call and should have been at home reviewing his notes, Dr. Hawthorne had decided to remain at work after he had received the call from one of his forensic pathologists, who had gone to the late-night crime scene, telling him about the bizarre nature surrounding a certain victim's death.

Hearing the voices of his two technicians, Dr. Hawthorne stood up from behind his desk, placed his thick folder of notes into his worn, brown leather shoulder bag and proceeded out of his office, down the hallway that led to the autopsy lab.

"Hi, Doc. We've got a weird one this time," the senior technician said as Evan Hawthorne walked into the chilled autopsy room, which housed the capacity to hold forty bodies in its multi-steel-drawer wall vault. In the center of the room stood four empty stainless steel autopsy tables and one exam table that was occupied by the new arrival.

Dr. Hawthorne walked up to the partially clothed male who had already been positioned supine on the cold steel table. He stared down at the victim's contorted face. His mouth remained twisted and open—frozen in time—with his final, anguished gaze. The victim's bloated face had a purplish hue, his eyes bulging like someone with a severe case of hyperthyroidism.

Dr. Hawthorne now focused on the victim's neck. A deep, reddish-blue groove cut into the flesh of the man's neck, revealing the probable cause of death. Strangulation. Proceeding with his external exam, Hawthorne put on a pair of vinyl gloves before gently separating the tattered, bloody shirt.

"What do you make of it, Evan?" the on-call forensic pathologist questioned as he entered the lab.

Staring down at the man's chest covered with thick, coagulated blood, Hawthorne was able to make out the familiar figure etched into the victim's skin. A dodecagon—the same figure with twelve sides that had been engraved into the chest of the slain friar who was found last week in the park along the Delaware River waterfront. Streaks of coagulated blood, which had oozed out from each of the twelve cuts, joined yet another familiar engraving in the middle of the twelve-sided geometrical design.

Four, wide, rectangular arms formed the shape of a cross.

"This guy was a priest," the assistant M.E. reported. "He was found hanging from the bell tower over at St. John's Church near Chestnut Street. And the engraving … we've seen that before, right?"

"Yes. And I don't like it. We have another victim killed, another priest, left with the same mark on his chest," Dr. Hawthorne answered.

He decided not to tell his assistant what really worried him. Hawthorne now realized the possibility that a serial killer was on the loose, responsible for not only the murders of the two priests in Philadelphia, but probably also the two deaths at the Renaissance Institute in Chester County. Hawthorne remembered that the chests of Farraday and Rafferty had been mutilated as well but the Chester County coroner wasn't sure what to make of it.

What did all of these victims have in common other than the markings? And what did those engravings mean? The cross, and two victims who were priests, clearly had some religious significance. But what was it? And why did the priests also receive the twelve-sided figure? Evan Hawthorne realized that Detective McManus needed to hear about this latest victim as soon as possible. Since it was already late in the evening, Hawthorne decided a call to the detective in the morning would be soon enough.

Hawthorne snapped off his gloves and left the lab with its new occupant in the capable hands of his assistant M.E. As he walked back to his office to retrieve his leather case, Hawthorne wondered if McManus had apprehended the young pharmaceutical researcher suspected of killing the two men at the institute.

Would McManus now think that his female suspect had also killed the two priests in Philadelphia? Hawthorne wondered.

It wouldn't be the first time that a serial killer turned out to be a woman.

Chapter Sixty

EVAN HAWTHORNE WALKED OUTSIDE TO his black Mercedes SUV parked in the chief medical examiner's space and noticed that the heavy rain that had fallen throughout the night was now replaced by a fine drizzle; still present, though, were strong, unrelenting winds gusting through the dark West Philadelphia neighborhood.

Hawthorne paused for a few seconds, thinking he had heard the sound of someone's muffled voice coming from the direction of the M.E.'s dimly lit building. Turning back toward the building and into the driving wind, he saw nothing but the wide shadow cast along the building's brick wall. Deciding it was just a city noise amplified by the wind, Hawthorne proceeded to his car and pressed the remote door-key button.

Suddenly, the small frame of a person wearing a hooded rain slicker stepped out from the building's shadow and firmly grabbed his arm.

"Dr. Hawthorne. I need your help," the soft voice pleaded.

Evan Hawthorne swung his body around. His heart skipped several beats as he struggled for his next breath amidst the damp, wind-swept parking lot.

"God, what the …" Hawthorne yelled as he dropped his leather bag and raised his fists in defense against his assailant.

"It's me, Meghan Cahill. I'm sorry I startled you, but I wasn't sure it was you leaving the building. Please … I need your help."

"Meghan Cahill? My God, it really is you," Hawthorne replied as he gently pulled back Meghan's hood from her face. "What are you doing here … and at this time of night?"

"I'm in trouble with the police. They think I've killed two people … two men that I worked with. It's not true, Dr. Hawthorne, I've been set up … I'm sure of it, but I have no one who believes me. Please … you've got to help me … I have no one else to turn to." Meghan pleaded her case, never looking away from Hawthorne's stare. She knew she spoke the truth. She only hoped he would read the honesty in her tired, burning eyes.

"Hold on … which police are after you?" questioned Hawthorne.

"Police in Chester County and in Ocean City. I just drove up from the Shore. The Ocean City Police have my house surrounded. There may be more. They're all after me … I don't know what to do." Meghan couldn't keep it in any longer. Suddenly, tears streamed down from her bloodshot eyes, and her anguished sobs echoed against the storm's wind gusts.

"Okay, Meghan, calm down. I will help you, but you have to calm yourself. Come inside, and we can talk in my office," Hawthorne said.

"No … no, it's not safe here. The Philadelphia Police might be looking for me, and we both know they sometimes stop off here unannounced," Meghan insisted as her body shook in the cold, damp air.

"You're probably right. It'll be safer at my house, and besides, your clothes are soaked. You can take a warm shower there and get a change of clothes. They may not fit, but they'll be dry. Now, where did you park your car?"

"In the lot off South Street at Penn Tower."

"And you walked the several blocks to get here in this crazy weather? No wonder you're soaked to the bone. All right, leave your car there for now and climb in." Evan Hawthorne motioned to his SUV.

"You can tell me everything that's been happening to you while we drive to my house."

As Evan Hawthorne drove his SUV out of the open-air M.E. parking lot, Stefan jumped down from the three-foot-high cement delivery platform along the side of the M.E.'s building where he had positioned himself to witness the monsignor's body escorted into its temporary home. This was the second time in just over a week that he had waited with each of his victims near their crime scene in Philadelphia and then had followed the victim to the M.E.'s building.

As the police had arrived at the crime scenes—Delaware River front and St. John's Church—Stefan reveled in their reaction to his work. He had enjoyed watching the wide range of behavior when they first examined the corpse. The younger, less experienced officers had to look away, often emptying their stomach contents at the scene. The more seasoned officers would then ridicule the rookies for their weak stomachs and brag to them how unaffected they were by the appearance of the mutilated priests.

Stefan, though, knew better. Everyone was affected by his work, even the ones experienced with investigating such crimes. It didn't matter in which country his victims had been found, or who had discovered them, Stefan had always witnessed the same reactions. Some behaved honestly. Others wore a facade, a self-protective cloak that shielded them from the horror of his work. He hated the dishonest ones—the pompous, holier-than-thou ones.

The guilty Church authority was also pompous, never once concerned about their abusive acts against children. Stefan's sworn allegiance was not only to God, but to the innocent faithful who were injured and abandoned by those in authority.

Stefan needed to meet with Professor Marguilies. It had been several days since they had spoken with each other. He was sure the professor would want to know about Meghan Cahill's new friend, Dr. Evan Hawthorne. He knew Jonathan Ashbridge would also want to hear about his former lover's activities.

Her survival tactics will surprise both of them, Stefan thought.

Stefan wasn't surprised, however. He had hoped Meghan Cahill would be a worthy adversary. So far, her resilience impressed him. Stefan was certain he would meet her soon. He could easily make it happen. He only wondered when and where their meeting would occur.

As Stefan hurried across University Avenue toward the Philadelphia V.A. Hospital parking lot where he had left his car, Stefan suddenly saw red and blue lights pulsate atop the M.E.'s van as it pulled away from the medical examiner's building and sped by him toward Chestnut Street.

Another autopsy waiting to happen. At least the monsignor won't be lonely tonight, Stefan mused.

Chapter Sixty-One

"HELLO ... HUH ... YEA, THIS IS Hawthorne. What time is it?" the chief M.E. mumbled.

"You've got to be kidding!" Hawthorne yelled as he pushed himself up against the bed's headboard. "I've only been in bed for a couple of hours. What's so God-damned important to call me about this early?" Hawthorne demanded from his on-call pathologist.

"What ... you've got a murdered seminarian on the table right now?" Hawthorne pushed the covers off and sat on the edge of his bed.

"Does he have the same design etched into his chest like the one we saw on the priest tonight?" Hawthorne questioned.

The chief M.E. remained silent for several minutes, which allowed his weary assistant M.E. to finish his detailed crime scene report that included his external examination of the seminarian's body.

The night security guard found the seminarian's body floating in the seminary's pool. A first-year seminarian student bludgeoned to death, the assistant M.E. reported.

"But nothing engraved into his chest," Hawthorne mumbled.

"All right, I've heard enough. I'll be back in my office sometime this afternoon to work on the two bodies brought in tonight." Hawthorne hung up and rubbed his eyes. They burned—and no wonder, he thought. It was just after 2:30 a.m. when he had shown Meghan the spare room and had given her his large sweatshirt with a Cape Cod logo on the front and medium-size lounge pants. These were the best that Evan could offer her on such short notice, or for that matter, at any time.

Evan Hawthorne was a bachelor and had been all of his fifty years. He had several relationships, but none felt good. Good enough to make it permanent.

Each woman had always told him that marriage was definitely something they did not want right now. But soon, each woman behaved as if suddenly time was of the essence, and they expected an immediate proposal. Usually, expressions like, *I'm not getting any younger,* or, *My clock is ticking,* were soon dominating their conversations.

Thank God he had his work, Hawthorne thought. But what was he going to do about Meghan? Technically, he was harboring a fugitive. McManus's fugitive. But, he had assured Meghan he would help her despite all of the incriminating evidence. It didn't look good for her, though. He would know. Before becoming Philadelphia's chief M.E., he had been one of the best criminal defense attorneys in Philadelphia. If there was a possible defense, however weak, he had always found a way to make it strong enough for an acquittal.

Hawthorne resolved to keep his word. He would help her. But first, right now, he desperately needed sleep. Tomorrow was already turning into a hellish day.

Chapter Sixty-Two

September 22
6:00 A.M.

MEGHAN COULDN'T TELL WHERE SHE was. The room was dark except for a nightlight that yielded a soft, yellow glow from within a wooden box that sat on a bureau across the room. Engraved on the box's wooden panel-face, in front of its internal light, was a figure.

A carved out figure of an angel.

As Meghan sat up in bed, she saw the angel's shadow fixed against the far wall, as if watching over her and protecting her. For the first time in several days, Meghan finally felt warm and safe. She never would have thought in her wildest dreams that she would be finding comfort in her former professor's home.

Pushing the warm bed covers off her, Meghan turned on the lamp on the nightstand. Dark plum curtains were drawn closed across two windows that faced her bed, preventing the impending early morning sun

from invading her hideaway. Meghan wanted to catch Dr. Hawthorne, or
Evan, as he had insisted last night she call him, before he left for court.
Getting out of bed, she stood and took one look at herself in the mirror
that hung over the bureau. Baggy sweatshirt, and even more baggy sweat
pants. Her hair flying in every direction. Not a fashion statement, but
certainly warm and comfortable.

But did she feel confident enough to face him this morning looking
like this? Meghan asked herself.

Why not? He certainly saw worse than this in his line of work,
Meghan decided.

Turning to leave her bedroom and find Evan, she looked down on
the nightstand and noticed a sheet of writing paper with his name, *Evan
Hawthorne*, scripted across the top. There was a message written, but the
words were somewhat blurry. Slowly the words came into focus.

Meghan—

*Left early for court. There's breakfast in the kitchen—help
yourself. Will call later today. Just one thing. Don't answer
the phone. I'll call you on my cell. I have caller ID at the
house so you'll know it's me.*

Best, Evan

Obviously, she had missed him. Probably just as well. Right now, she
felt all talked out. Last night, she had told him everything. She had to.
He was the only one who could help her now.

She told him about her work at the institute, her stormy relationship
with Jonathan, and the incriminating evidence against her. What had
impressed her the most was not his willingness to help, even though
that in itself overwhelmed her with heartfelt gratitude. Rather, it was
his silence. Evan was patient enough to listen to her ramble on and on,
and not interrupt her once.

And, he didn't judge her.

Meghan was grateful for that.

Meghan walked over to the covered windows and pulled apart the curtains to assess what kind of day it would be. She looked down onto the dark and quiet cobblestone street and noticed a pair of headlights slowly navigating its way between the cars parked on both sides of the narrow city street. As the car passed by, Meghan's attention was drawn to a black sports car parked about halfway down the street. A tiny, orange glow appeared and then disappeared near the driver's window. Soon, puffs of smoke exited through a crack at the top of the window and then quickly disappeared into the early warm autumn morning.

Meghan stepped back from the windows and shielded herself behind the lace curtains. She then hurried across the room to the nightstand and turned off the light. Meghan took a deep breath. She slowly walked back toward the windows and stopped several feet away. She could still see the black sports car, but this time there was no orange glow from inside.

She decided to walk closer to the window. As she carefully parted the lace curtains, Meghan looked out through the window and down onto the street, which remained dark and quiet. Was it her imagination? Did she really think that there was someone sitting outside watching her? She was tired. Tired and hungry. Meghan decided it was all in her head. No one was sitting outside watching her.

As she turned to walk away, she caught a quick glimpse of something outside. An orange glow engulfed in puffs of smoke, down on the sidewalk, right beneath her window.

My God, there is someone out there watching me.

Chapter Sixty-Three

STEFAN CRUSHED THE BURNING CIGARETTE between his thumb and forefinger and placed it deep inside his coat pocket. He turned away from the front of the three-story Williamsburg townhouse and walked back to his black 765Ci sports car parked some twenty yards away.

Stefan still had time before his mid-morning meeting with Professor Marguilies. He had been up all night and wasn't tired. On many occasions when performing his duties as a Knights Templar for Imago Dei, Stefan would be without sleep for more than twenty-four hours; his burning desire to fight for the oppressed was his inspiration. His sleep-deprived body always successfully completed his missions.

The Pegasus Project mission was no exception.

Stefan was confident Meghan Cahill never caught a glimpse of his face. She had only seen a figure sitting in a car and then standing outside, just below her third-story window. Neither turning out her lamp light nor hiding behind the curtains were enough to keep her hidden.

Or safe.

Even though Stefan did not have a contract on Meghan Cahill, he still enjoyed the game-playing. Stefan decided, for now, he had done enough. Meghan Cahill knew, Stefan felt sure, that although she had escaped the police and had gained the help of Philadelphia's chief M.E., she still was not safe.

With or without a contract, *he* would decide her fate.

As he had done with so many others before her.

Chapter Sixty-Four

STANDING BENEATH THE TWELVE-FOOT-HIGH GRANITE statue of an angel erected in the park along Philadelphia's Kelly Drive near Boathouse Row, Professor Marguilies watched Stefan walk up toward him from the sloping bank that led down to the Schuylkill River.

It was 10:00 a.m., and Stefan was punctual as usual. The professor had been waiting for almost twenty minutes beneath the granite angel statue where Stefan had requested they meet; the professor never wanted to keep Stefan waiting.

"How are things progressing?" Marguilies called out.

Stefan remained silent until he stood directly in front of the professor.

"Inform Imago Dei the monsignor has been appropriately punished. The bishop is another matter, however," Stefan declared, staring into the professor's eyes.

"Yes, I heard the news reports this morning about the monsignor.

Hanging by the church's bell tower rope was quite effective. The news media is all over it. Even got CNN's attention."

"Our drug worked well on the monsignor. Its effects differed somewhat, though, from the effects seen in my clinical trials. You know, with the street people."

"What do you mean?" the professor asked.

"With each human subject, our drug did in fact arrive in that part of the brain that controls behavior and impulses. The only difference was with the clinical outcome. As you know, our drug caused the street people to become very aggressive and demonstrate strength they normally didn't possess. The monsignor's reaction was different."

"How so?" Professor Marguilies asked.

"With the help of your virus gene-carrier, the drug you created at the Renaissance Institute was taken to the emotional or impulse center of the brain. But remember, our clinical subjects, the homeless, and our targets, the bishop and monsignor, are humans that possess different underlying thoughts and emotions. The monsignor was not aggressive. Rather, he was distraught. Not at all lucid when I faced him in the bell tower. For some time before his death last night, I believe he agonized over what he had done to those children."

"You mean he felt guilty?"

"Right, and the drug drove him further into despair. If I hadn't come along when I did, I'll bet the monsignor would have committed suicide. I merely facilitated his fate."

"And Bishop Torrey?" Marguilies questioned.

"Only some of the drug got into him. The bishop's brain didn't receive the drug in the same concentration as what was delivered to the monsignor."

"Why not? Your plan was for both of them to inhale the incense along with the drug. I don't understand."

"The bishop was fortunate. He has bronchitis, and it apparently saved him last night. It prevented him from inhaling the full drug dose," Stefan replied.

"I understand. If the lungs don't get the full dose, the brain won't either. I almost forgot about the intimacy shared between the lung's blood circulation and the brain. Not enough drug flowed from the lung to the brain," the professor concluded.

"Right. Like I said, the bishop's chest cold saved him last night. After killing the student, the bishop was able to control his behavior and escape police detection. However, it didn't save the young seminarian."

"Wait a minute. I heard about that coming over here. You mean the bishop had something to do with that murder?"

"No question about it. I'm sure the bishop got some of the drug, though. Its effect was just delayed and somewhat diminished."

"Do you know where Bishop Torrey is now?" Marguilies asked.

"On his way to Rome. I confirmed his departure this morning through one of my computer access codes. Surprisingly, the Philadelphia airport's security system isn't that difficult to get around."

The professor stood silent for a few moments reflecting on Stefan's news about the bishop's escape.

"What are your plans now for Bishop Torrey?"

"I'm booked on Friday night's 7:50 flight to Rome. I'll take care of him there."

Once again, Professor Marguilies remained quiet. He was carefully organizing his thoughts and preparing his words for what he now needed to tell Stefan. The professor only hoped that Stefan would have the time before his flight tomorrow night to deal with this new problem.

One that involved Jonathan Ashbridge.

And threatened Imago Dei's Pegasus Project.

Chapter Sixty-Five

"OUR PROJECT HAS A PROBLEM. It's Ashbridge." The professor paused and waited to see some reaction from Stefan. He knew Stefan didn't think much of Jonathan and therefore expected an immediate "I told you so" from him.

Instead, Stefan ran his fingers through his hair. His eyes, slightly bloodshot from lack of sleep, continued their cold stare into the professor's gaze. Stefan's face remained frozen, devoid of any expression, as if posing like another granite statue along the bank of the Schuylkill River.

The professor continued. "The problem is this. Ashbridge called me early this morning and informed me that he intends to publicize our drug's effects on humans. He insists the scientific community needs to hear about his breakthrough research discovery. He claims that by showing the success his drug has achieved in producing uncontrollable impulses, he can convince his scientific peers that he can also manipulate the chemical composition of his drug and permanently block the creation of all abnormal impulses."

"What ... even provide a definitive cure for all criminally compulsive behavior ... like child abuse?" Stefan mused.

"Actually, he did mention that, along with all obsessive-compulsive behavior. In fact, Ashbridge also insisted his research was vital to the future work of Imago Dei."

"Interesting." Stefan grinned.

"You realize that if he tells the scientific community everything he knows about the Pegasus Project, he'll threaten Imago Dei's noble work, here in the United States and throughout the world. The world is not ready yet to hear about our society. Even though its basic tenets are well-founded in the Bible's Old and New Testaments, many people would unfairly challenge and condemn our methods for carrying out Imago Dei's teachings.

"You realize, however, that despite these numerous biblical references to Imago Dei, there is really no definitive theological explanation offered by the biblical authors regarding what is meant by the term Image of God. Also, it's a mystery what the authors would have recommended as specific actions to promulgate this historic doctrine ... the doctrine of man created in the Imago Dei," Stefan said.

"I agree. But Genesis does quote God, who commands us, as men made in the image of God, to rule over all things—and remember, Stefan, specifically, *over every creeping thing that creeps on the earth*. Our society, Imago Dei, has a mandate, we have decided, to support all organizations and governments in their good-faith efforts to nurture mankind, as a creation in God's image, toward loving one another as God loves them," said the professor.

"And when those organizations ignore that responsibility and intentionally harm the weak, that's when I'm asked to serve."

"And serve well, I may add." The professor looked up at the granite angel figure that held firm to a sword that pointed up toward the gray sky. "We must protect the secrecy of Imago Dei," the professor urged.

"I agree. Disclosure would be a problem for us," Stefan replied.

For the first time, Stefan took his eyes off the professor. He now stared out at the brown racing river that continued to swell up along its bank, claiming more ground by the minute. Even though the storm had stopped for several hours, the Schuylkill River was still engorged with the Nor'easter's heavy rains, which had created numerous whirlpools along the river current's path.

"Do you see the tree limb out there? The one caught in that whirlpool?" Stefan asked.

"I do," the professor replied, staring out at the raging muddy water.

"Well, that will be Jonathan Ashbridge. By the time I leave for Vatican City tomorrow evening, he will no longer be a threat to us or Imago Dei," Stefan assured.

Chapter Sixty-Six

"**N**o. I can't hold. Tell Detective McManus that this is Dr. Hawthorne, and it's urgent!" Hawthorne shouted, knowing McManus's secretary was just trying to do her job.

Hawthorne did not have to wait long. "All right, Evan ... what's so important? My secretary was a bit frazzled by your aggressive tone."

"Spare me the guilt trip. I need to know what evidence you've got on your murder suspect," Hawthorne insisted.

"I'm not sure I know what you mean, Evan."

"Physical evidence ... what have you found that points to your suspect?"

"Well, we got lucky. We used a private lab in Harrisburg that only needed seventy-two hours to analyze the DNA samples we sent to them from our crime scene. The lab compared DNA from hair and skin samples found on the two victims with the DNA of all Renaissance Institute employees. And they came up with a positive match. Meghan Cahill. She's a researcher whom we also discovered had the motive and the opportunity to commit these two murders. Why do you want to know?"

"Listen. Didn't you tell me a few days ago that the county coroner noticed a strange engraving on each victim's chest?" Hawthorne asked.

"Yes. We weren't sure what to make of it. At first, we thought the markings were made by the assailant's knife during the victim's struggle. Then the coroner looked closer. His report states that the victims have similar knife wounds carved on their chests. Almost in the shape of—"

"A cross, right?"

"Christ—how do you know about this?" McManus said.

"Like I said, you had told me something about strange markings found on your victims' chests. Listen, I've had two victims brought into my lab within the last few days, each with the same wide-shaped cross. But their crosses were inside a dodecagon figure carved into each victim's chest. One victim was a Capuchin friar, the one murdered down along the Delaware River. The other was a monsignor. This one was found hanging from a bell tower rope over at St. John's in Center City."

"Sounds like we have a connection with all the victims. Do you have any leads?" McManus asked.

"No. But let me ask you something about your suspect. The Renaissance Institute researcher—what's her name, Cahill? Do you really think she murdered those two at the institute and then carved that figure into their skin?"

"Anything is possible … I don't know. Maybe."

"Because if you do, are you also thinking now she had something to do with the two murdered priests that I have in the city morgue?" Hawthorne challenged.

"I know what you're driving at. Do I think she's a serial killer?"

"Exactly," Hawthorne replied.

"I don't know, Evan. I just don't know. What I do know, however, is that she is quite resourceful. She escaped the Ocean City Police late last night when they had her surrounded at her beach house. What time did the monsignor die?"

"Between 11:00 and 11:45 p.m."

"That's an impressive narrow time frame, even for your office."

"It's easy when the victim signaled his own demise. The bell rope that was tied around his neck rang the church bells at 11:45p.m., fifteen minutes too early that night," Hawthorne replied.

"Meghan Cahill could have driven up from the Shore and had enough time to hang the priest," McManus asserted.

"Hold on. I think you're reaching. What was her motive, and what about the friar?" Hawthorne paused a few seconds so as not to appear too defensive of Meghan.

"Do you mind if I examine your physical evidence?" Hawthorne finally asked in a somewhat detached tone.

"No, not at all. When do you want to review it?"

"How about this afternoon?" Hawthorne suggested.

"Sure. Then afterwards I'll treat you to dinner," McManus offered.

"Thanks. I should be in Chester County in a couple of hours. I have two autopsies waiting for me at the city morgue." Hawthorne hung up. He had just testified all morning in the murder trial that he had prepared for up until late last night, and he was now exhausted. He knew he would not be recalled in the afternoon as a witness. Despite his distraction with Meghan, he was confident he had nailed his testimony for the prosecution's case.

As Dr. Evan Hawthorne exited City Hall, he pulled out his cell phone and dialed his home number. He hadn't spoken to Meghan since last night. He would have preferred having dinner with her tonight, as it would have been a good time to review with her his examination of the physical evidence that McManus had against her. Maybe having dinner with McManus instead and talking about his case against Meghan would be beneficial, Hawthorne hoped.

Despite his strong gut feeling that Meghan was innocent and

was somehow being framed, he still could not erase one truth. Evan Hawthorne, Philadelphia's chief medical examiner, was harboring a fugitive. If he was wrong about Meghan's innocence, he would not only lose his career, but his own freedom as well.

Evan Hawthorne was willing to take that chance.

Chapter Sixty-Seven

MEGHAN LOOKED DOWN AT THE phone's handle flashing the caller ID.

It was Evan. *Thank God*. Meghan sighed.

All morning she had checked and rechecked, and then checked again the front and back door locks, as well as the locks on each window of Hawthorne's three-story townhouse. Hours ago, she had seen a male figure get into a black sports car and drive off down Pine Street. Only now did she have some feeling of security when she realized Evan was on the phone.

"Hello, Evan?" Meghan whispered.

"Are you all right?" Evan answered.

"I need you here. Where are you?"

"I'm still down at the courthouse. What's wrong?"

"I'm being watched. Someone was lingering outside your house early this morning. Please ... you've got to get home."

"Meghan ... relax ... it's all right. It was probably just a neighbor.

The police are the only ones looking for you, and they don't know you're staying with me. Right?"

Meghan took a deep breath. Evan was right, of course. The figure in the shadows below her window was probably a neighbor finishing his cigarette before he left for work. But her fear was understandable. She was on the run. Trying to escape the police and also find some way to exonerate herself. Meghan knew she would feel much better when Evan came home.

"Listen, Meghan. I know you're worried, but you're all right. There's just one thing ... I won't be home until late tonight. I'm meeting a Chester County detective later this afternoon. I want to see firsthand the evidence they have on you."

"What's the detective's name?"

"McManus. Why?"

"He's the detective who's after me. You can't meet with him. He'll know you're helping me." Meghan's breath hastened as she paced the living room floor.

"Listen. McManus is an old friend, and he won't know about you. I promise."

"I don't know. I just don't know ..." Meghan sighed as her eyes searched the room for a quick escape. She knew her wet clothes from last night were dry by now. Evan had seen to that.

Sensing her hesitation, Evan spoke. "Did you hear me? You are safe. Stay right where you are. You don't need to run anymore. I promise I'll help you."

Meghan sat down on the nearby leather ottoman.

"What time do you think you'll be home tonight?" Meghan whispered.

"Not too late for an evening drink with you. I'm sure I'll have a lot to tell you after I examine the evidence."

"Okay. I'll wait for you. Just be careful of him. McManus and the Ocean City Police almost caught me last night."

"Try not to worry. We'll be having that drink tonight before you know it," Evan reassured.

Meghan hung up the phone and dialed information for a local cab. She then gathered her dried clothes and quickly changed, trying to wait patiently for the next available cab.

Meghan couldn't just wait around and let Evan fight for her innocence. She realized he was taking a risk for her.

She decided she must find the truth for herself.

Meghan knew what she had to do—return to the Renaissance Institute.

And somehow search Jonathan's office.

Meghan believed it was the only place where she could find the truth and prove her innocence.

Chapter Sixty-Eight

"SHE'S THE ONE. ALL OF the evidence at the scene matches her DNA. The strands of hair ... the skin samples from under the victims' nails. All of it shows Meghan Cahill killed Farraday and Rafferty," McManus said.

"What about the knife wound? Do you really think she was capable of making the exact same entry wound into both victims' chests?" Hawthorne questioned skeptically.

"Why not? She *is* a medical researcher with training in pathology, compliments of Penn's doctorate program. She knows anatomy and therefore knows precisely where and how to kill her victim."

"Did you ever find the murder weapon?" Hawthorne asked.

"No. Our one hunch was that she used an ice pick—the type used to break apart ice blocks in a Renaissance lab freezer. We found one in her lab, examined it for evidence."

"And?"

"Nothing. No trace of blood or tissue was found on it. Not even

DNA from Cahill's skin oil. The ice pick was pristine. Don't you think that's odd? She must have at least on one occasion grabbed the thing and thereby would have left fragments of oil residue on the handle. Right?"

Hawthorne remained silent, taking several more seconds to stare down at the forensic reports that detailed each piece of incriminating evidence that, in the chief medical examiner's opinion, would easily lead to Meghan's conviction.

"I know you've given this a lot of thought, but I have an idea why there's no trace of Meghan's DNA on the ice pick," Hawthorne offered.

"Okay. I'm listening. Anyway, you are the forensic expert."

Hawthorne agreed but chose not to acknowledge his friend's compliment, however facetious it sounded. He definitely did not want to appear to McManus as the expert trying to tell him how to run his investigation.

He had to think of Meghan. He couldn't afford to act like he was defending McManus's lead suspect. Meghan was right. He had to be careful around McManus. Hawthorne had worked with him in Philadelphia for enough years to know that McManus could easily become suspicious over the most subtle clue.

"Well, Evan, what do you think?"

"Gloves. She wore gloves when she used the ice pick. She was a researcher, right? Probably got used to wearing gloves whenever she worked in her lab."

"Yeah, maybe."

"So where's the weapon?"

"I don't know, and I don't care. As you know, we don't need to find one to convict her. Like I told you already, we have her motive established in the computer e-mails, and we have her placed at the murder scene according to Farraday's 911 call to the security department. We just need to find her."

"Do you think you will?" Hawthorne asked.

"I can promise you one thing—we will find her, sooner or later."

Chapter Sixty-Nine

SEPTEMBER 22

9:30 P.M.

"**J**EFFREY, WHAT ARE YOU DOING sitting behind my desk? Get the hell away from there!" Jonathan Ashbridge yelled out as he walked into his office.

The room was dimly lit by a corner desk lamp whose cream, linen-covered shade cast a soft glow across the floor and against Jeffrey slouched in the leather desk chair.

"Did you hear me? I told you to get the hell away from my desk," Jonathan demanded as he now stood in front of his desk.

"He can't hear you, Jonathan. And he certainly won't be getting up from your chair."

Jonathan froze; the voice was familiar. He quickly turned toward the direction of the voice and saw Stefan step out from the shadows just beyond the illuminated table lamp.

"You look startled. Did you think you were meeting Jeffrey alone tonight?" Stefan asked.

"What are you doing here? I had a meeting with him in my office. He called me … told me it was crucial that I meet with him right away." Jonathan turned around back toward his desk. He now remembered what he had seen when he had first come into the room.

"Yes, I know about your meeting. I called your assistant this evening and told him to set up this meeting," Stefan said.

"What?"

"I told him we, the professor and I, that is, were concerned about your loyalty to the group. Actually, I found it quite easy to convince him that you considered yourself more important than our mission and that you were a threat to the Pegasus Project. The fact that I also told him his own life was in danger guaranteed his trust in me. It seemed Jeffrey did not feel entirely safe around you." Stefan grinned as he walked behind Jonathan and placed a hand on his shoulder.

"Go ahead. Say hello to your loyal assistant," Stefan prodded.

Jonathan slowly walked around the desk and turned the chair toward him.

Jeffrey Manion's lifeless body slumped forward away from the chair and fell across the glass-covered desk. Jonathan fell back. Thick, red liquid oozed from his assistant's temple and slowly coursed its way through the victim's thick, matted hair and down across the glass desktop.

"Christ—what have you done?" Jonathan cried out.

"It's not what I've done, but rather, what *you* have done, Jonathan," Stefan accused.

"What do you mean?"

"Let me show you the e-mail Jeffrey had prepared to send to the Valley Creek Police Department." Stefan turned the computer flat screen toward Jonathan.

As Jonathan read aloud Jeffrey's e-mail implicating him with the murders of both Farraday and Rafferty, he realized what was happening. The professor had contacted Stefan to punish him for his success with his drug study. As he had told the professor, the scientific community deserved to hear about his work. Now, Stefan was here to prevent that from ever happening.

"Listen. Are you thinking of framing me with my assistant's murder like I framed Cahill with the Farraday and Rafferty murders? Well, you've got a lot to learn about me and what I'm capable of doing. Just because you're some kind of international hit-man doesn't mean you're infallible," Ashbridge rebuked.

"Is that so?" Stefan replied, calmly moving closer to Jonathan.

"Yes. The Pegasus Project, my drug study, was designed to destroy the lives of Bishop Torrey and his monsignor. The murders of Farraday and Rafferty were required to achieve the success of the project. I know the monsignor is dead. My question to you, however, is what happened with Bishop Torrey? You do remember, don't you, that the bishop intends to travel to Rome and become appointed as Philadelphia's new cardinal. Once named cardinal, he would become Imago Dei's appointed successor to Pope Luke, who is dying. Or have you forgotten that part of your assignment?" Ashbridge challenged.

"Forgotten? Certainly not. The monsignor has been punished for his sins of abuse against the innocent children. The bishop who enabled the abusive transgressions of priests to continue in the Philadelphia Archdiocese will also be punished. But why should this concern you?"

"Because I'm a part of the project. Without me, there would be no drug to make them suffer the intense pain and anguish that Imago Dei ordered as part of their punishment. Without my drug, Imago Dei would not have its revenge against these child abusers," Ashbridge argued.

Stefan stood next to Jonathan and looked into his eyes. He placed one hand against the researcher's face and gave him a gentle caress.

"That's just it. You are no longer a part of this mission," Stefan whispered into Jonathan's left ear and then pulled away.

Stefan raised his right hand and firmly positioned the steel nozzle of his Beretta 92A1 against Jonathan's right temple.

"I hope you enjoy this," Stefan mused as he squeezed the trigger, sending the bullet through the silencer and into Jonathan's brain.

Chapter Seventy

"GOD ... OH MY GOD," MEGHAN stammered as she reeled back against the wall just outside Jonathan's office.

She had heard it all. Everything. The plot behind the Pegasus Project. Her DNA evidence planted on Farraday and Rafferty. The monsignor's murder and the plan to kill Bishop Torrey. She had to get away. As far away as possible from Jonathan's office and the two murdered victims.

Jeffrey Manion.

Jonathan Ashbridge.

If the police found her here, she was certain McManus would charge her with these crimes as well. But who was Jonathan's killer? His name was never mentioned; she didn't even get a glimpse of his face. The room was too dark. Just his voice. Cold and detached.

A voice she would remember forever.

Meghan took a deep breath, turned her head to one side, and found her escape. The red EXIT sign, atop the stairway door at the end of the hallway, was only about fifty yards away.

Suddenly she heard the killer's footsteps approach from Ashbridge's office; the EXIT sign now seemed miles away. Meghan pushed off from the wall and raced down the dimly lit corridor. Thank God for the backup generator's lighting; maybe the killer wouldn't be able to ID her.

Meghan had realized something had tripped the electric power to the building when she arrived earlier at the institute. During her hour-long cab ride from Philadelphia to Chester County, she wasn't sure how she was going to get inside the Renaissance Building. When she had arrived at the west wing doorway, which was normally unattended by security at night, the building had suddenly become dark. She then realized she had a way inside the institute; the power failure had also unlocked the door.

As she fled down the dark hallway and neared the steel stairway door, her gratitude for whatever it was that had interrupted the building's security system and allowed her entry now turned to fear. The killer, a professional hit-man, had created her access to the building and to Jonathan's office, Meghan realized. If she didn't know better, Meghan thought, Jonathan's killer had lured her inside.

Just as Meghan pulled open the heavy steel door, a cold, detached voice echoed down the empty hallway.

"Don't run away, Meghan. I'd like to get to know you."

As she heard her name called out, she suddenly felt intense pain rip through her thigh. She fell against the stairway railing and heard the door close behind her. She grabbed her leg, trying to stop the burning pain from tearing into her flesh. What happened to her? Meghan tried to reason the cause, but it was no use. Her thoughts were confused, her heart raced, and Meghan felt a moist and sticky fluid ooze between her fingers.

My God—I was shot. Freeing one hand, she grabbed the cold, steel rail that quickly became slippery from her bloody fingers and dragged herself down two flights of stairs that brought her to the west wing emergency exit.

Don't look back, Meghan kept telling herself. She had to get away.

But how? It was going to hurt horribly, but she had to run. Hiding in the nearby cornfield was an option, she thought; she forced the emergency exit door open and started running toward the field. The lake was just beyond it. While struggling to gain ground, she traveled only a short distance before her body suddenly slammed forward against the macadam parking lot. Breaking her fall, her outstretched palms burned as the rough surface tore off layers of skin and exposed her raw flesh. Meghan slowly pushed herself up to a kneeling position and searched the area for an alternate escape.

The water basin. It was another forty, maybe fifty yards away, she thought. She could make it there. *She had to.*

Reaching the basin that already had several feet of water in it from the Nor'easter's heavy rains, Meghan slid down the wet, grassy embankment and entered the dark, cold water.

Dark and cold. Three feet, maybe four feet deep; the water quickly encircled her waist. Within seconds, her body began to twitch. Then shiver uncontrollably. The cold would be good for her gunshot wound. Cause vasoconstriction and slow down the bleeding, she thought.

The cold would not be good, however, for the rest of her body, she feared.

Hypothermia.

Cardiac failure.

Death.

Her knowledge of physiology was not comforting, she knew, but if she had remained back on the parking lot, her fate would be the same. Death—but at the hands of a professional killer.

Suddenly, Meghan heard the voice.

"Where are you? I know you can't go far with your injury. You realize, of course, Meghan, I always hit what I aim for. I could easily have killed you but decided to give you just a flesh wound. Nothing too traumatic."

His voice was getting closer. Meghan dragged her body through the dark, murky water and finally reached the far end of the basin, the farthest point away from the killer that she could possibly move to.

Meghan turned around and caught only a glimpse of a figure moving toward her through the darkness from around the other side of the water basin.

She couldn't remain here.

She had to act quickly.

She had to move now.

Reaching through the blackness that surrounded her, Meghan suddenly felt the opening to a circular cement drainage pipe that had several steel rods running up and down across its face. She remembered having seen these pipes in each of the basins surrounding the institute property. If the water became too high in the basin, the pipes were constructed to carry the excess water approximately one-half mile down toward the lake.

This would be her escape route; climb up into the cement pipe and somehow follow it down to the lake.

Meghan grabbed two cold steel rods with her numb fingers and stared into the black emptiness.

She had to go in there. There was no other way. But could she do it? Could she crawl inside this small, dark tunnel and then inch her way along the half-mile cement conduit? Even if it was her only possible escape from her pursuer, Meghan still couldn't move forward; her frozen fingers locked around the steel rods.

Meghan breathed deeply. She knew she was on her own now. She resolved not to allow Jonathan, even when now dead, to control her life anymore.

Meghan took another deep breath, exhaled, and then slowly squeezed between the steel rods that guarded the opening of the drainage pipe. As she moved forward, Meghan felt as if her legs were no longer a part of her. Numb and heavy, they were merely following the rest of her body as she crawled into the darkness.

If she could just make it out to the lake, Meghan thought, she could then regroup and decide her next move. She hoped Jonathan's killer didn't see her in the basin and then slipping away into the pipe.

One thing was certain though. Meghan had to call Evan. She would've used her cell phone now but knew she probably couldn't get a signal from inside the underground drainage pipe. She would just have to wait to call him.

God, he was going to be furious with her.

Chapter Seventy-One

THE FULL MOON BROKE THROUGH the dark autumn clouds and beamed through the pine trees and across the lake's still surface.

She was almost there. She could see it now. The moonlight signaled the end of the underground pipe; it was only a short distance away. Soon she would be outside, free from her escape tunnel and Jonathan's killer.

As she reached the opening, she stared out onto the lake's bank and scrutinized as much ground as she could possibly see without leaving the pipe. She was alone.

The cacophonous honking sounds of geese echoed across the lake and signaled their impending descent upon the moonlit water. If the approaching geese felt it was safe to land, then it should also be safe for her to exit the pipe.

As Meghan crawled out, her arms and legs immediately sank into the cool, thick mud. She struggled to find solid ground, trying to keep her face away from the stagnant odor that seeped out from the black mud around her.

She had almost forgotten about her gunshot wound—her thigh was numb from the cold basin water. Her struggling, however, soon brought back the burning pain. It was almost unbearable, but she had to free herself from the quagmire that was quickly engulfing her.

Finally, Meghan felt a section of dry land beneath her fingers and slowly dragged her body to a much needed rest. Her leg ached. Her heart pounded within her chest as she lay breathless against a pine tree. Meghan reached into her inside raincoat pocket and pulled out her cell phone. Thank God it was still dry. She dialed Evan's cell phone number, which she had retrieved from his house phone caller ID memory when he had called her earlier today.

God, his phone call from outside City Hall's courthouse seemed like an eternity ago when he had told her he was meeting Detective McManus.

Meghan prayed Evan was still nearby in Chester County.

"Hello," the voice crackled.

"Evan, is that you?" Meghan looked down at her weak battery signal. Damn it. Maybe just enough time to tell him where she was.

"Yes it is. Who is this?"

"It's Meghan … now don't be angry. Something has happened. I need your help."

"Meghan? Where are you? And why aren't you at my house?"

"I'm sorry. I saw things tonight … Jonathan is dead."

"What?"

"Ashbridge. Jonathan Ashbridge was killed tonight. I saw it."

"Where?"

"At the institute. At Jonathan's office."

"What? I don't understand. Why were you at—"

"Evan, stop. I said I'm sorry. I had to find the truth for myself. Somebody is setting me up. The only place I could think of was back at the institute. I went back to search Jonathan's office." Meghan's breath hastened.

"All right. Just relax. Are you okay?"

Meghan reached down and grabbed her thigh. Her muscles were cramped. Probably in spasm from the cold. She instinctively felt the popliteal pulse behind her knee. Strong. Blood flow to her leg and foot wasn't compromised yet, she thought.

"I'm okay. Can you come get me?"

"Yes. Tell me exactly where you are."

"At the lake near the institute."

"What … what the hell are you doing there?"

"It's a long story. I'll meet you on the dirt road that runs near the lake. You can get on that road off of Ship Road, just past Ship Inn."

"All right, but don't move. I'll be there in minutes." Hawthorne assured her.

Evan didn't know where the dirt path was located, but he did know where Ship Inn was. He had been sitting at the Inn's bar when he took Meghan's call.

Meghan reached inside her rain slicker and dropped her cell phone into her pocket. Evan didn't tell her where he was, but she hoped he was nearby. She wasn't sure how much more she could endure tonight. And for how long.

Stefan witnessed everything. He remained standing behind the cloak of several holly-evergreen trees that grew wild among the dense pine tree cover surrounding the lake. He had seen Meghan slide out from her escape route only to fall prey to the quicksand-like mud that had greeted her. Even though he couldn't hear her phone conversation, Stefan knew whom it was with.

Dr. Evan Hawthorne. She had no one else in her life to help her now.

Stefan grinned as he saw Meghan's worn body slowly limp toward the undulating headlights from a car that sped down the bumpy dirt path.

Did she really think she had escaped him? Stefan mused.

Chapter Seventy-Two

"My God, look at you. You're covered with mud ... and you've been shot. I've got to get you to a hospital!" Evan shouted as he helped Meghan into his SUV.

"No. You must listen to me. First, get us away from here. I think Ashbridge's killer is nearby," Meghan urged.

"We have to call the police. McManus has to know about this," Evan demanded.

"Please, Evan, just drive. The killer is some kind of hit-man. A professional guy hired by some secret Catholic Church organization. It's not safe here," Meghan pleaded, her voice finding some way to speak despite the agonizing spasm in her wounded thigh.

"All right ... hold on," Evan shouted as he floored the accelerator and executed a 180-degree turn, churning up the gravel dirt path beneath his vehicle's wheels.

Turning onto Ship Road toward Ship Inn and then making a left onto Lincoln Avenue heading toward Route 202, Evan heard every detail of Meghan's ordeal.

"Are you sure it's only a flesh wound?" Evan asked skeptically.

"Yes, I think so. Remember, I do know something about anatomy. And, please, turn down the heat. I know I'm soaked to the bone, but you're suffocating me with this hot air." Meghan's hand quivered as she reached for the automatic window control and lowered her window.

"Listen. You may know something about anatomy, but I'm the medical doctor. You're hypothermic—I don't want you to go into shock."

"I'll be fine. Just get us back to your place. Does Dr. Hawthorne, the chief medical examiner, have any medical supplies there that could help a gunshot victim who is still alive?" Meghan forced a smile.

"I don't like your humor."

"It's the only thing I have right now. With what I've been through tonight, it's a wonder I even have that left." Meghan sighed as her head fell back against the headrest; her eyes slowly closed. Right now, they ached worse than her leg.

Evan approached the on-ramp to Route 202 North, which would eventually take them onto the Schuylkill Expressway and to Philadelphia's Society Hill section where his townhouse was located. But was this the right thing to do? Continue to harbor a fugitive and drive her away from a crime scene? Assuming she was not guilty of anything, not the murders a week ago at the institute and not the murders tonight, still Evan asked himself the same question.

Am I doing the right thing by protecting Meghan?

He knew he had a professional responsibility as Philadelphia's medical examiner not to obstruct a police investigation. He was already guilty of that offense. Now he was aiding and abetting a fugitive ... assisting her escape once again. Looking over at her, he reminded himself that he had promised he would help her.

He believed in her. He wanted Meghan to be innocent. He needed her to be innocent. After tonight, however, things were getting too complicated. McManus needed to hear from Meghan firsthand about everything she had heard tonight at Ashbridge's office. McManus had to believe her story … she was shot and pursued by a hit-man. McManus couldn't accuse her of lying about this.

Evan drove past the on-ramp for 202 North and instead turned off Lincoln Avenue and into the Sheraton Hotel complex. Evan decided he would get a room there tonight. He could provide a warm shower for Meghan and then use the medical supplies that he always kept in his car for emergencies to clean her wound. He couldn't think of a better emergency than this one to open up his medical bag. Then, after he treated Meghan's gunshot wound, he would help her as a professional with the police. It had been a while, but Evan decided now was the time.

Dr. Evan Hawthorne would become the criminal defense attorney that he once was, now that he had a client who was truly innocent and in desperate need of his legal expertise.

Chapter Seventy-Three

STEAM FROM MEGHAN'S SHOWER FLOWED beneath the bathroom door and spread its warm dampness into the bedroom where Evan lay sprawled out across the king-size bed. Evan looked at the nightstand clock. She had been in there for over thirty minutes. He knew he had made the right decision. Meghan needed this time to relax and unwind.

Evan dialed McManus's cell phone number. He was prepared for McManus's accusations of obstruction of justice, aiding and abetting, and any other crime he wanted to throw at him. Evan had a defense. He had used it many times in the past for his clients, not always feeling right about it.

Staying within the gray legal boundaries afforded a criminal defense attorney, Evan had many times manipulated the justice system on behalf of a client, and it was always effective.

For Meghan, it felt right this time. He was now her attorney and had placed her under his temporary protective custody as an officer of the court.

Meghan Cahill was the victim. Shot by a professional hit-man. Her safety as a material witness was also in jeopardy. McManus wouldn't like it, but it was legal.

"Hello, McManus here." Evan could tell his friend was tired; his voice was terse and barely audible.

"This is Hawthorne. Sorry about the late hour, but there's something important you need to know. It's about your investigation."

"God, I thought we already went over all this tonight. What else could be—"

"Just listen, will you? I'm with Cahill."

"What?"

"She's been shot tonight. There's a professional guy stalking her … she saw him kill Ashbridge in his office within the past hour."

"Where are you?" McManus demanded.

"I'll tell you in a minute, but you've got to listen carefully to what I'm about to tell you. Okay?"

"Go ahead, I'm listening," McManus replied. Evan could tell he probably had about three minutes before McManus could get a trace on the call.

"Your theory about Cahill … it's all wrong. She didn't kill anyone. Ashbridge set her up. He was working with some professionals on a secret project called Pegasus Project at the Renaissance Institute where he had developed a drug that would make targeted Catholic priests become psychotic. Certain priests who were child abusers."

"You're crazy," McManus challenged.

"No, I'm not. Trust me, there's more. Cahill went back to Ashbridge's office tonight to get evidence that would clear her name. While standing outside the office, she heard some guy and Ashbridge argue. Ashbridge admitted everything. Falsifying the e-mails between Farraday and her, and get this … Ashbridge planted hair and skin samples from Meghan on your victims."

Evan paused a few seconds. McManus was silent. So far, so good, Evan thought.

"And there's more. Apparently, a secret organization inside the Catholic Church designed the Pegasus Project to seek retribution against certain priests who were child abusers."

"That's an amazing story. How do you know it's true? And how the hell did you find her?"

"Listen, McManus, I know her and trust her. She used to be one of my graduate students at Penn. She called me for help. Okay?"

"I want to see her. And I want to see her *now*."

"We're at the Sheraton on Lincoln Avenue, just down from the institute."

"I know the place. My officers will be there in minutes."

"Just one more thing, McManus."

"What's that?"

"I'm representing her, and as an officer of the court, I have placed her in my protective custody. There's a hit-man out there watching her. She's not safe."

"Protective custody? You've got to be kidding."

"I'm serious, McManus. Don't forget, I used to be a damn good criminal defense attorney. You don't want to tangle with me," Hawthorne warned.

"Okay. We need to talk … I can be at the hotel in a few minutes, and I'll be alone."

Chapter Seventy-Four

Monsignor Hans Reuss led Bishop Torrey down the hallway of the papal apartments located on the top floor of the Apostolic Palace Building that stood along St. Peter's Square. The papal apartments were comprised of several private and official rooms that had served since the seventeenth century as the religious residence of the Catholic Church pontiff.

Stopping halfway down the plush, purple-carpeted hallway, the monsignor opened the mahogany double-doors that brought them into a sitting room. The monsignor turned to the bishop and motioned him to follow across the room and through yet another doorway that was already opened and guarded by a man wearing a black suit and a barely visible earpiece. Monsignor Reuss nodded to the plainclothes Swiss

Guard as they now entered Pope Luke's private chambers—a room dimly lit with several flickering candles where the ailing pontiff's labored breaths resounded against the tapestried bedroom walls.

Standing around the pontiff's bed were several members of his private staff, including Cardinal Peter Grossi—the pope's Camerlengo—who witnessed each day the gradual and painful deterioration in the pontiff's health. What had amazed Cardinal Grossi and others closest to the pope, including his medical staff, was the heroic dying process—obviously painful and yet silent suffering experienced for many months since his diagnosis of pancreatic cancer.

How much more could His Holiness endure? No one could be certain, not even the medical experts. Each time a physician predicted when the final day would occur, Pope Luke would prove the prognosis wrong. For several weeks at a time, he would rally and regain enough strength to attend to his official duties. Thousands had flocked to Vatican Square to pray for his recovery. He was the "loved one."

"Your Holiness, may I present Bishop Torrey." Cardinal Grossi placed a hand on the bishop's back and guided him closer to the pope. Slowly turning his head, covered in a white linen cloth, Pope Luke looked into the bishop's face. Bishop Torrey could not help but see suffering etched across the pontiff's face and deep inside his jaundiced eyes.

Bishop Torrey fell to his knees and lowered his head. "I am your humble servant, Holy Father. Do unto me as you wish. Not my will, but your will be done," the bishop whispered.

The burning candles filled the room with a heavy almond-scented fragrance that blended with the scent of incense recently burned as a prayer offering. *If I stay here any longer, I'm going to puke*, the bishop thought. *The odor in here is sickening … I've got to hold on. Just a few more minutes. That's all … just until I get his God-damned blessing. Then I become Cardinal Torrey.*

The bishop refused to breathe through his nose. Rather, he took a deep breath through his mouth, hoping to lessen the pungent smell. It was no use. He tasted the dense candle and incense odors as they coated his tongue and worked their way down his parched throat and into his lungs. He couldn't breathe. Each new breath was harder to take. The bishop tried to swallow but realized he had no saliva left in his mouth to quench his throat.

He had to hang on. *Just get it done … give me the papal blessing and anoint me. Make me cardinal, and then you can die*, the bishop thought.

Pope Luke extended his arm, and with the help of an aide, he placed his shaking hand to the top of Bishop Torrey's still-bowed head. Barely audible prayers stumbled across the pope's lips. As he withdrew his hand, Pope Luke struggled to keep his arm outstretched, offered an abridged sign of the cross, and then dropped his weak arm back onto the bed's purple, satin comforter.

The ceremony was complete. It was official. Cardinal Torrey rose to his feet and bowed to his Holy See. It was just a matter of time now until the churches in Rome, and all churches around the world, would toll the death of Pope Luke, the new cardinal reflected.

Cardinal Torrey was now prepared to become the next pope. He was certain his papal reign would overshadow the few accomplishments made by his predecessor. True, Pope Luke would be remembered as the kind and loving shepherd of his flock, always forgiving and never willing to challenge other countries' political agendas.

Torrey, however, would remember Pope Luke as the weak pope who almost destroyed the Catholic Church.

As the new pope, Torrey would be ready to take on those countries that challenged the conservative Catholic Church doctrines. His Church would not be docile and forgiving like it was under Pope Luke's rule. Instead, using the Catholic Church's wealth and power, he would challenge any person, organization, or country who disagreed with his dogma.

His authority would be infallible; Imago Dei had assured him of this. Any opposition to him would be destroyed. Imago Dei would see to that.

Chapter Seventy-Five

Exiting the pope's sitting room and closing the mahogany double-doors behind them, Monsignor Reuss grabbed Cardinal Torrey's arm and stared into his face.

"We need to talk," the monsignor advised.

"Yes, we do. There is a lot of preparation we now need to do so that we are ready when Luke dies," Cardinal Torrey responded.

Walking down the quiet hallway, the monsignor realized they were alone but still wanted absolute privacy before he discussed anything further about Imago Dei's plan for the cardinal.

"Let's go in here. I can guarantee we won't be disturbed." The monsignor opened the door of his office at the end of the hallway. Locking the door behind them, he motioned Cardinal Torrey toward a pair of crimson upholstered chairs that faced each other beneath an oil painting depicting the coat of arms of Cardinal Scipione Borghese, an early seventeenth-century librarian of the Holy Roman Church.

"Interesting painting," Cardinal Torrey noted as he stood scanning the entire 5'x7' work. "I particularly like the detailed work done on the brown crowned eagle, painted against a gold background, and poised atop the gold-winged dragon. I think, though, the use of the cherubs holding the coat of arms is a bit much."

The monsignor offered a smile. He would have guessed, rather, that Torrey would have been drawn to the cherubs. He was a child abuser. He knew Torrey was also an enabler who had permitted many other priests under his authority in the Philadelphia Archdiocese to commit similar acts of abuse. He also knew the new cardinal would not like what he was about to tell him.

"Please, have a seat, Your Excellency."

"Thank you, Monsignor. Now before you begin with what you have to say, I want to tell you that I'll be relying on you very much after I become pope. You've been most helpful to me with my appointment as cardinal. I know that. You will have a bright future with me in the Vatican."

"Thank you … but I don't think I will be in a position to serve you."

"What do you mean?"

"Imago Dei considers you a liability. Your acts of abuse and your tolerance of similar acts by priests under your authority do not make you suitable as a papal candidate. If your actions were made public, the ensuing scandal would destroy Imago Dei and its ability to do good in the world." The monsignor paused and took a few moments to study the cardinal's stone-faced reaction. Monsignor Reuss continued.

"Imago Dei was willing to help you become cardinal and then allow you to return to Philadelphia. But that's it. Nothing more."

"What are you saying, Monsignor?" demanded the cardinal as he leaned forward in his chair.

"Stated simply, Cardinal Torrey, Imago Dei will not arrange for you to become the next pope."

"Don't give me that crap. Do you and your organization forget what I know about *your* activities? Or shall I enumerate them for you now?"

"I know you're upset, but we have made you—"

"Listen to me, and listen very carefully. If I don't become pope, I will report everything I know to the authorities. Everything, Monsignor ... the circumstances behind Pope John Paul I's mysterious death, Imago Dei's hidden finances in the Cayman Islands, and much more. No, Monsignor, I'm not upset. I'll be happy to tell all."

Monsignor Reuss stood up and walked across the floor to the *window loggia* of the papal apartment study where every pope greeted pilgrims in St. Peter's Square. He gently parted the curtain and gazed out at the thousands of concerned visitors who continued their vigil since Pope Luke's most recent relapse over a week ago. The monsignor shared their concern for Pope Luke's health. He was always a kind and compassionate man. A loving pope who carried the pains and sufferings of all mankind in his heart. He would miss Pope Luke when it was time for him to leave this world.

Turning back to face Cardinal Torrey, the monsignor finally spoke. "I've listened to what you have said, and I understand. I will report your reply to Imago Dei. But I must be honest with you. They will not like it at all. In fact, they have already advised me to speak for them should you refuse to return to Philadelphia."

"Oh, have they?" the cardinal scoffed.

"Yes. And now it's time for you to listen carefully. Imago Dei will not be threatened by you or anyone else. You cannot touch them. What you have to understand is this ... should you attempt to carry out your threat, then your life will not be safe here in Vatican City or anywhere else in the world."

The cardinal pushed himself out of the chair and walked over to the monsignor. Even though the cardinal had documentation that could prove his allegations against Imago Dei, he also knew what this organization was capable of doing to him.

"I may have spoken incorrectly, Monsignor. Perhaps, I can have a day or two to think over everything. A lot has happened to me today. Would you be gracious enough to give me that time?"

Monsignor Reuss saw a change in the cardinal's demeanor. Not the pompous man he usually was, but now someone who was somewhat humbled.

A good act, the monsignor admitted to himself. But he wasn't fooled.

"Of course. Please take as much time as you need. Can I arrange for an aide to take you back to your guest quarters at St. Martha's house?"

"No. That won't be necessary. It's just a short walk. In fact, I may stop inside St. Peter's Basilica on the way to meditate for a while."

The monsignor nodded and accompanied Cardinal Torrey to the study door.

It was unfortunate Stefan had missed his opportunity to take care of the cardinal in the United States, the monsignor thought. He would allow Stefan one more chance to finish his contract on the cardinal.

It must happen in Vatican City.

And Stefan would be given just twenty-four hours to make it right.

Chapter Seventy-Six

"YOU'RE WALKING A THIN LINE between making an aggressive legal defense and obstruction of justice."

Detective McManus glared at Evan Hawthorne as he entered the hotel room and walked toward Meghan Cahill, who was sitting on the edge of the bed.

"Didn't you hear Ev … Dr. Hawthorne tell you there's a hit-man after me?" Meghan was glad she caught herself. "My God, look … he actually shot me in the leg. Or do you think I made all of this up and shot myself?" Meghan shouted.

"That thought did cross my mind," McManus smirked.

"God-damn you," Meghan rebuked.

"Hold on, McManus, and, Meghan, keep quiet." The last thing Evan

Hawthorne wanted was for Meghan, now his client, to engage in a verbal scuffle with McManus. Evan knew who would win.

"But it's not right that he's accusing you—"

"Relax, Meghan. He's just playing with me," Evan assured her.

"Oh, you think so," McManus challenged.

"Yes, I do. In fact, you're lucky I haven't yet called in the feds. I can see the headlines now: *Philadelphia's chief M.E. alerts FBI to examine negligent police investigation of two prominent Chester County murder victims.*"

"Don't be a jerk," McManus countered.

"I'm just a criminal defense attorney zealously representing my client who is a material witness to murders committed by an international killer."

"All right, I get your point. So, where do we go from here?" McManus questioned.

"The way I see it … you've got two options. You could arrest my client right now based on your tainted evidence that was planted on the victims at the lake to incriminate her … or you can believe her story and try to find the assassin who shot her and who is still after her. Either way, I'm not leaving her alone. Up until now, she's been on her own too long. It's now time for you guys to do something for her." Hawthorne took a breath and continued.

"We've told you about the Pegasus Project and the plot to execute priests who were child abusers. Your job is to find this guy, prevent any future hits, and protect my client."

Evan Hawthorne stood between Meghan and Detective McManus. If he knew his friend the way he thought he did, Meghan would not be spending the night in a Chester County cell.

McManus sighed.

"Fine, will you take responsibility for Dr. Cahill's safety or do you expect us to give her twenty-four-hour police protection?"

"I know you, McManus. You'll sleep better at night knowing your guys are watching over her," Evan mused.

"You're right about that. Now, Dr. Cahill, tell me everything you heard tonight in Ashbridge's office. Especially the part about the next victim … a certain bishop in Vatican City."

Chapter Seventy-Seven

S TEFAN DROVE AWAY FROM THE Hotel Flora where he had checked
in several hours ago. Rome was only ten kilometers away; one
main reason why he had chosen to stay here was its proximity to Vatican
City.

He also favored the hotel's discreet layout of having only three suites,
out of thirty-seven rooms, located on the top floor and overlooking
Frascati's vineyard countryside. His suite was the only one that offered
an outdoor patio area off the bedroom; Stefan already had plans for his
late evening dinner on the patio when he returned from his assignment
at St. Martha's House.

Monsignor Hans Reuss was emphatic during his call to Stefan
when he had arrived at the Rome/Fiumicino Airport. Pope Luke was
near death. Bishop Torrey had been made a cardinal. If Torrey wasn't

311

eliminated before Luke's death, then upon the pope's death, Cardinal Torrey, now a member of the College of Cardinals, would be a participant in the papal conclave to select a new pope.

And, Cardinal Torrey expected to become the next pope. Monsignor Reuss insisted that this was never to happen. Torrey was a security risk.

A threat to Imago Dei.

The American cardinal knew too much.

Stefan walked up to the street-level double-glass entrance doors that stood beneath the stucco plaque that read *Domus Santae Marthae*, checked his watch—it was already 10:45 p.m.—and proceeded into the building.

Stefan wasn't surprised by the security guard's immediate demand for identification, which the guard checked against his approved guest list. He quickly found a match with a name that Monsignor Reuss had provided earlier.

Monsignor Klaas.

Just one of the many false identities Stefan had used. His work had been required in the Vatican before, and Monsignor Klaas had been very useful to Imago Dei. After tonight though, Stefan knew that Monsignor Klaas would never surface again. Or, at least not that identity.

Standing in the hallway outside Cardinal Torrey's room, Stefan checked the time again. According to Monsignor Reuss's plan, the cardinal was to receive the complimentary nightcap, Chambourd— Cardinal Torrey's favorite—delivered to him by one of the monsignor's associates. This particular nightcap was actually a blessing, as Monsignor Reuss had pointed out to Stefan that the strong liqueur's sweet taste would mask the bitter taste of the sedative—Midazolam—that was mixed in the drink.

It was now 11:00 p.m. The Midazolam dose was strong enough to send Cardinal Torrey into a deep and undisturbed sleep.

Stefan easily unlocked the door and slowly pushed it open. Sitting up against pillows positioned against the headboard, Cardinal Torrey was sound asleep, his chin resting on his chest and each hand still holding open a leather-bound book.

Stefan stood still for a moment. The high-pitched metallic clicking sound of the door locking behind him was in sharp contrast to the cardinal's deep, guttural breathing efforts.

His victim remained motionless.

Stefan moved closer.

From within his overcoat pocket, Stefan removed a compact leather case that contained a .25-gauge butterfly needle with a 10-ml. filled syringe attached to the butterfly's plastic tubing.

The combination of succinylcholine and potassium chloride was Stefan's favorite.

Quick and effective.

First, lethal cardiac arrhythmia from the potassium. Then, muscle paralysis from succinylcholine.

Stefan added the paralyzing drug since he once had a victim who, despite the sedative, woke up with chest pain from the heart palpitations and tried to call for help. Stefan preferred silence and cooperation from his victims.

Stefan gently pulled off the bed covers and tied a vinyl tourniquet around the cardinal's leg. Several veins became engorged with a dark bluish hue, pushing up from beneath the cardinal's pale, leathery skin.

Usually he used the saphenous vein, a reliable and sturdy ankle vein; he never wanted to leave a bruise at the injection site. With the cardinal's death, however, there was sure to be an autopsy, and so he decided to choose a smaller, less prominent vein.

Stefan flicked his finger several times against each toe. Soon, several smaller blue lines grew in size, but he had to be careful. The slightest bruise caused by a vein collapsing under the pressure of his injection or from his needle damaging the blood vessel wall would alert a medical examiner to suspect foul play.

So far, Stefan's drugs had always escaped detection from toxicology analysis. That was mainly due to the fact that his victims' cause of death was always attributed to cardiac arrest. There had never been a reason to suspect otherwise. And, even if his victims' blood was analyzed for lethal drugs, the presence of high levels of potassium would reasonably be attributed to cell death from heart failure. And the paralyzing drug—succinylcholine—would go undetected; the medical examiner could detect traces of succinylcholine only if he was looking for it.

Stefan turned the cardinal's foot on its side and palpated a vein that coursed behind his heel. If he left a small bruise there, the onset of rigor mortis would camouflage such a mark, he thought. Stefan guided the tiny needle through the thick, aging skin and knew he penetrated the vein as he saw blood flow back into the butterfly tubing. The cardinal never stirred.

Cardinal Torrey's execution sentence commenced.

The syringe slowly relinquished its lethal contents into the vein and into the cardinal's circulation, which quickly delivered the drugs to their final destination.

The cardinal's heart and muscles.

After several seconds, the cardinal's arms and legs twitched, which told Stefan that succinylcholine was already at work depolarizing the muscular system. Soon, such over-stimulation of each muscle in the cardinal's body would result in paralysis and thereby suffocate his victim's attempt to breathe.

Cardinal Torrey slumped to his side; his leather-bound Bible closing shut. Stefan placed his finger to his victim's neck. No carotid pulse.

Stefan then raised each eyelid. Pupils: fixed and dilated.

Stefan's work was finished here. He was hungry and was already thinking about what wine to drink with his late-night dinner out on his hotel patio.

Stefan hurried down the four flights of stairs that brought him to the lobby where the same guard who had approved his credentials now sat reading the Vatican's newspaper, *L'Osservatore Romano*. The sound of Stefan's footsteps across the marble floor echoed across the foyer as Stefan moved closer to the security desk.

The guard lowered the paper and smiled at Monsignor Klaas, who challenged the friendly acknowledgment with a cold stare. Stefan reached inside his jacket and withdrew his Italian-made Beretta. The muffled sound of the bullet passing through the Beretta's specially designed silencer was quickly replaced by the loud crash of the guard's aluminum chair slamming against the marble floor as the guard's body jerked violently against the desktop.

Stefan reached across the guard's lifeless body and picked up the visitor log book. He tore out the page documenting his visit tonight. No evidence of Monsignor Klaas's visit with the cardinal would exist.

Within minutes, Stefan entered his car, which he had parked around the corner of St. Peter's Basilica, adjacent to St. Martha's House, and looked into his rearview mirror. He was tired, and his eyes burned from lack of sleep. He had only slept several hours over the last three days and needed rest.

Suddenly, red and blue lights pulsated in his rearview mirror and were quickly getting closer with each passing second. Instinctively, Stefan fell against the front passenger seat as Rome's police raced past him and tore around the corner where they screeched to a stop at the entrance to St. Martha's House.

Stefan thought of only one person who would have reported his presence in Vatican City.

Meghan Cahill.

She was probably listening outside Ashbridge's office longer than he had thought. *My, my, Meghan … you certainly are proving yourself to be a worthy adversary,* Stefan thought.

But first, a well-deserved dinner and good night's rest. Tomorrow afternoon, he had a meeting with Monsignor Reuss. After that, Stefan had no other commitments that would keep him from her.

Chapter Seventy-Eight

SHERATON HOTEL

VALLEY CREEK TOWNSHIP, CHESTER COUNTY

IT WAS EARLY SATURDAY MORNING, almost 7:00 a.m., and Meghan knew Valley Creek's dayshift police officers would be arriving soon to relieve the nightshift squad.

McManus was not taking any chances with her safety, he had told her, and therefore positioned numerous officers, some of whom had volunteered to work overtime, around the Sheraton Hotel's outside perimeter as well as inside the lobby and outside her hotel door. Even though Meghan didn't entirely trust his motives, still she felt somewhat confident that McManus was finally starting to believe her story and was committed to protecting her.

Meghan sat on the edge of her bed, having already changed into a nylon running suit that Evan had given her. She ran her hands through her hair and took a deep sigh. God, she had to get out of this room. She had been here since Thursday night, and the walls covered with Andrew Wyeth prints were closing in on her. If she couldn't run with her injury, she would settle for a brisk walk. Anything but staying here closed in for another minute.

Meghan heard the usual exchanges made outside her door between the two shifts. As she released the deadbolt and opened her door, she was suddenly confronted by one of her uniformed guardians.

"Pardon me, Dr. Cahill, but where do you think you're going?" a tall, clean-shaven, muscular-framed officer questioned.

"What does it look like I'm doing, Officer? I'm going out for a run. You can join me if you like."

"I'm sorry, but I need to get clearance for you to leave."

"Well, you'd better start getting your *clearance* because I'm leaving now. By the way, since I'm not under arrest, don't try to stop me."

Meghan moved around the young patrolman who had just come on duty and, she could sense, was in no mood for such an early morning confrontation.

"Dr. Cahill, can you at least give me a few minutes until I can get a hold of Detective McManus? It shouldn't take long."

Meghan paused at the elevator and smiled back at the officer.

"All right, you've got three minutes. Then I'm pressing the down button." Meghan realized the Valley Creek Township police officer was only doing his job—and a great job at that. But she also liked asserting some control in her life.

It was Saturday, and a week had already gone by since Dan Rafferty and Farraday had been killed. A lot had happened to her in that brief time. Her whole life had been changed forever. Two trusted friends, Dan Rafferty and Emily DeHaven, had been killed. She was convinced Emily was yet another innocent victim of the Pegasus Project.

Meghan didn't have to wait long for an answer. She saw the young officer approach her while he was still speaking into the cell phone.

"Just a minute, Detective, you can tell her yourself. She's standing right here." The officer handed the phone to Meghan.

"Hello, Meghan? It's McManus. What's this I hear about you giving my officers a hard time?"

"Listen to me, I've had enough. Enough of you and enough of being cooped up in a hotel room. I'm leaving for a run ... with or without your blessing."

"All right. Just relax. You can go outside, but an officer must be with you at all times. There's something you need to know." Meghan didn't hear the usual sarcasm that she was used to hearing from McManus. Instead, she heard a softer tone, one filled with concern and urgency.

"What is it?" Meghan asked.

"It's about the guy who shot you."

"Did you find him?" Meghan's voice grew excited.

"No. After you told us about his plan to travel to Vatican City to kill Bishop Torrey, we immediately notified Interpol and Rome's Police Department." McManus paused, making sure that Meghan heard and processed each word.

"And ...?" Meghan asked.

"It's not good news. Your information was accurate. Bishop Torrey, actually it's Cardinal Torrey now, was found dead in his apartment in Vatican City. By the time Rome's police arrived, they also found the building's security guard dead. Shot at close range. They called it a professional job. They also think they missed the killer by only several minutes. I'm sorry, Meghan."

Meghan looked up at the young officer still standing next to her. She noticed his facial muscles had grown taut. He must have heard the same report from McManus. She realized the officer knew what she now feared. The same man who had shot her and was responsible for multiple murders, including the two victims at St. Martha's House in Vatican City, was still at large and unpredictable.

Her life was still in danger.

"Thank you, Detective. Have you told Dr. Hawthorne?"

"Not yet. I was about to call him when I got this urgent call from your protection unit. Do you still insist on going outside?"

"I do. Now more than ever. I need some fresh air."

"I understand. Just stick close to my men. This killer is probably still in Europe. For all we know, he doesn't plan to return to this area. You never saw his face or heard a name. You're not a threat to him, Dr. Cahill. He should still consider his identity protected."

"Thanks. I hope you're right." Meghan sighed and managed a forced smile. She handed the cell phone to the Valley Creek Officer and pressed the elevator's down button.

"Yes, sir, I understand. We won't leave her side," the officer assured. The elevator door opened, and Meghan stepped inside where two other clean-shaven and well-built Valley Creek police officers stood towering over her. For the first time since she had started receiving her twenty-four-hour protection, Meghan felt a deep sense of gratitude to her protectors. She realized they were keeping her safe not just from some local thug, but from a highly successful and experienced professional killer.

Meghan believed these officers were very well aware of the risks involved. It was possible her assailant would return to Chester County to kill her.

Chapter Seventy-Nine

"Thank you ... thank you for everything." Meghan touched the sleeve of Evan's brown corduroy jacket and stared up into his grayish-blue eyes while they stood at the bottom of the gray stone steps that led up to her home in Ocean City.

It was a crisp late-Saturday afternoon in mid-October, exactly four weeks since Dan Rafferty and CEO Farraday were murdered at the Renaissance Institute lake. Signature autumn clouds—ones shaded with gray and indigo hues—hurried across the blue sky canvas, at times covering the soft, warm glow of a tired, setting sun.

"Are you sure you'll be okay?" Evan asked as he reached down and held Meghan's cold hands.

"I think so ... at least for tonight. I just have to take one day at a time."

"Well, I don't like leaving you here alone. Even though McManus and the feds don't think you're in any danger, I have to say, I don't share their opinion."

"My, you sound like you really care for me," Meghan teased as she offered Evan an appreciative smile.

"Stop kidding around …"

"Who says I'm kidding. I think Dr. Evan Hawthorne is afraid to show his true feelings," Meghan said in a confident tone. In fact, she was surprised at her confidence as she heard her own words spoken. For the first time in a while, she did feel sure and confident, and it was a wonder that she did, given everything she had been through during the past month.

But how could she feel this secure? Was it the assurances given to her by the police? Or that she was finally cleared of all criminal charges and was now standing in front of Nana's home?

Meghan thought those facts did have something to do with how she now felt. But they weren't the real reason.

It was Evan Hawthorne. He had risked everything—his career, his freedom—to save her. He had always believed in her innocence. It was Evan who gave her this new feeling of security. In fact, he shared this certain quality with Dan Rafferty. Not that she wanted to compare Evan to Dan, but these two men were sincere and had committed themselves to her.

Dan was gone, but Meghan would forever keep him alive in her thoughts. Even though she had no factual evidence, somehow Meghan knew Dan Rafferty was murdered that night trying to keep her safe. He must have returned to the institute that night to make sure no harm would come to her. He didn't trust Ashbridge and hated what he had done to her.

Dan Rafferty was a gentle spirit who had tried to make her world safe. Meghan promised to keep the memory of their friendship alive as long as she lived.

"Earth to Meghan," Evan announced. "Where were you?"

"Right here all the time. Though sometimes, I guess, I've been accused of daydreaming. That's right, Evan, I was daydreaming about you."

"All right, I give up. You win. I do care about you—I just don't like you kidding me about it."

"Okay. Truce. No more joking—I promise. But you have to promise me something."

"Name it."

"Don't be too quick to agree."

"I'm listening, Dr. Cahill."

"Promise me you'll drive back here to Ocean City next weekend for one of my special dinners. Remember, you've never tasted my cooking." Meghan smiled.

"It's a deal. Just remember that if anything happens to me because of your cooking, the Philadelphia medical examiner's office will find the cause. You won't be able to poison Philadelphia's M.E. and get away with it," Evan mused.

"Fine. Let's say, next Saturday—4:00 p.m. Before dinner, we can take a walk along the beach."

"Great. I'll be early," Evan assured her.

Chapter Eighty

MEGHAN STOOD ON THE WRAP-AROUND porch of her beach house and waved good-bye to Evan as he drove down Gull Road toward the Ocean City-Longport Bridge. Even though at first she wanted to drive herself back to Ocean City and to her beach house that she so desperately missed, Meghan was now glad Evan had insisted that he drive her instead.

She was already anticipating Evan's visit next weekend.

As Evan's SUV drove around the bend and out of sight, Meghan walked to the front door and unlocked it. A strange feeling suddenly came over her. The last time she was here was on September 21, the two-year anniversary of her grandmother's death, and the night she narrowly escaped the police.

Meghan carried her clothes bag through the living room and entered the kitchen. The house had been closed up for a month. Even though a cool autumn breeze flowed across the porch and encircled her Victorian house, the air inside was warm and stale. Meghan dropped the bag on the kitchen table and walked toward the double atrium doors that led out to her second-story deck. Meghan paused. This was where she had jumped and had escaped capture from the Ocean City Police. But now, she was safe.

Meghan opened the atrium doors, and a gush of salt air blew against her face. It felt good. Familiar and refreshing. Meghan Cahill was glad to finally be back at her house.

Standing outside on her deck, next to the black wrought-iron gate that formed a perimeter around the Williamsburg brick patio floor, Meghan stared up into the cloudy sky and watched as a solitary herring gull hovered instinctively and effortlessly within the turbulent ocean breeze. Meghan had been like that seagull, instinctively surviving the many forces that had threatened her life. The one difference, though, was that unlike the gull who found a safe milieu amidst the ocean's constantly changing wind currents, Meghan couldn't rely on instincts alone but desperately needed help.

Thank God for Evan, Meghan thought.

And yet, Meghan also knew that someone else had sustained her through her ordeal.

Another force.

Her kindred spirit.

Nana.

Meghan firmly believed even when she had felt alone and abandoned, her grandmother had never left her side. Meghan's every decision, her every action during the past several weeks, were all experienced with Nana's spirit at her side.

There were still, however, many unanswered questions left for Meghan to ponder. Too many questions, she thought. But, Meghan didn't want to think anymore. All she knew for certain now was that she was finally at her beach house.

There was one question that she needed to answer for herself. It concerned one room in her house that Meghan still needed to visit.

Her haven.

The last time she was there, she remembered, was the night she was filled with despair. She remembered that she had tried to feel Nana's presence in her special room that night, but it was no use. She was gone. Now, several weeks later, she had to return to that room and see if Nana's spirit was there.

Turning back toward the deck's atrium doors, Meghan walked through the doorway, across the kitchen, and down the single oak step that brought her into her haven.

Nothing was disturbed. Everything was still in the same place.

Thank God, the Ocean City Police didn't ravage her home when they had come for her that night only to find the house unoccupied. Or was she giving the O.C. Police too much credit? It wasn't as if they were in search of drugs or other contraband that would have required a thorough search of each room.

Rather, their search had focused on one person.

A fugitive.

And she had been that person.

Meghan walked across the room and now stood in front of her easel that was positioned near the east wall that ran between two corner windows. The lighting was perfect there. The one window allowed the sun's early morning rays to gently bathe her canvas; the other window permitted an afternoon and early evening light to flow across her palette.

Meghan reached down and picked up her paintbrush. The bristles were soft and not frayed. They felt good against her fingers.

Meghan turned around and gazed at Nana's oil painting above the mahogany-wood piano. Everything that Nana had taught her since she was a child was depicted in that oil of the double-mast schooner coursing confidently through the ocean's white-capped waves. The sky's clouds were painted with a mixture of dark gray and indigo tones that foretold an impending storm.

Nothing was impossible to accomplish if you believed in yourself.

And, never allow your subject to control your painting.

Like the schooner, adapting to nature's threatening environment, the artist, as well, must strive to remain honest with her creativity and not simply create the subject matter as if the work was a photographic image.

Also, in life, Nana had gently reminded Meghan that her artistic creativity and her inner spirit must never permit another person to control her. And always try to surround herself with supportive people who were genuinely concerned with her personal development and growth.

All of Nana's teachings were brought to life once again as Meghan stared at the oil painting.

Meghan sighed deeply.

Her breathing slowed, and her muscles relaxed.

She was at peace here.

Meghan sighed again. She finally allowed her inner spirit to speak with her grandmother …

Nana, I love you, and God knows I miss you terribly.

But, I know you're here with me.

I can feel you with me now in this room. And I know you will always watch over me.

Nana, I want to tell you something very important.

I met someone—someone who risked everything to save me. He's kind, giving, and he deeply cares for me.

Nana, if I sometimes become a little preoccupied in my life and don't think of you as often as I have in the past, please understand. Each day of my life, I love you more and more. And, I miss you.

But I realize now, ever since you left this world, each day my love for you grew out of my feelings of sadness and loneliness over losing you. I couldn't help that. I'm sorry.

We were so close.

But now, Nana, this man—Evan Hawthorne—has eased the pain in my life. When I'm with him and hear him speak, I'm reminded of the many things you taught me about life.

And about myself.

My love for you, Nana, I truly believe, will actually grow stronger. I see that now.

By allowing my pain to ebb away, I am actually making more room for unconditional love to grow and nourish and strengthen my inner spirit.

Nana, if you could be with me now, I know you would like Evan.

I believe he is the person whom you often spoke of when you tried to guide me toward that someone special you knew I would one day meet in my life.

Another kindred spirit for me ...

Meghan walked closer to the piano and picked up the black and white photo of her grandmother. She then sat on the piano seat and slowly ran her fingers across her grandmother's face.

Tears welled in Meghan's eyes. Her grandmother's portrait was blurry. But Meghan saw her more clearly than she could ever remember since she had died.

More clearly inside her mind and thoughts.

Stronger than ever within her inner spirit.

Nana was smiling at her and gently holding Meghan's face between her loving hands.

Meghan was truly at *home* now.

Chapter Eighty-One

"WELCOME TO VICKERS TAVERN. CAN I help you?" inquired a slender, mid-twenties hostess with aquamarine eyes and sandy blonde hair tightly pulled back into a ponytail.

She was attractive, thought Stefan, but not as striking and suitable to him as the hostess who had greeted him here several weeks ago in this historic Chester County restaurant.

"Dinner for one. Preferably a table in one of your more secluded rooms," Stefan replied, observing the young woman's every move. Her repeated and certainly not needed hand gestures that swept behind her ears and along the side of her tightly pulled-back hair were out of habit, he thought, to ensure that any loose strands were returned to their proper place.

"Please follow me." The young woman guided Stefan past the lounge, empty except for a female bartender who was busily restocking several bottles atop the oak shelves that ran across the back wall behind the bar.

Stefan stood still. He only saw the young bartender's profile. But it was enough.

It was the hostess who had greeted him at his earlier visit to Vickers Tavern several weeks ago. There was no mistake about it.

"Is there something wrong?" Stefan's guide asked.

"What? No. Everything's fine ... now," Stefan replied, gesturing the hostess to continue showing him to his table.

"I hope this room is okay. I don't expect to seat anyone else in here this evening."

Stefan seated himself in one of four wooden high-back Amish chairs positioned around one of only three tables tucked away in a dark, mahogany-walled room that the hostess referred to as the Study. Across two of the four walls were floor-to-ceiling bookcases that provided homes for hundreds of leather-bound books whose exposed spine covers gave the authentic appearance of nineteenth-century origin.

Stefan faced a floor-level Williamsburg brick fireplace that had already begun to surrender its remaining embers to the late autumnal evening. It was October 16, the first month when the constellation Pegasus dominated the evening sky, and Stefan reflected on his successful and timely completion of his Pegasus assignment. Just as he had assured the professor and Monsignor Reuss last August—except, for a few unplanned killings. But that was okay. In his line of work, he had grown accustomed to taking care of those extra annoyances. For some clients, he would expect and receive additional compensation for such work. For a few select others, like Imago Dei's devoted corporate officers, Professor Marguilies and Monsignor Reuss, Stefan had chosen to comp the additional work. It was good for his reputation. He was thorough but not greedy.

The hostess remained in the room for a few minutes longer to encourage the fire with a wrought-iron stoker. Within seconds, her expert touch produced a moderate blaze, and soon Stefan felt a warm rush of heated air move across his face.

"Excuse me. Can you tell me when the lounge will be closed?" Stefan inquired.

"If it's not busy, like tonight, maybe around 10:00 p.m."

"Thank you." Stefan examined his watch. He had ninety minutes to order, receive his meal, and eat it. He wanted to be sure he had enough time to go to the lounge while it was still open.

While *she* was still there.

Chapter Eighty-Two

"You're not closing yet, are you? It's only 9:30," Stefan said as he entered the lounge and settled himself on a barstool.

The young woman suddenly turned around. She stood and faced Stefan, who was leaning forward against the thick oak bar counter. Her pale green eyes wide open, her tan face momentarily flushed with surprise.

"No ... no, we're not closed. Soon, though. It hasn't been very busy tonight. In fact, you're the first one in here since 7:00."

"I guess Sunday evenings aren't very busy," Stefan observed.

"At least not in the fall. The summer, well, that's a different story. Except, maybe, about a month or so ago."

"What do you mean?"

"I guess you're not from around here. But we had two murders occur only about three miles from here. When the word got out about them, we had the curious ones and a lot of media come in here to have a drink and share stories with one another. Especially the Sunday after the killings.

They occurred about a month ago on a Saturday evening. But, I suppose you haven't heard about them."

"No. I haven't. Did they catch the killer?"

"No. And this is the best part of the whole story. The police don't say much, but the papers printed a story that says a professional killer, some kind of international hit-man, was responsible."

"Really? That is quite interesting."

"The police think he's still in Europe somewhere. They think he had something to do with the death of a Philadelphia cardinal. His body was found in some Vatican City apartment. I know, it all sounds so surreal—a professional hit-man in Chester County."

"I see what you mean. It really sounds like something you would read about in a spy novel."

"Well, it is real, and it kept this place quite busy even on a Sunday evening. But, listen to me going on and on. I'm sorry, what can I get for you?"

"That's okay. I think I'll have an Amaretto di Sarona, straight up."

The young bartender turned around and looked up at the top shelf, only to realize there was probably just one drink left in the bottle.

"Let's see. There's a full one down in the cellar. I'll be back in a sec."

Stefan enjoyed the intimacy, the one-on-one attention he was receiving without making any effort. He wasn't surprised she hadn't remembered him. Probably too much time had elapsed since his last visit—or, too much hype had been given to the murders, which served as a distraction to her. Either way, Stefan preferred to remain a stranger. A first-time visitor to Chester County and to Vickers Tavern.

And, how was Meghan Cahill doing?

Had she forgotten him as well? Stefan doubted that very much. He knew the sting of his bullet, intentionally missing a vital part of her body and instead only tearing a superficial crease through her flesh, still reminded her of him.

But what should he do about her?

She was not like the rest. Not like Ashbridge or his assistant.

And, certainly not like Cardinal Torrey and his assistant, Monsignor Brannigan.

Meghan Cahill was different. In a way, he admired her. The way she had stood up to Ashbridge, escaped police capture, and especially, fought her way to freedom and finally convinced the police she was innocent.

Stefan also knew Meghan had help. Help that *he* had given her. She couldn't have survived to tell the police about the Vatican City hit if it weren't for *him*. But that was okay. She deserved her freedom. She was like the many innocent children who were abused victims of Cardinal Torrey and Monsignor Brannigan. Meghan was also an abused victim of Ashbridge. He had been a bastard. Jonathan Ashbridge had manipulated her and abused the trust that she had placed in him. Since the first day he had met Ashbridge here in Vickers Tavern, Stefan knew what type of person he was. Just like Cardinal Torrey, Ashbridge would never allow anyone to stand in his way or prevent him from achieving greatness.

Stefan was a Knights Templar sworn to protect the innocent and to deliver justice on their behalf. His sworn allegiance as a Knight to Imago Dei was also a sworn commitment to seek revenge against the victims' oppressors. Before leaving Italy, Stefan had met with Monsignor Reuss, who had given him his next assignment. There were others that needed to be found. Defrocked priests from the Philadelphia Archdiocese who had escaped prosecution because of Pennsylvania's statute of limitations. Because of this law, there were dozens of Catholic priests who were no longer with the church but who were now free to roam neighborhoods and prey on innocent children.

These priests were his next assignment for Imago Dei.

Where were these defrocked priests living now? No one knew. Supposedly, not the Catholic Church, and certainly not the legal authorities. Even after the Catholic Church had removed them from their ministries, the Catholic Church technically was not required to report the names and locations of these men to the police. Stefan knew that the Catholic Church had used the technicalities of Meghan's Law to avoid reporting their names and locations to the authorities. Under

Meghan's Law, only those individuals who were arrested and found guilty for crimes of abuse toward children had to be reported to the authorities so that their daily activities would be monitored.

Not so for these priests. Even though Imago Dei did not know the location of these priests, Stefan was certain he would find them.

Find them and punish them.

As a Knights Templar, Stefan had wanted to protect Meghan Cahill from Ashbridge's abusive behavior and his plan to destroy her. He had ensured that Ashbridge received his just punishment. Stefan also had enabled Meghan to regain her freedom.

It was the honorable thing to do.

Stefan would always remember Meghan Cahill for her resilience and strong-willed determination. He also hoped her new life without Ashbridge would be filled with happiness and fulfillment. Stefan believed she deserved such a life.

That is, as long as Dr. Cahill no longer interfered with his work for Imago Dei.

Stefan examined his watch. It was nearly 10:00 p.m. Now, where was his friendly bartender? Stefan was anxious to begin his evening with her.

Made in the USA
Lexington, KY
30 December 2013